Charles Rollin Burdick

Before the dawn

a poem

Charles Rollin Burdick

Before the dawn
a poem

ISBN/EAN: 9783743657861

Printed in Europe, USA, Canada, Australia, Japan

Cover: Foto ©Andreas Hilbeck / pixelio.de

More available books at **www.hansebooks.com**

BEFORE THE DAWN:

A POEM;

WITH

INTRODUCTORY LECTURES

ON PROPHETIC SYMBOLS:

PORTRAYING THE LAST GREAT CONFLICTS WHICH RESULT IN THE

DOWNFALL OF PAPAL DOMINATION

THE DESTRUCTION OF POLITICAL AND ECCLESIASTICAL DESPOTISM, AND THE
REMOVAL OF OTHER HINDRANCES TO CHRISTIANITY IN THE
NINETEENTH CENTURY.

BY

REV. C. R. BURDICK, M. A.

———————

BUFFALO:
BREED, LENT AND COMPANY.
1872.

Warren, Johnson & Co.
Stereotypers, Printers and Binders,
Buffalo, N. Y.

CONTENTS.

PREFACE.

THE object of the author in presenting the following volume to the public, is to call increased attention to the wonderful book from which the theme of the poem is drawn, and, if possible, to awaken interest in the great subjects there shadowed forth, in the minds of those who have hitherto rejected the claims of Christianity as a divine revelation. He is well aware that the book of Revelation has been quite generally regarded as a sealed book, whose mysteries might not be pierced by the inquiring or the curious; but if "all scripture is profitable for doctrine, for reproof, for correction, for instruction in righteousness," surely it cannot have been the Divine plan that this book should remain unstudied. Its sublime symbols, finding their fulfillment in the passing events of history, were designed to rebuke skepticism and strengthen the Christian's faith.

The author has made no attempt to be critical in his exposition. Neither does he claim that his views are, in the main, original. His chief object has been to

enforce the views taken by our recent standard expositors, and, by vivid pictures, to impress them permanently upon the mind and heart of the reader, while,
at the same time, he has felt at liberty to depart
from the authorities in some particulars.

The lectures were presented, in course, to his congre-
gation in the city of Joliet, Ill., in the fall of 1870 and
spring of 1871.

The poem has occupied all the time he could devote
to it, without interfering with his pastoral duties, for
more than two years past. He wrote it because he
loves to sing, in his humble way, of those great struggles
and glorious triumphs of his Master's Kingdom, which
precede the blessed Millennium.

He feels sure that he cherishes no unworthy ambition, if he would attempt to consecrate the noble
Spenserian stanza to the uses of Christianity.

He offers his first book to an intelligent public,
humbly wishing, hardly daring to hope, that he may
thus be instrumental in hastening the final triumph
of the Messiah's Kingdom in the world. If the Church
wants it and it helps her in any degree, he will be more
than rewarded for all his toil.

INTRODUCTORY LECTURES.

I.

THE GREAT WAR IN EUROPE, 1870.

And oh! this night brings tempests in its train.—Canto I, Stanza 11.

And I looked, and behold, a white cloud, and upon the cloud one sat like unto the Son of man, having on his head a golden crown, and in his hand a sharp sickle.

And another angel came out of the temple, crying with a loud voice to him that sat on the cloud, Thrust in thy sickle, and reap: for the time is come for thee to reap; for the harvest of the earth is ripe.

And he that sat on the cloud thrust in his sickle on the earth; and the earth was reaped.

And another angel came out of the temple.which is in heaven, he also having a sharp sickle.

And another angel came out from the altar, which had power over fire; and cried with a loud cry to him that had the sharp sickle, saying, Thrust in thy sharp sickle, and gather the clusters of the vine of the earth; for her grapes are fully ripe.

And the angel thrust in his sickle into the earth, and gathered the vine of the earth, and cast it into the great wine-press of the wrath of God.

And the wine-press was trodden without the city, and blood came out of the wine-press, even unto the horse-bridles, by the space of a thousand and six hundred furlongs.—Rev. xiv. 14-20.

This is an epitome of what follows, until Satan is bound for a thousand years, as represented in the twentieth chapter. Under the startling and awful symbols of our text, the apostle makes a general statement, and then goes on, in the following chapters, to particularize. It is a synopsis of what is contained under the symbolism of the seven vials. I do not, therefore, pretend to find a specific fulfillment of these awful prophecies in the events of the present time. Yet I do believe that a general history, in its relation to Christianity, of the latter part of the eighteenth and of the nineteenth centuries, up to the present time, is shadowed forth in the symbols of this part of the Word of God.   I have given the subject a great deal of thought, and my conclusions are not founded on mere fancies.   The resemblance of these symbols to what I believe to be their substance, is too striking to pass unnoticed by the careful student of the Bible.

After much study I have adopted, so far as I dare, what seems to me to be the most rational interpretation of the symbols of the beast and of the woman who sat upon his back, clothed in scarlet, as described in the seventeenth chapter; though, of course, I do not pretend that the events, when they transpire, may not furnish a better, and, perhaps, an essentially different, interpretation.   As it seems to me, the beast with seven heads and ten horns symbolizes Political Despotism—Monarchism, Imperialism, Absolutism—as found in the seven principal countries of Europe—England, France, Spain, Italy, Austria, Russia, and Prussia.   I will not strenuously contend that those seven kingdoms are the specific ones shadowed forth by the heads of this monster, nor that the ten horns are the kings increased by the subordinate kings of Germany.   Yet all will agree that there is some resemblance.   But I *am* convinced that the woman symbolizes Ecclesiastical Despotism, seated on the back of political power, without which she could not, in our day, execute her decrees.   You will find Ecclesiastical Despotism chiefly among the Papal powers, but not exclusively.   The English and Greek churches have had some share in ecclesiastical domination, and their garments are not entirely free from the blood of persecution.   So even the Presbyterians and Puritans have had some share in persecution.   But as religious despotism has been chiefly confined to Rome, John locates its throne upon the seven hills.

When the student of history sees that all the great wars that have shaken the world for a hundred years, have resulted in weakening these two powers, sweeping away one after another of their supports, even when the thunders have not been directly launched upon either of them, he must be skeptical, indeed, if he cannot see Eternal Providence riding on the storm, and directing the winds where to blow, and the bolts where to fall.

We find in prophecy that the woman fell first. Babylon is first proclaimed fallen, then "the beast which was and is not, and yet is," goes down in the last great battle, when the angel standing in the sun calls to the fowls of heaven to "Come and gather themselves together to the supper of the great God, to eat the flesh of kings, and the flesh of captains, and the flesh of mighty men, and the flesh of horses and of them that sit on them, and the flesh of all men, both free and bond, both small and great."

Ecclesiastical Despotism to-day trembles when she sees her defenders march away to a distant land to be swallowed up in the maelstrom which ambition has stirred up on the stormy waters of strife, and turns pale when she hears the murmur of rising peoples and the tramp of armies hastening to hurl her down from her seat on the seven hills. I say ecclesiastical despotism; I do not say the Roman Catholic Church, for it would be a great calamity if that should be destroyed; but the power that dominates her shall be cast down, and she, like the nations, shall be enfranchised.

You remember how the revolution of 1789 rolled its surges, not only against the throne of kings, but also that of religious despotism, and bore away some of their strongest supports. Then the wars of Napoleon Bonaparte, though in the service of the most absolute despotism, launched their thunders upon the head of this power, and under their shocks it almost went down. True, it raised its head again above the waves, but it was shorn of much of its prestige. Then during the revolutions in Italy, where the fifth vial was poured out upon the throne of the beast, and especially in Italian unity, so hopefully initiated by the battles of Magenta and Solferino, and thus far perfected by the battle of Sadowa— the same event liberalizing Austria, its chief bulwark—ecclesiastical despotism received most stunning blows. The abolition of serfdom in Russia, and the destruction of slavery in this country, after one of the most tremendous struggles of history, are great events bearing directly on political despotism, and more remotely on religious. I refer the reader to my poem further on, which embodies my thoughts on this subject, rendering it unnecessary to repeat them here.

1*

It is not for me to say that Louis Napoleon stands forth in the foreground of history to-day, as the fulfillment of any distinct prophetic symbol. I do not see him in any symbol, nor anything, as it seems to me, that would suggest him to any unprejudiced mind; yet, doubtless, his form was seen by the prophet, blended with other forms which crowd the great canvas of Eternal Providence, as objects are blended by distance on a landscape, and I do not doubt but he has had an important part in the fulfillment of prophecy, and I have never doubted what the termination of his reign would be. In prosecuting my work on the poem which follows these lectures, about a year ago, (October, 1869,) I sketched the campaigns of the first Napoleon, in northern Italy, as the highly probable fulfillment of the symbolism of the third vial. At the close of the sketch I introduced what seemed to me to be a still further fulfillment of this terrible symbolism, a short sketch of the Franco-Italian campaign against the power of Austria, in that same country of rivers and fountains. I quote a few lines, as they will not appear, in this form, in the poem:

> But all that vial was not spent,
> Though many streams with blood were blent,
> Till fifty years, when in that land,
> Another scourge of God should stand.
> Exalted to his uncle's throne
>   By revolution's shifting tide,
> He grasped a scepter not his own,
>   But for a season to abide,
> To beat the nations, as a rod,
> In hand of an avenging God;
>   Then to be vilely cast aside,
>   All shorn of power and crushed in pride.
> That fate is thine, Napoleon,
> Of Rome, self-styled, the eldest son.

Of course I make no claim to prophetic vision, nor, indeed, to any extraordinary sagacity; but I wrote the above when there was no political cloud in the heavens to portend the fearful storm that is now sweeping over France; because I believed in God, in his revelation, in eternal right and in the final triumph of civil liberty along with a pure religion; both of which are grandly shadowed forth in the prophetic symbols we are considering — of both of which Louis Napoleon, with all his large professions, has shown himself a most unscrupulous enemy. It is true that none of us are yet certain as to what his ultimate fate may be; yet it now looks very much as if he had been "vilely cast aside, all shorn of power and crushed in pride," by the swirls of the whirlwind which he himself has evoked from the stormy elements.

Contemplate the fearful campaign whose thunders have startled the world for the last two months, and tell me if ever the hand of God was more distinctly visible in human affairs. Everything about it has disappointed ordinary human calculation. The world was astonished and indignant when Napoleon, on the most flimsy pretext possible, declared war and hurried his army away to invade Prussian territory. All have been astonished at the amazing rapidity of the mobilization of the Prussian army, so rapid that William was ready to strike the first blow. Who ever heard of three-quarters of a million of men drawn so quickly from every part of the kingdom, and hurled so furiously against the would-be invaders? We were astonished to see the tables turned, and a great host invading France, instead of Germany. We have been filled with admiration at the wondrous unity of the German people; and the sagacity of statesmen has been put to fault by the course which the South German States have taken in the conflict. The world has been filled with amazement at the unbroken series of brilliant victories that have crowned the German arms, and at the rapidity with which the magnificent army of France has melted away under the steady but terrific assaults of her invincible foes. And we are bewildered at the unparalleled spectacle of a hundred thousand Frenchmen surrendering in Sedan at discretion, with the emperor himself, and his generals, arms, munitions and standards. We instinctively exclaim: Where are the valor and generalship of Austerlitz, of Jena and Auerstadt? And so, when the veil of the conflict lifts and displays more perfectly the gory wrecks of the battle-field, no doubt the world will be astonished and appalled at the fearful slaughter of victims by the terrible engines of destruction which civilization, or barbarism, has introduced into the warfare of the nineteenth century. To cap the climax, the world is amazed at the rapidity and apparent hopelessness of the downfall of the most formidable despotism of the age.

I have read with wonder and awe about the rapid advance of Alexander into the East, when, before his invincible phalanxes, the Persian legions went down on the fearful fields of the Granicus, of Isus, of Arbela, and other fields, which in twelve years erected the great Macedonian Empire, with Babylon for its capital. With wonder I have followed Hannibal, the Carthaginian general, across Gibraltar, through Spain, over the Pyrenees, through Gaul, and over the Alps into Italy, his wonderful campaign culminating in the terrific battle of Lake Thrasymene, in whose roar an earthquake which shook the continent and overthrew cities, passed unheeded by the opponents. I know something of the campaigns of Julius Cæsar, who spread the Roman Empire over Switzerland, Gaul, Germany, and a large part of Britain. I have studied quite carefully the campaigns of Napoleon. But I find nothing in all these that can equal this campaign, not even in Napoleon's masterpiece, as it has been called, the campaign of Austerlitz. Results which formerly would have required years to accomplish, have been achieved in two short months. What but the hand of God is hurrying up affairs to make room for the grand coming events whose greatness casts their shadows before? He hath said of the world, "I will overturn, overturn, overturn it," to prepare the way for the reign of his Son.

Of course it is too early to speak with certainty in reference to the ultimate results of this fearful campaign. But one thing seems to be taken for granted by all: the Empire of Louis Napoleon Bonaparte is at an end. There are none among the nations, and few even in France, so poor as to do him reverence. Held as a prisoner in a German fortress, which at the same time affords an asylum to him from the fury of his quondam subjects, he is to-day an object of commiseration, rather than of fear.

But one of the impending results of the fall of the French Empire is the destruction of the temporal power of the Pope, and the end of ecclesiastical despotism in Italy. Imperial

France was its last powerful supporter. When her armies embarked from Rome, the city was left at the mercy of Italian troops, which, beyond all doubt, will soon occupy it, and make it the capital of United Italy. The Papacy has nothing to hope from a French Republic; and should that fail, as many of its friends fear it will, years must elapse, if the time ever comes, when France will have gained anything like the position she has lately occupied among the nations. Ere that time the last vestige of ecclesiastical despotism may have been swept from the earth forever; or other nations may so far outstrip France that she cannot afford protection to the Papal power, should she have any inclination that way. So this great war has knocked another strong pillar from beneath that colossal power which, at one time, dominated the world, and even now, in its dotage, shows immense vitality. True, it is not destroyed, but it hastens to its downfall.

And so there can be no doubt that this dreadful war will strike an equally strong blow upon political despotism. We know that Sadowa liberalized Austria, whatever may have been the intentions of Prussia. We see that this war has overthrown imperialism in France and erected a French Republic, whatever may be its future fate. It cannot be that such expense of blood and treasure, solely in the interests of despotism, will fail to open the eyes of nations, and to hasten the time when it shall be an established maxim that government is for the people, and not for those who hold its reins.

However this may be, we may rest in the conclusion that the destinies of Europe, and, so far as it goes, of the world, will be safer under German, than under French leadership. We may hope for a more liberal international policy, so far as German influence can establish it. German ideas are more nearly abreast of the age than French; and, in all good conscience, we hope and believe that the tone of public morality is much higher in Germany. If she stands at the head of the nations of Europe, these things must have their influence, and they will help to shape its international policy.

The greatness of Prussia is not so much in the diplomacy of her statesmen, nor in the strategy, generalship and bravery of her armies, as in the universal education of her masses. When the predecessor of William nobly resolved, at the risk of his throne, to instruct the masses by a system of free schools, he laid the foundation of the greatness of Prussia. Her people thus have an immense advantage over the uneducated masses of France. While the French soldier, only inspired to battle by the vision of glory, little capable of realizing the moral aspects of the struggle he may be engaged in, is demoralized when his bubble is pierced by the bayonets of defeat, the German, having decided that he is fighting for a principle, and capable of reasoning on the subject, esteems temporary defeat an honor, and, with more unyielding determination, nerves himself anew for the conflict whose success with him is a moral certainty, because it is right. Had the armies of Napoleon the First met the soldiers of William on the tremendous fields of Jena and Auerstadt, the result of that awful day of battles would, undoubtedly, have been different. That the Germans believe that they have been repelling unprovoked aggression in this conflict, no one doubts; and all thinking men will admit that this is one great secret of their success. So one great lesson of this war, to rulers and statesmen, is, to educate the masses. It is time to dismiss the idea that ignorance in the common soldier promotes obedience—that the thinking bayonet is not the ready instrument of thorough military discipline. It *is*, doubtless, true that the soldier must be ignorant to be the ready tool of an unmitigated despotism. But if he is to fight for humanity, and not to decide the quarrels of kings, in which he really has very little interest, he must be educated. Religious, moral and intellectual instruction for the masses, is the great want of France to-day. Without it, we have little hope of her maintaining a republican form of government. If the Republic can retain its power until the light of science and of a pure religion beams upon the darkened masses, we may hope that it will become permanent, but not without.

The sympathizers with France—and it is a little curious that these are nearly all Catholics—claim that this struggle has none of the features of a religious war. They refer, by way of proof of the correctness of their claim, to the example of the Catholic States of Germany. If Catholicism, they ask, were arrayed against Protestant Prussia, why should not these States be against her? But this is no proof. The Emperor calculated upon their siding with him, and all thinking men will see that Catholicism was the chief ground of this expectation. But he reckoned without his host. The Ecumenical Council had been in session at Rome; the dogma of Papal Infallibility had been proclaimed, against the protests of German bishops. Estranged, to a great extent, by this, from Rome, these States would naturally follow their national sympathies. So, the folly of the Pope has aided in the downfall of Napoleon, and hastened his own. And it does not appear that Jesuitism did not connive with Napoleon's ambition to cripple the strongest Protestant power on the continent, thus to forward its own schemes of ambition. The result appears in a dethroned and captive. Emperor, the great army of France defeated, demoralized, almost annihilated, and a victorious Prussian army, swarming like grasshoppers around doomed and trembling Paris, and thundering at her gates. Future historians will place William among the champions of Protestantism, along with Frederick the Great. Thus, in our day, Providence has raised up the German power, a granite mountain, against which Latinism has been dashed to pieces in the behalf of human liberty.

The moral lessons of these great events cannot be enumerated here. We can only glance at some of them. One is Providential retribution in the affairs of nations. Jesus Christ said, long ago, "All they that take the sword shall perish by the sword." We have seen this verified in history too often to be skeptical. The first Napoleon carved his way to the Empire of France, and to the dictatorship of Rome and of Europe, with his merciless sword. The star of his destiny began to wane on the frozen steppes of Russia; it was shaken from its hight on the tremendous field of Leipsic, to rise again, to blaze for a hundred days in the eyes of an astonished world, but it set in blood on the awful field of Waterloo. The third Napoleon followed in his uncle's steps, so far as his genius and the spirit of the age would permit—wading through the blood of revolution to an imperial throne. The sword of execution raised him to his throne; the sword of Jehovah, in the hand of Germany, has laid him low. And the last act in this drama is the most striking illustration of all. He took the sword, on the most shallow pretext, to humble an envied rival; it is turned against his own bosom, and he is smitten from his throne.

Here is another astonishing lesson of Providence. The Pope had just arrived at the summit of his earthly ambition; he had just procured the pompous proclamation of his own infallibility, when lo! the shifting scene! The bayonets which have upheld his waning power are withdrawn from his support; his last imperial defender is crushed under the avalanche which his own hand had loosened, and His Holiness is left drifting on the sea of revolution, with Italian nationality and unity knocking at the gates of Rome. Will his infallibility save him? We shall see.

Here, too, is another lesson on the vanity of human greatness. It was but yesterday that the third Napoleon sat upon the throne of the greatest nation in Europe, wielding the destiny of millions, dictating the policy of nations—the dread of the civilized world. To-day, where is the pride of his greatness! Where is the glittering crown which begirt his ambitious temples! Where the pomp and splendor of his imperial court! Where are the purple robes of state! Where the adulation of millions whose thundering "Vive l'Empereurs" were wont to tingle in his ears! Where is that magnificent martial array which poured through the gates of Paris, with waving banners, and dancing plumes, and gleaming armor, the tramp of whose splendid cavalry shook the earth around? They went gaily, *boastfully* forth, joyful with life and vigor, as if to a summer pic-nic on the fair banks of the Rhine. Where are they now? Their mangled carcases lie weltering in gore upon the battle-fields of the frontier; horse and rider have gone down in the shock of battle; the fowls of heaven swarm to their feasts upon the unburied slain, and the wail of the widows of France goes up from the length and breadth of that unhappy land. Napoleon a prisoner in a German fortress! His Empress flying for her life from the multitudes which once fawned upon her footsteps! His child an exile in a foreign land! He himself proscribed by his own countrymen, and covered with their curses! His palaces invaded by the mob! His royal tables feasting the palates of the *sans-culottes*! The symbols of his imperial sway indignantly torn down and trampled in the dust! How have the mighty fallen! "*Sic transit gloria mundi!*" Will ambitious men learn a lesson? Will the worldly learn to "set their affections on things above, and not on things on the earth"?

II.

THE FRENCH REVOLUTION IN PROPHECY.

Wide o'er the astonished world an angel soars.—CANTO I, STANZA 35.

And the first [angel] went and poured out his vial upon the earth ; and there fell a noisome and grievous sore upon the men which had the mark of the beast and upon them which worshiped his image.—REV. XVI. 2.

THIS is the beginning of one of the most solemn and awful delineations of the Word of God. Such startling symbols must be portentous of great calamities upon the class of men here designated, whoever they may be. Of course, no wise man will be very positive that he has found their true meaning. Yet they are in the Word of God, in the Revelation of Jesus Christ, which God gave to him, to show unto his servants. They must have been designed to be understood at some time, or they could not be called revelations, for that is no revelation which conveys no meaning with it. It must have been designed for study and meditation; and if we engage in it with a humble and teachable spirit, there can be no doubt but it will be profitable for us.

It was, undoubtedly, the intention of this symbolism to shadow forth something falling upon a large class of men which might be called a plague or sore. Any thing which would produce such an effect would answer the conditions of the symbols. Whatever the contents of the vial might symbolize, whether something in itself good or evil, if it produced such an effect upon them, they would certainly call it evil; to them it would be a plague, a sore. The beast is, beyond all question, a symbol for the same things which the woman and the monster on which she rode symbolize, to which I alluded last Sabbath evening, viz.: civil and religious despotism. Mr. Barnes calls them the civil and ecclesiastical powers of Rome; but as Rome has not been the only power which has wielded a despotic sway over the bodies and souls of men, it must appear that his exposition is not broad enough. Yet if we could take from the pages of history the record of Roman political and ecclesiastical despotism, especially the latter, we should take away the greater part of history for fifteen hundred years. These two powers are so nearly allied that they have usually gone in company. Ecclesiastical despotism could never have done much hurt in the world, if she had not been supported by political despotism—if she had not been able to catch and ride that beast into power. Hence, what affects one must directly or indirectly affect the other. We have concluded that the whole seven vials symbolize those influences of one kind and another which are crippling, and finally destined to destroy, these forms of despotism which we find shadowed forth under the symbols of the dragon, the first and second beasts, the abandoned woman, the false prophet, the Great River Euphrates, and the three unclean spirits which proceeded out of the mouth of the dragon, out of the mouth of the beast, and out of the mouth of the false prophet. All these disclose forms of evil at war with human advancement, spiritual and temporal, and hence, despotism, in its various forms and modes, seeking to destroy both political and religious freedom. Hence, whatever goes to cripple despotism, of any form, and especially ecclesiastical, may be fitly symbolized by a vial of wrath poured out upon the supporters of oppression by a God who "created all men free and equal, and endowed them with certain inalienable rights, among which are life, liberty, and the pursuit of happiness." So any thing which may be called a plague or sore upon the supporters of despotism, may be fittingly symbolized by the effects of this vial of wrath. It was poured out upon the earth, and it produced "a noisome and grievous sore upon the men which had the mark of the beast, and upon them which worshiped his image." This describes two classes of adherents to these forms of despotism. Those who bore the mark of the beast are, undoubtedly, those who gave him their external support for mere personal ends, without any particular regard for him, only as he could promote their own selfish purposes. Among this class must be ranked many of the Roman Catholic sovereigns of the past century. Those who worship his image are those who, body and soul, believe in, and worship the monster. But it should be observed that both classes are involved in consequences which follow the outpouring of the vial.

At the risk of being considered, perhaps, a fanciful innovator, I shall make the suggestion that modern Republicanism may be fittingly symbolized by the contents of this vial. Poured out upon the earth, it operates as a healthful medicine often does upon a patient whose blood has long been corrupted, by bringing the corruption to the surface in the form of grievous sores. The rude shocks which political despotism experienced from the American Revolution —whose successful issue was followed, in less than seven years, by that of France—showed its insecure tenure of existence in modern civilization. The scenes that followed are the sores which broke out upon its upholders. France*† thought to improve the medicine by mingling that with it which proved to be a fatal poison, and that was French atheism. But the compound acted with special potency upon ecclesiastical despotism. This was the offspring of long years of tyranny and abuse. God and heavenly things were so wretchedly represented by their accredited earthly exponents, that a natural, though most disastrous result, was, that many, in throwing off the abuses, repudiated all religion. And however terrible French atheism proved to be, however impious its upholders, though they cannot be held at all excusable, yet political and ecclesiastical despotism are mainly responsible for it. It is little wonder, then, that so unseemly an offspring should turn and rend its equally unseemly parents. The French Revolution was a tremendous upheaval of human society, resulting largely from the republican leaven which had long been working there. While it did incalculable service to the cause of human progress, like the whirlwind and thunder-gust—which are often necessary to purify the stagnant air, shaking from it its poisonous malarias—it did a great deal of harm. While it struck most staggering blows upon kingly and priestly prerogative, it

---

* Note 3, Canto I, stanza 36.

swept away much of the beneficent fruits of a pure Christianity not yet entirely dead in France, which, if preserved and nurtured, might have rendered their republican institutions enduring.

The nation has not yet recovered from that storm of good and evil, so strangely blended. All authorities admit that she had been the victim of shameful abuses, under monarchical rule. The people had groaned, for a long time, under them. They had loudly and justly clamored for redress. The imbecile Louis obstinately persisted in refusing it, until he drove them into open revolt. Then, when they had taken redress into their own hands, he offered to make concessions, but it was too late. In 1789 the Revolution triumphed, and he was virtually stripped of power, though he nominally held the reins until some time after. But he was finally deposed, amid great indignities, and ultimately guillotined, with several of his family, including his Queen. A French Republic was thus established. It was sustained for a number of years. Napoleon the First subverted it, while uttering the most enthusiastic protestations of attachment to liberty. Yea, in the name of civil liberty, his usurpations were accomplished, liberty strangled, and an unlimited despotism enthroned. But while the Republic lasted, it was the plague—the sore of despotism. It proclaimed universal war on kings of every degree, and too generously offered the right hand, to help all who would hoist the flag of rebellion against kingcraft and priestcraft. French emissaries were in all parts of Europe, secretly, if not openly, stirring up the people to rebellion. They had numerous sympathizers everywhere, and kings, feeling the heavings of the earthquake, trembled for their crowns, sceptres and royal prerogatives. French influence established republics in Belgium, Holland and Italy. Republican armies hung like thunderclouds in the passes of the Pyrenees, and even rolled the tide of invasion into Spain. Republican cannon thundered across the Rhine, at the gates of Germany; and their echoes were heard across the Straits of Dover. Republican armies defied the world, and, for a time, faced the combined powers of Europe. Had the Republic been less inclined to proselyte other nations, by intrigue and by arms, and, content with achieving the liberties of France, acted purely on the defensive, she might have remained unto this day, in spite of the opposition of kings. It is conceded that republicanism gave to the nation that tremendous military prowess which, under Napoleon, carried the eagles of France to Berlin, Vienna, Moscow, Madrid, and the Eternal City. Could it have been directed by such pure and patriotic men as our own dear Washington, the history of France, and of Europe, would have been different. But her leaders were either wrong-headed or corrupt men, and they led her to destruction.

The Roman Catholic Church,* the instinctive enemy of republican institutions, so recognized and so treated by the French Republic, felt the heaviest blows. All church property was confiscated, priests were banished under the severest penalties, and the Roman Catholic religion publicly abjured.† But the terrible misfortune and fatal mistake was, that, with this, she abjured all religion.‡ Her chamber of deputies published the awful blasphemy: "Resolved, that there is no God, and death is an eternal sleep." The Republic then became a more bitter persecutor than Rome had been in France for centuries. The Reign of Terror, the most terrible outbreak of human passion on the records of civilized nations, began soon after this. The Girondists first held the power, and ruled the nation with high-handed tyranny; but they were soon hurled by violence from their seats in the national assembly by the Jacobins, and hurried away to the guillotine, under the leadership of Marat, Danton, Robespierre and others. The rule of the Girondists was mildness and mercy, compared with that of the Jacobins. Political murders became the order of the day. Tens of thousands, on the merest suspicion of being inimical to the Republic, as was claimed, but really to the reigning faction, became the victims of midnight arrest by *gens d'armes*, and, with scarcely a form of trial, were sentenced to death, and, without a decent delay, were hurried away to the guillotine. The streets of Paris swam with the blood of her citizens. Whole hecatombs of victims, men, women, and

* Note 4, Canto I, stanza 38.   † Note 5, stanza 39.   ‡ Note 6, stanza 40.
§ Note 7, ibid.

even children, were slaughtered by the executioner, under the very shadow of the statue of Liberty, which Frenchmen boasted to worship. The most high-handed and bloody deeds of tyranny were enacted in the name of Liberty. Excesses of the most horrid kind were perpetrated. An unchaste woman, of rare beauty and symmetry of form, was brought naked before the assembly, and proclaimed the Goddess of Reason, and thence carried on the shoulders of some Jacobins to the Church of Notre Dame, she was placed in the same condition upon the altar, where she was worshiped by the crowd which filled the cathedral. The corruption of morals was general and deplorable. It spread over the whole nation. All the cities and large towns were scenes of civil murder, enacted in ways which fill the mind with horror to think of them. No man was safe, especially if he had any wealth which could be confiscated for the use of the fiends that ruled France. Thus events continued to grow worse, until Marat fell by the dagger of Charlotte Corday, for which she was sent to the guillotine. The jealousy of Robespierre sent Danton the same way, a few months after. The former recreant fell soon after, before a counter revolution, and the Reign of Terror ended. All these terrible calamities, and especially the infatuation which seemed to fill the whole nation, are justly symbolized by a noisome and grievous sore falling upon the men who had upheld political and religious despotism, and no one can for a moment doubt the effect they had upon these powers. Under the supposition that the contents of this vial were meant to symbolize republicanism, the plague of despotism, poured out upon the earth, it will be admitted that these events meet the conditions. The symbols of the text are strikingly satisfied, if not actually fulfilled.

I do not claim to be supported by authority in this exposition, precisely as I have given it. More generally, the noisome and grievous sore is supposed to symbolize French atheism, with no endeavor to find a meaning for the contents of the vial. Mr. Barnes adopts the latter exposition. My own view differs from this only that it makes the contents of the vial symbolize republicanism, while French atheism is only one among the plagues which fell upon the nations, as a consequence of pouring out the first vial. But it may justly be considered a chief one, as it was not confined to France. It broke out, with more or less malignancy, over the whole world; and it has been one of the great hindrances to the progress and triumph of republican institutions; for it must be admitted that infidelity and republicanism have gone in company too much for the good of the latter. But it will not be so when men have learned to distinguish between true and false religion—when the church becomes entirely divorced from her paramour, the political power.

I have been studying the prophetic symbols in this part of the Word of God for some months past; and, should the unfolding of the great schemes of Providence prove that the above exposition is correct, I should not be disappointed, for I have much faith in its correctness. While, on the other hand, should the true exposition be found in something entirely different, it would equally confirm my faith in the prophecy as from God, for I am not so presumptious as to suppose that it must be this or nothing.

Admitting the reasonableness of the supposition that we have found the fulfillment of the symbols of the text, you will, I trust, allow me a single reflection. The thought, that these old prophecies are being fulfilled in our day, is intensely interesting and startling. More than eighteen hundred years ago, an old exile sat among the rocks of Patmos, a barren island in the eastern Mediterranean Sea. He had been driven there, in his old age, by persecution; but, in the scheme of Providence, he was to receive, amid those solitudes, the most interesting book of the whole Bible, if we except the history of Jesus. Then the book of the future history of the Church was opened by the Lamb, and disclosed to the old prophet, by symbols always striking, sometimes sweet and beautiful, sometimes terrific in their significance, and sometimes sublime and awful in their portrayal. With his spiritual vision sharpened, he gazes down the shadowy vista of the future. These striking and thrilling symbols rise upon his view. Seal after seal of the great book is opened, and the wondrous events are passed before him. When the seventh seal is opened, the seven trumpeters prepare to sound. Under their successive blasts, he sees innumerable men and horses rushing to battle; the bottomless pit opened, evil powers, like locusts, swarming over the world, and desolating it; hears earthquakes shaking continents, sees the terrified mountains and islands flying away; heaven opened—angelic contending with evil powers, symbolized by fearful monsters—and hears the loud heavenly anthems of triumph rolling up, like the voice of many waters, from that vast multitude whose number is ten thousand times ten thousand and thousands of thousands. Then, when the seventh angel sounds, the seven angels having the seven last plagues come forth from the temple, prepared for their fearful tasks. Seventeen hundred years have passed. The darkness is deep, but the dawn approaches. The first angel goes and pours out his vial upon the earth. A plague and sore follows. The subtle influence shakes the thrones of kings and ecclesiastical hierarchies, and they totter to their fall. We look on with awe and wonder as we see these events transpiring almost in our own day and before our eyes. We see God in history. He has taught us to expect these terrible wars and commotions, and their coming meets our expectation, and assures our faith in His Word.

It is the conviction of your speaker, that in the millennium, for which the events of this period are preparing the way, republican institutions will prevail. Hence, any question affecting the possibility of such institutions, is properly discussed here. It is sometimes charged upon republics that they are inherently aggressive, and that they can only flourish by nurturing and giving activity to the military spirit, as if it must necessarily co-exist with them. Hence, no such form of government can exist when "wars shall cease to the ends of the earth." Such, it is contended, was the history of the Roman Republic; such, the democracies of Greece; such, the French Republic. The fallacy consists in assuming that the aggressive spirit which confessedly distinguished the peoples alluded to, is an offspring of their form of government, and not of something else. We could make a stronger argument against monarchism, in the same way, but we do not propose to do it, as both arguments would be fallacious. There is no such connection. The Roman

Republic and Grecian democracies existed in ages when the aggressive spirit was universal among all nations, and a pacific spirit, in connection with power to make aggression, was scarcely known. That republican Rome, or democratic Greece, should partake of the same spirit, is nothing strange. Indeed, the Empire of Rome was even more aggressive than the Republic. It can be shown that so far from a military spirit being necessary to their existence, it is that which usually destroys republics. It was that which subverted the Roman Republic. It was that which destroyed the French Republic.* The great mistake of France was her emulation of those old, warlike nations, leading her to suppose that her mission was to conquer the world by arms. Her danger would have been great enough if she had only used her military power to repel aggression. But in throwing down the gauntlet to the nations of Europe, to meet her on the field of Mars, she assured her own destruction. We may be safe in saying that as long as our own nation adheres to the pacific policy recommended by her founders, she will be safe. Existing thus for almost a hundred years, she furnishes an unanswerable refutation of the charge thus made against republican institutions.

* Note 8, Canto I, stanza 41.

III.

ENGLAND AND ITALY IN PROPHECY.

Ere the first woe is spent, another comes.—CANTO I, STANZA 44.

And the second angel poured out his vial upon the sea, and it became as the blood of dead men ; and every living thing died in the sea.

And the third angel poured out his vial upon the rivers and fountains of waters: and they became blood.

And I heard the angel of the waters say, Thou art righteous, O Lord, which art, and wast, and shalt be, because thou hast judged thus.

For they have shed the blood of saints and prophets, and thou hast given them blood to drink ; for they are worthy.

And I heard another out of the altar say, Even so, Lord God Almighty, true and righteous are thy judgments.—REV. XVI. 3-7.

IF our interpretation of the symbolism of the first vial be received, of course, we must look for the fulfillment of the second and third in events closely connected and nearly contemporaneous.

We should look for that of the second in events mainly transpiring upon the sea—some terrible naval war, which would result disastrously to the supporters of political and ecclesiastical despotism. And as France and Spain had been the chief naval powers which had, hitherto, supported the despotism of Rome, we should naturally expect that the disasters would fall mainly on them. While, on the other hand, we should expect that success, in any such struggle, would strengthen the hands of them who fought most in the interest of liberty. In studying the history of those times, we find, such were the complications of affairs, that England—though a monarchy, and much of the time fighting against the French Republic, and a declared enemy of republican institutions—was contending mainly for the rights of man. The sympathies of a disinterested lover of his race, therefore, naturally incline toward her. The naval war which she waged, about this time, was one of the most fearful, if not *the* most fearful, of history.   It lasted twenty years.   Her chief opponents were France and Spain, though Holland, Denmark, Prussia, Russia and Sweden were, at different times, arrayed against her.

We purpose to show that, supposing it was the design of revelation to foretell, by a fitting symbolism, the events of this terrible period, a vial of wrath poured out upon the ocean, by an angel of vengeance, taken in connection with other fearful symbols disclosing contemporaneous events, would be a most striking and appropriate method of doing it.   If John's prophetic vision should catch, through the vista of distant ages, the gloom, the fires, the thundergust and the flowing blood of naval warfare,* such as this period discloses, a mighty angel—rushing over the sea on the wings of the storm, throwing into it some potent substance, which raises the winds, the waves, and the thunders, and tinges its waters with the blood of living creatures, slain in the commotion—would, best of anything, carry to the mind an adequate image.   Seeing scores of great naval battles, as it were, condensed into one view, in the glass of prophecy, what better conclusion could be formed of it than that it was the result of some tremendous outpouring of wrath upon an offending world?

We may observe that it is not necessary to suppose that John meant to say that all the sea became as the blood of dead men.   If that portion of it which was affected by the vial, assumed such an appearance, it would justify his language.   The expression, "Every living soul died in the sea," is designed to convey to the mind an image of the dreadful destruction of life in this war.   It commenced between England and France, at Toulon, where a large French fleet was destroyed by the English, soon after the French Republic had risen to power.   Then followed the great battle of Ushant, under Admiral Howe, in which the French were completely routed.   The West Indies were, one by one, wrenched from the hands of France, by successful naval expeditions.   The capture of the Cape of Good Hope from the Dutch, added South Africa to the British Empire, and

---

* Note 10, Canto I, stanza 45.

increased her resources for the further struggle that awaited her, really, as the event has proved, for the destruction of Papal domination, ostensibly, in part, for self-defense, and for the promotion of liberty, but largely—it must be admitted—for self-aggrandizement. The French and Dutch fleet sent to retake the Cape, soon after this, were also entirely routed. The tremendous battle off Cape St. Vincent, was a disastrous and crushing defeat of the naval powers of France and Spain. Then, soon after this, the great battle of Camperdown added its blaze and rack to the smoke and conflagration which had but just lifted from the sea; all adding nerve and sinew to the already gigantic power of England, whom invisible hands were preparing for still mightier struggles. Napoleon had now begun his career, as one of the generals of the Republic. His known ambition and increasing popularity with the armies of the Republic made the chamber of deputies afraid of him, and they were glad to assent to his desire to go on an expedition to Egypt, that they might be rid of his influence at home. He went, revolving vast schemes of ambition in his mind. The career of Alexander was before him. Perhaps he might pursue the same victorious path to the Indies, erect another great oriental empire, and thwart the English there. With vast naval and land forces, he landed at Aboukir, in Egypt. But scarcely were the latter disembarked and well under way, inland, when the British fleet, under Nelson, hove in sight. The cloud burst in thunder and hail upon the fated French,* and in the awful battle which followed—the battle of the Nile—their noble fleet became a complete wreck, or captive to the English—the tricolor of the Republic torn down, and the flag of England floating at the mast-head of the men-of-war that had escaped the wreck of battle. Thousands went down in the terrible battle, and the water "became as the blood of dead men," for miles around.† It was a fatal blow to Napoleon's career in the East, crippling his resources, and interfering with all his future plans. So, after a brilliant, but, on the whole, unsuccessful campaign, he returned home to figure still more largely in those terrible events foreshown by

---

* Note 11, Canto I, stanza 45.   † Note 12, Canto I, stanza 46.

other prophetic symbols. But the naval wars continued. The northern nations, Russia, Prussia, Denmark and Sweden, became jealous of England's increasing power. They leagued against her to cripple it. The awful battle of Copenhagen soon after followed, again a great success to English arms. This gave her power and prestige for striking a last terrible and crushing blow upon the Papal powers of France and Spain. This occurred soon after, at the terrific naval battle off Cape Trafalgar, when their great navies (embracing all their marine forces) were wrecked, and England stood the acknowledged mistress of the world, on the sea, though at the price of the death of her gallant Nelson.* Elliott, as quoted by Barnes, remarks, with regard to these battles: "Altogether, in this naval war, from its beginning in 1793, to its end in 1815, there were destroyed near two hundred ships of the line, three hundred to four hun dred frigates, and an almost incalculable number of smaller vessels of war and ships of commerce. The whole history of the world does not present such a period of naval war, destruction, and blood-shed." The reader can readily see the bearing they had upon the Papacy.† No Papal power has ever since had any commanding influence upon the ocean;—a circumstance which has proved fatal to the ambitious designs of Rome, as without the supremacy of the sea she can never gain what she has evidently hoped to do—the supremacy of the world. As things now look, the prospect of any maritime power ever coming to the succor of the fallen Pope is exceedingly dubious.

Thus the events foreshadowed in the symbolism of the second vial put a decisive and irrevocable check upon the progress of Rome; yea, I may say, with other things, made her downfall, as a political power, inevitable.

But almost contemporaneous with the outpouring of the second vial, using John's language,‡ "The third angel poured out his vial upon the rivers and fountains and they became blood." Then comes the response of the two angels. This evidently foreshadows great calamities upon the power in question, in a country where her crimes against the

---

* Note 13, Canto I, stanza 47.   † Note 14, Canto I, stanza 47.
‡ Note 15, Canto I, stanza 48.

world had been more especially atrocious. Do we find a country meeting the demands of this symbolism? Northern Italy* is composed chiefly of the basin of the Po and its tributaries. If you look at the map, you will not fail to note how numerous are the rivers and small streams which rise in the Appenines, on the south, and the Alps, on the west and north, forming the Po, the Adige, and other smaller streams which empty into the Adriatic sea. You cannot find a country which could be more properly called a land of rivers and fountains. Lakes Garda, Como, Maggiore, and other smaller bodies of water in the mountains, supplied by the melting of snows which rest perpetually upon those lofty peaks, give rise to beautiful streams which flow, clear and perennial, through the vales of Piedmont and Lombardy, and make them the most delightful places on earth. It must be remembered that it was along the banks of the Po where Pagan Rome heaped up some of her greatest holocausts of the martyrs of Jesus, on the shrines of her Pagan deities. It was upon these same rivers and fountains that the burning star, called Wormwood, fell, when the third angel sounded, where the Pagan oppressors of the Church sunk beneath the tempest which Jehovah of hosts rolled down upon them from the northern wilds. It was here where, during the long, dark night of Papal supremacy, the faithful churches of the Albigenses and the Waldenses lived and suffered. The cruelties which Papal Rome inflicted upon these people have scarcely a parallel in all the long, dark history of martyrology. Even Smithfield pales before the horrors of the sunny vales of Piedmont. Rome was determined to have these regions to herself, even at the price of extermination of their population. Those rivers and fountains had been repeatedly stained with their blood. But the time of reckoning came, when those valleys became the theatre of some of Napoleon's fiercest campaigns. They are described as having been unnecessarily cruel and bloody, and his exactions of the conquered people unwarrantably harsh, under the sternest codes of military law. But the march of the great conqueror over that land was the pouring out of the

* Note 16, Canto I, stanza 50.

wrath of God upon the supporters of Rome, and the calamities must have been severe, to justify the symbolism of the third vial.   (See Poem, Canto I, stanzas 49-62.)

It must go for something to the student of prophecy, that all these fearful campaigns in Piedmont and Lombardy, hastened the fall of the declining political power of the Pope.   Nopoleon's rude assaults destroyed his prestige among the nations, and crippled his government, and that of Austria, one of his chief supporters.   You will also remember that the battles of Magenta and Solferino tinged these same rivers and fountains with blood, and hastened still further the downfall of ecclesiastical despotism.   This last war wrested a large part of the States of the Church from Rome, established the Kingdom of Sardinia, and laid the foundations of that United Italy which we behold to-day.   Could any power, short of the ALMIGHTY'S, have caused that these awful retributions should fall on Rome, in the very land where she had shed so much martyr blood?   Look at the awful record of those Italian campaigns, and see how appropriate is the symbolism.   Monte Notte, Milessimo, Diego, Lodi, Milan, Mantua, Castigleone, Caldero, Arcole, a second Mantua, the fall of Venice, the Senio, Faenza, Ancona, Loretto, Rome, Trebbia, Marengo, Magenta, and Solferino. Think of all these battles on a territory not larger than the State of Illinois, and most of them in the short space of five years, and tell me if you can find a more fitting prophetic symbol than a vial of wrath poured out upon the rivers and fountains, and changing them to blood.   See how the military powers which supported Rome were crippled, and mark how the leaven of republicanism, scattered in Italy by the armies of the French Republic, has spread and borne fruit, until Italy is united in a constitutional monarchy, with Rome for its capital, and religious liberty for its motto, while the temporal power of the Pope is hopelessly gone, and see if you are able to doubt that this third vial foreshadows these events, and was destined to aid in the destruction of the Papal domination.

IV.

NAPOLEON BONAPARTE IN PROPHECY.

Yet over the sun a dread angel arises.—NOTE 17, CANTO I, STANZA 64.

And the fourth angel poured out his vial upon the sun ; and power was given him to scorch men with fire.

And men were scorched with great heat, and blasphemed the name of God, which hath power over these plagues : and they repented not to give him glory.—REV. XVI. 8–9.

THE use of this symbolism would seem to be suggested by a quite popular belief, in the days of John, that the sun, moon and stars had a great influence upon the destiny of nations. Particular conjunctions and occultations of the planets, eclipses of the sun and moon, and especially the appearance of comets, were supposed to foreshadow some great national event—generally some calamity. Some dread angel of wrath, in the form of a blazing comet, casting its shadow across the sun, and eclipsing its splendors, while, at the same time, it might impart some of its substance to the sun, to increase its power of combustion, would well lead men to forebode some awful calamity.

As to the meaning of the passage, of course, we are not to suppose that a literal vial was poured into the sun. It is but a symbol, forewarning of fearful calamities. We remark,

1. There must be something in the calamities when they come, to justify the use of such a startling symbolism—in other words, the effect must be somewhat like what might be supposed if a great angel should pour some combustible into the sun, and by the increased combustion, so intensify its heat that it would scorch men.

2. These calamities must be more widespread and general than those foreshadowed by the former vials. There is no inconsistency in limiting the application of the third vial

2*

to Northern Italy. But, as the influence of the sun is universal, we should expect this symbolism would have a much broader application, and that the calamities would be much more widespread.

3. Scorching men with fire is one of the strongest symbols of suffering which we can find in the Word of God. We should therefore, expect that these calamities, whether similar, or not, to anything which had already occurred, would be far severer.

4. We should not expect that the principal actors and sufferers would be made any better by them. John says, "they blasphemed the name of God which hath the power of these plagues, and they repented not to give him glory."

5. Comparing this with the third vial, we should conclude that, while the main object of these calamities was to weaken despotism, they would not fall so directly upon the supporters of ecclesiastical prerogative. Blood was given them to drink who had slain God's saints and prophets, by having their rivers and fountains filled with the blood of the slain. But in these calamities, *men* are scorched. The more general term is used to indicate a more general application.

I now invite your attention to the question, "Have we anything in history which will answer the conditions of the above symbolism?" To show that we have, will be my next object. I do not say, however, that I cannot be mistaken. I follow the suggestions of our ablest commentators, having been confirmed in them by examinations of my own. I will seek to enforce them, also, with arguments of my own. I will say, also, that I have very great confidence that we have found here the fulfillment of this prophetic symbolism.

We may make the preliminary remark, that in searching for events that meet the demands of this symbolism, we should expect to find them in close connection with the events predicted in the third vial. Indeed, we need not be surprised if we find the fourth vial was poured out before the third, and even the second and first had spent themselves upon the earth. That the events predicted in former vials may, as it were, flow into, and be contemporaneous with, the events of this. For instance, if we find the sore of the first still upon men, and some of the battles on the sea and in Italy occurring after the train of events here predicted, has opened, we need not consider it as causing any confusion, or any objection to our interpretation. The object of the seven vials was not so much to trace distinctively marked consecutive events in the order here introduced, as to show how different opposing powers, and the same powers in different localities and under different circumstances, are to be put out of the way. Even if the vials should not follow each other exactly as they are named chronologically, it would not particularly interfere with a clearly marked fulfillment in other respects; though we must expect that the general chronological order must be the same.

On the supposition, then, that our interpretation of the third vial is correct, we shall, as a fulfillment of this, look for wars more widespread, more destructive, more terrible, than any we have yet contemplated. We find them in the wars of Napoleon Bonaparte,* in other portions of the world. There is no more terrible period in the whole history of the civilized world, than that marked by Napoleon's accession to the Chief Consulship, in 1799, beginning with the battles of Marengo and Hohenlinden, in 1800, and ending on the field of Waterloo, in June, 1815. Though the most Titanic powers were not unchained, its fiercest blaze did not scorch men, until, after the *coup d'etat*, the Emperor met the combined powers of Europe, first at Ulm, and then at Austerlitz, in 1804.

1.   Let us then see if we can find anything in these wars which meets the first demand of this symbolism. Is there any resemblance between scorching men in the intensified blaze of the sun,† and, in the blaze of battle, as presented to the world during the existence of the French Empire? We are to remember that John knew nothing about the use of gunpowder in modern warfare. God did not see fit to reveal, beforehand, any of the great discoveries and inventions of science and art. His sole purpose seems to have been to disclose to men his great scheme of redemption, leaving it for the progress of human genius to discover and utilize the great and wondrous secrets of nature. But he

---

* Note 18, Canto I, stanza 65.   † See Poem, Canto I, stanzas 65-80.

might disclose to his prophets, by appropriate symbols, some of the effects of great scientific inventions, long before they were brought to light. Such, we contend, he has done in this case. For, supposing John, without the knowledge in question, should have had his prophetic vision so sharpened that he could have looked down through the vista of coming ages, and have seen such a battle, for instance, as Marengo or Hohenlinden, seeing the blaze of cannon and the flash of musketry,

" Where the red fires of battle glowed,"

with men fighting and falling amid the glare, what better idea could he have formed of it, than that the fire-demon had been let loose among men, and was slaying them by the thousand? What if his ear could have caught the dreadful clamor of battle, and the blasphemies of the infuriated soldiery rising above the groans of the dying, would it not have added force to the impression thus made? Supposing a hundred battles, on as many different fields, some of them five times as destructive as either of these, all occurring within the short space of eleven or twelve years, could have been condensed into a single view, and to it should be added the glare of the conflagration of towns and cities, which so frightfully attended some of Napoleon's wars, what a fearfully thrilling picture would have been in his mind! Would it not have been the most natural thing in the world for him to compare the terrible commotion, glare, blaze, rack and destruction, to some supermundane agent—even to some potent influence flowing down from the sun, the source of heat, and scorching the world in its blaze? Would not the resemblance be sufficiently striking to warrant the use of the symbolism of our text? We are sure that it would be, and it will appear even more obvious as we proceed with our discussion.

2. Our second remark was, that the calamities should be general, not limited, as in the third vial, to a comparatively small territory. As the sun affects the whole world, they ought to, or, at least, a very large proportion of it. So the work and influence of Napoleon did affect the whole civil-

ized world, and even further than this. Many half civilized nations were scorched in the blaze of his genius. There was not a nation in Europe that did not feel the weight of his arms, and but one whose plains and mountains were not shaken by the tramp of his invading hosts. His genius displayed the imperial standards from the ramparts of Lisbon and Madrid, from the grim heights of Smolensko, and from the magnificent Kremlin of Moscow, from the towers of Vienna and Berlin, on the defenses of Copenhagen and Stockholm, and amid the Alp-bound vales of Switzerland. And he did not scorn to flesh the blades of the imperial legions on the half-naked barbarians of San Domingo. England, at one time, dreaded the flash of his merciless sword over her territory, leading on his invading hosts, more than any other conceivable calamity. Even our own country was not wholly exempt from fear, lest, having broken down all the barriers to his ambition in the old world, the greedy conqueror should attempt to plant the imperial standards in the new. A wider influence was never attained by one man, nor a wider waste and desolation under one leader. So this demand of the symbolism of the fourth vial is satisfied by the events we are considering.

3. Our third remark was to the effect that scorching men in the fire would indicate unusual severity in the calamities predicted. We should expect that the suffering and destruction of life and property would be unusually severe. This was the case. To get an adequate conception of this terrible drama in the world's history, you must become familiar with all the awful battles of that period. You must witness the fearful onslaught of Moreau, in the woods of Hohenlinden, when, before the battle,

> "All bloodless lay the untrodden snow,"

and see, amid the gloom of a winter's storm, the smoke of battle, and the blaze of firearms,

> "Where furious Frank and fiery Hun
> Shout in their sulphurous canopy;"

and the legions of Austria shattered in the fray, amid fearful slaughter, and the power of the chief consul extended.

You must see the imperial armies of Austria surrounded and captured at Ulm, and, soon after, behold the victorious Corsican on the heights of Austerlitz,* directing the most brilliant battle of his extraordinary career. There three of the greatest armies of Europe, each led by an emperor, (viz.: of France, Russia and Austria,) contended for the supremacy of Europe. See how the "Sun of Austerlitz," as Napoleon always afterwards designated that day, lighted up the fires of a conflict hitherto unparalleled. Napoleon won the day, but twenty thousand men went down in the conflict. As one instance of terrible destruction of life, in these wars, during this battle, the eagle eye of the Emporor discovered two thousand fugitives flying across a frozen lake, to join their friends; he ordered his gunners to elevate their pieces and pour a plunging fire of shot and shell on the ice; it was broken both by the falling missles and the explosion of shells beneath it, and the whole flying multitude perished.

> "Amidst the shriek and gurgling groan,
> The water claims them as its own."

You must see the two stupendous battles which crushed Prussia, and ground her monarchy in the dust; see

> Jena and Auerstadt blaze next on the sight,
> Twin furies of the same tremendous day.†

Then, soon after this, you must see the French eagle face the Russian bear at Pultusk, Golymin, Hielsberg, Lansberg and Liebstadt, where, in all, the Russian armies retired before the victorious French. Then, as the awful climax of this winter campaign of 1806–7, you must see these two gigantic powers grapple with each other, on the thunder-scarred and lightning-scorched field of Eylau,‡ where a drawn battle left the field in the possession of fifty thousand dead and wounded soldiers. Then a few months after, you should see the army of Napoleon, reinforced by a vast array of two hundred thousand men, and, in June, 1807, see the two great powers again in a death struggle on the terrific field of Friedland, where twenty-five thousand men went down in the shock of arms,

* Note 19, Canto I, stanza 65.   † See Poem, Canto I, stanza 66.
‡ Note 20, Canto I, stanza 67.

and the Czar was forced to the terms of the peace of Tilsit. Then you must see the blaze of Napoleon's wars beyond the Pyrenees,* in the long and bloody campaigns of the Peninsula. See the fires of battle at the two sieges of Saragossa,† in which sixty thousand men are said to have perished‡— Baylen, Reynosa, Burgos, Tuedela, and Corunna—where Sir John Moore fell, mortally wounded — Talevera, Albuera, Badajos, Salamanca, and red Vittoria, and other battles, which set the whole peninsula ablaze with the fires of war.§ These latter battles resulted disastrously to the arms of France, because Napoleon was called to face more formidable foes in the North, in 1809. Austria‖ had sent forward large bodies of troops into the Tyrol and into Italy, and Napoleon must meet her again. So, in harmony with his usual tactics, instead of meeting them on the old fields of his glory, where his young laurels had blossomed at Lodi and Arcole, he aims at the heart of his foe, by pushing his mighty armies, like an inundation of flood and flame, down the valley of the Danube. The armies of Austria go down before him at Abensberg, Landshut, Echmuhl,¶ and other minor points. As a consequence of this series of brilliant victories, the great conqueror enters Vienna in triumph, a second time. But the Austrians rally nobly, to crush the invaders, and, at Aspern and Essling,** towns on the flanks of the battle-field, he lost the first great battle of his life. He retreated, by his bridges, back to an island in the Danube, where he fortified himself, and, though in the extremest peril, recuperated and concentrated his armies, from the other side of the river and from Vienna, which still remained in his possession, and prepared for the awful battle of Wagram,†† where he annihilated the Austrian Empire, and put fifty thousand men *hors du combat*. From this point you must see the horrors of war increasing. You must follow Napoleon in his fearful campaign to Moscow,‡‡ in which, during both the advance and retreat, by battle, cold and hunger, he lost over four hundred and fifty thousand men, besides destroying many thousands of his foes. Ninety thousand fell in the awful battle of Borodino alone. Follow that vast inun-

* Note 21, Canto I, stanza 68.   † Note 22, Canto I, stanza 68.
‡ See Canto I, stanzas 68–70.   § Stanzas 70–72.   ‖ Note 23, stanza 73.
¶ Note 24, ibid.   ** Note 25, ibid.   †† Note 26, Canto I, stanza 74.
‡‡ Note 27, Canto I, stanza 75.

dation, its van wrapped in the flames of battle and of burning towns set on fire by the Russians themselves, to prevent them from giving aid to the enemy, see its climax capped with the wide glare of the flames of burning Moscow, and tell me, if some malign power had not been commissioned to scorch the world. Napoleon returned, humbled, to France. The sun of his glory was waning. But it had not yet lost its power to scorch men.* He repented not of his great ambition. He levied another army in France, vast in numbers, though he had to "rob the cradle and the grave" to do it. The powers of Europe combined to crush him. Yet he won brilliant battles at Lutzen, Bautzen, Dresden, and others of less importance. At length, at Leipsic, more than half a million men met in the awful shock of battle. For three terrific days the conflict raged, and one hundred and ten thousand soldiers fell in the strife. Napoleon was defeated. His retreat was fearfully destructive, as he, having been so universally successful, took little precaution to guard against disasters on a retreat. But many more battles were fought, and he still dazzled the world with his victories. Nevertheless, the allies closed in on Paris, and March 31, 1814, Alexander entered the city. The little island of Elba,† in the Mediterranean Sea, was given him in exchange *for the Empire of Europe.* He staid there but eleven months, when an uprising in *France recalled him.‡* The nation rallied around him again.§ Louis XVIII. left his throne, without a blow struck in its defense. Napoleon took possession, and the famous hundred days of the restored Empire astonished the world. He soon after met and defeated Blucher on the field of Ligny. But, in a few days after,‖ his sun, which had scorched men so fearfully, went down in the cloud and flame and tempest of Waterloo.¶ His retreat was a worse defeat than the battle, and, in a few days more, the allies were again in possession of Paris. The greatest military genius the world ever saw, was now banished for life to that desert island in middle of the Southern Atlantic.** Look at the foregoing picture, and tell me, if the

* Note 28, Canto I, stanza 77.   † Note 29, Canto I, stanza 78.
‡ Note 30, Canto I, stanza 78.   § Note 31, Canto I, stanza 79.
‖ Note 32, Canto I, stanza 80.   ¶ Note 33, Canto I, stanza 81.
** See Poem, Canto I, stanzas 81–83

demand of the symbolism of our text is not fully met—if scorching men with a great heat be any too strong a figure.

4. Our fourth point: Were the nations on whom these calamities fell, made any better by them? They blasphemed the name of God, which had the power over these plagues, and repented not, to give him glory. It is a well known fact of history, that impiety, blasphemy and atheism were never more prevalent than in the republican, and afterwards imperial, armies of France. It was France that "Resolved, that there is no God, and that death is an eternal sleep." Has she repented of her sins? Has Paris, the great Sodom of modern times, repented of her sins? Behold her infatuated people abandoning themselves to the furies of a popular insurrection! Before the thunder-cloud has rolled away, which has desolated her provinces, dismembered her territory, and laid a quarter of a million of Frenchmen in bloody graves, or left their unburied bones to bleach on the field, those infatuated multitudes are tearing each other. Read the history of Paris during the last half century. Have her people brought forth fruits meet for repentance? Ah! gay and licentious city, the curse of God is upon thee. Has the nation repented of its mad ambition to dominate the world? Have Germany and Switzerland repented of their atheism, infidelity and profanity? Does a nation of Sabbath breakers afford good and satisfactory evidence that they have humbled themselves under the mighty hand of God? Has Russia repented of her grasping ambition? She affords little evidence. Have supporters of ecclesiastical despotism repented of their pretensions and purposes? Let the history of their recent councils and decrees answer. When the Pope is exalting himself into the place of God, and proclaiming his own infallibility, it looks very little like repentance. When many are revolving another crusade to enforce papal rule upon the unwilling necks of the people of the Papal States, it shows that the supporters of ecclesiastical despotism have not yet relinquished their insane idea of propagating the religion of Jesus with the sword. They repented not, to give him glory. Ah! no, ye despots of the world, your tottering thrones and upheaving kingdoms must receive other vials of wrath, before ye repent. Your tiaras

and scarlet robes must be scorched by other fires, before ye relinquish your insane ambition. I shall speak further on this topic under the next vial.

5. My last remark on the symbolism of the fourth vial was, that, while these calamities would tend toward the destruction of religious despotism, they would not tend to that exclusively. They have affected other interests, and avenged other sins. The campaigns in Italy were mainly battles between Roman Catholic powers, so that, whichever side was beaten, the defeat fell on such a power. But these wider campaigns smote Protestant as well as Catholic countries, while all tended, at the same time, to the destruction of despotism. But we shall study this point, also, more on a future occasion, so we will leave it here.

V.

ROME, THE SEAT OF THE BEAST, IN PROPHECY; OR, DESPOTISM AS A HINDRANCE TO CHRISTIANITY.

Now turn, my muse, to that old throne of power.—Note 33, Canto I, Stanza 81.

And the fifth angel* poured out his vial upon the seat of the beast;† and his kingdom was full of darkness: and they gnawed their tongues for pain,
And blasphemed the God of heaven, because of their pains and their sores.—Rev. xvi. 10–11.

This passage will furnish us with a wide range of topics that are of great interest to us now, as, if our former interpretations are correct, we are now seeing the effects of the outpouring of the fifth vial. To present the subject as its interest demands, I shall have to spend several evenings upon it.

As this vial, being poured out upon the throne of the beast, was to affect despotism, directly, we will now speak of that, and some of its prophetic symbols, as used in other parts of the book of Revelation. We will ascertain the meaning of the phrase, Σπι τον θρονον του θηρίου. We shall show that του θηρίου symbolizes despotism.

1. We remark, then, in the first place, if we were looking for a symbol to shadow forth despotism, in all its forms, modes and extent, we could not find anything in nature, that would meet the demand. We must resort to some monster of the imagination, to find an adequate symbol. What principle has been more influential and varied? We speak of it as a principle, and not as a form of government. It is the disposition to tyrannize over others—to hold their lives, property and conscience in the power of another. It is the

---

* Note 35, Canto I, stanza 88.   † Note 36, Canto I, stanza 89.

same principle, whether we find it in the heart of the absolute monarch, or in that of the king, whose power is limited by the forms of a constitutional government. It is the same, whether it exist in the heart of a single man, or of a class of men; the same, when it assumes control of the conscience, as when it restrains the body; the same in church as in state; and the same in a republic as in a monarchy; so far as it enters into and controls these various forms of polity. We find it sometimes, in its most odious forms, in social life, and in the family. The history of the world is one, almost uninterrupted story of one man, or class of men, or one nation, striving to conquer and enslave another. The greed of power lies at the bottom. It adopts the code of the wild beast, viz.: that might makes right. Three-quarters of all the wars in history have been undertaken at its instigation. It was that which launched so many mighty armies from the gates of old Babylon, and bound the chain around so many nations, to form the old Assyrian Empire. The greed of power stimulated the frightful wars of Alexander the Great, so called. This was the animus of Antiochus, who figured so largely in the fulfillment of the prophecies of the Old Testament. It fired the zeal, falsely called patriotism, of the Carthaginians, in their wars of conquest. It spread the Roman power over nearly the entire known world. It exercised the vast genius of Julius Cæsar. The love of power propagated the religion of Mahomet. Fourteen millions perished at the shrine of the ambition of a Jenghiz Khan.

So we may conclude that it must be a potent influence for dreaded evil, that will spur men to do such deeds as have been done against it. Look at little Greece, rolling back, before the spears of her valor, the vast tides of Xerxes' army, numbering three millions of souls. Stand among the Alps and witness the brave Switzers' unending struggle for the maintenance of civil liberty. Go down into Piedmont, and see what the Albigenses and Waldenses suffered. See what battles the Dutch fought, for liberty, with the armies of Philip II. of Spain. On the other hand, when despotism is aroused to crush out liberty and true religion, and clothes herself with a false religion, what nameless deeds of horror has she not perpetrated! The rise of the Dutch Republic tells you a story, which fills every generous heart with indignation against the despot, and with admiration for the brave Netherlanders. See the Huguenots of France crushed down under the heel of political and religious despotism; witness the horrors of St. Bartholomew's day,—and then, if you will, turn and see France suffering the frightful penalty of those crimes against humanity and religion to-day. Hear the pibroch of Scotland, sounding among her valleys, and calling her sons, from age to age, to repel her invaders from the south. Follow the armies of Cromwell through their desperate struggles with the despotism of Charles I., while the nation was suffering the throes of the birth of constitutional government. Condense three-quarters of all the wars of the world, with all their tears, and groans, and blood, and death, with their desolation of provinces and their flaming cities, towns and hamlets, into one horrid picture, conceive of despotism as being the presiding genius of such a picture, and see if you can think of a symbol horrid enough to represent it. Think what a hell it has created in this world, and you will have to ransack the infernal regions, and study its nameless shapes of horror to find a fitting symbol for it. Do you wonder, if John says this monster ascended from perdition? Do you wonder when he says it shall go into perdition? To see it, along with death and hell, plunged into the lake of fire, was the culmination of John's mysterious vision. Millions are now looking for the millennium. Shall despotism cease during that happy period? Yes, and before it can commence; for it must be taken out of the way of the progress of the world toward that happy day. With this impression of despotism as a hindrance to the progress of Christian civilization in your minds, look at John's symbolism, and see if it is adequate. He first introduces it to our notice, in the twelfth chapter, as the great red dragon, having seven heads and ten horns, standing ready to devour the woman's offspring as soon as it should be born. He had seven crowns upon his heads, and his tail drew after him a third of the stars of heaven, and cast them down. I have no doubt but this monster represents political despotism, with that of Pagan Rome for its prototype, in its attempt to subvert Christianity with the sword. When the Empire became nominally Christian, the form of despotism changed, and another symbol is employed. This you find in the thirteenth chapter. A beast rose up out of the sea, having seven heads and ten horns, and upon his horns ten crowns, and upon his heads the names of blasphemy. He was like a leopard, and his feet were like the feet of a bear, and his mouth as the mouth of a lion; and the dragon gave him power and his seat, and great authority. This symbolizes some power taking the place of the dragon, as the possessive pronoun αυτος, referring to power and seat, belongs to the dragon, *i. e.*, it was the dragon's power and seat that were given to the beast. Thus, Pagan despotism resigned its power and throne to another form. No doubt, this symbolizes the despotism of the Empire, after it abandoned Paganism, and professed Christianity, but perverted it to the purposes of despotism, to crushing down, with an iron heel, all that did not subscribe to the creed of the Empire—Pagan Rome surrendering the sword of persecution into the hands of Christian Rome. Nearly the same symbols are used, the seven heads in both monsters denoting the seven mountains on which Rome stands; the ten horns denoting the ten tributary kingdoms, or, as some have it, ten forms of administration; the seven crowns denoting seven kings, in the one instance, and the ten crowns denoting ten kings in the other. Thus it was through the Empire that ecclesiastical despotism controlled the consciences of men. But, again, when the Empire was subverted, it is plain that some other symbol should be used to designate the persecuting power principally at Rome; for this power gained in influence as the secular power of the Empire waned. So, further on in the chapter, we have a symbol of this power, in the second beast, which came up out of the earth, "And it had two horns, like a lamb, and he spake like a dragon. And he exercised all the power of the first beast before him." But you will observe that he must do it in a different manner. Before the destruction of the Empire, the political and ecclesiastical powers were one, in both Pagan and Christian Rome, but, afterwards, when it was divided into a number of smaller empires and kingdoms, the despotism of Rome must exercise its political jurisdiction, through different channels, and by different appliances, though none the less effectually. It is now the one beast, but the ecclesiastical idea seems to predominate. Its mode of administration is suggested in the symbolism, the two horns of a lamb. The lamb signifies the appearance of gentleness and meekness, which the Papacy has always put on, in the exercise of its tyrannical and sanguinary powers; while the two horns symbolize the political and ecclesiastical prerogatives exercised by Rome. The ecclesiastical administration was nearly the same as under the Empire, while the civil must be wielded through the many kings which owned the supremacy of the Pope. Its hold, however, was upon the people, rather than upon their rulers, as it always has been. The second beast spake just as the dragon had spoken, decreed extermination upon all that questioned its exorbitant pretensions. The one beast is all-sufficient to symbolize that terrible power. What it decreed, was inexorable law, and must be unrelentingly executed, alike under the Empire and under the administration of the second beast. The kings of the earth were its servile ministers. Yea, they were compelled to it, for the Papacy had more influence over the superstitious masses of Europe, than the most popular kings ever could have. An interdict laid upon a kingdom, outlawed the king, and made it, not only the privilege, but the duty, of his subjects to kill him. Instances of such licensed regicide are not wanting in the annals of the Papacy.

But in the lapse of time, the assaults of the Reformers, and the progress of the age, very much modified the prerogatives of this power, so that it could not be symbolized by one beast, wielding two administrations. The hierarchy has lost much of its influence over kings, so that, instead of their being subject to its dictation, it has become a creature of their sufferance. Now, a different symbol is required. That is furnished in the seventeenth chapter, in the summary of the history of ecclesiastical despotism, there furnished. The Prophet is carried away, in the spirit, into the wilderness, and he sees a woman sitting upon a scarlet-colored beast, full of the names of blasphemy, having seven heads and ten horns; and the woman was arrayed in purple and scarlet color, decked with gold, and precious stones, and pearls, having a golden cup in her hand, full of abominations and filthiness of her fornication, and upon her forehead was a name written, "MYSTERY, BABYLON, THE GREAT, THE MOTHER OF HARLOTS AND ABOMINATIONS OF THE EARTH." The prophet also sees the woman drunken with the blood of the saints, and with the blood of the martyrs of Jesus. This woman represents ecclesiastical despotism, intolerance, the same power which had its principal seat upon the seven mountains of Rome. Yet, how changed in its form! From a furious beast, with the paws of a bear, and the jaws of a lion, with which, in its own power, it could grapple with the nations, and rend and devour them, to a beautiful, abandoned woman, dependent, for her influence, upon her charms and wiles, her lures, traps, and intrigues, by which she ensnares and holds her victims, sitting upon the back of political despotism, supported by it, dependent upon it, bolstered up by its bayonets. This describes religious despotism for two or three hundred years past. It has been dependent upon the will of various sovereigns, for the execution of its decrees. Let me ask if there could be a better symbol of the Papacy, as it now exists, than is afforded by this abandoned woman, dependent, for her influence, upon the display of her ornaments, and borne on the back of civil power. But this figure, taken in connection with others, shows that the ecclesiastical power is being separated from the civil. There was no way of separating the two in the symbol of the beast. But there is a very obvious way in which it can be done in this symbolism. The monster may fling the rider from his back. He has done this several times, already, and the Pope has been compelled to fly from Rome. And the time will come when the rider will be forever cast down, for the ten kings shall finally hate the woman, and make war upon her.*   Then shall the strong angel cry, amid the jubilation of disenthralled millions, and the hosannahs of those souls, upon whose blood the woman had made herself drunken, "Babylon, the Great, is fallen, is fallen!" and this shall be the end of religious despotism. No religious body shall ever thereafter persecute. The followers of Christ will then have learned better—learned that the peaceful religion of

* Rev. xvii. 16.

Jesus is not to be, and cannot be, propagated with the sword. But it will not be the end of civil despotism, as a hindrance to the progress of Christianity. We find a beast alluded to in this chapter, as "the beast that was, and is not, and yet is." As the old red dragon of Pagan Rome, it was, and is not; but, as the same power, under different administrations, it yet is. Mortally wounded on a thousand fields, its deadly wounds are healed. Cast down to hell, it rises again from the Stygian waves, and curses men with its presence. This old dragon appears again in the nineteenth chapter, as Satan himself rallying the kings of the earth to his bloody standard, armed with hell's furies, fires, and thunders, burning with wrath, that the empire of the world is slipping from his grasp. The man upon the white horse appears in heaven, with "vesture dipped in blood." Then comes the cry of the angel standing in the sun, to the fowls of heaven, "Come and gather yourselves together to the supper of the Great God." The man on the white horse descends; the armies of heaven follow him, on white horses. They rally all the armies of the church militant to the war. Angels, men and devils are arrayed, with hostile front, against each other. They stake the supremacy of the world on one great battle. The last tempest before the dawn breaks over the world—the beast and false prophet are taken and cast, alive, into the lake of fire, burning with brimstone—myriad myriads of their followers are slain with the sword; the fowls of heaven are filled with their flesh; the devil is bound and cast into hell a thousand years, and earth salutes her descending Lord and King. This is a brief synopsis of the history of despotism, as foreshown in the symbols of this prophecy. There are points in it, which I shall call up and discuss more fully, as I proceed. But I desired to bring before your minds, *the one power, despotism*, running through the whole history of the Church, until the commencement of the millennium.

To trace some of the effects of the outpouring of the fifth vial, in history, shall be my next business.

Let us then remark on this vial:

1. The calamities foreshadowed by it must come in immediate connection with those already noticed, and be a part in the chain of events tending to the same general result.

2.   We should expect that they would fall directly upon the source, common center, or seat of influence of the evil powers at which all these vials are aimed.   Therefore, as Rome has been, and is, the chief center of despotism—as the most disastrous forms of it in modern times have been stimulated by the example of old Rome, in the desire of ambitious men to restore the old Empire—and as it is now the seat of the most formidable ecclesiastical despotism the world ever saw, we should expect that the disasters would first fall upon that city—or more directly, upon the powers having their seat there.

3.   That, as the Pope is the head of despotic influence there, they must affect him very disastrously.

4.   That there must be something in them to suggest the propriety of the symbolism—something which, in some sense, resembles darkness.

5.   That revolution and war would constitute important features of the calamities.

6.   But that, while this is so, they must consist, widely and deeply, in something else, and proceed, not only from the influence of the fifth vial, but from all the rest combined, as allusion is made, even back to the first, as a cause for them.

7.   That they must be very severe, as they gnawed their tongues for pain.

8.   That, as the two forms of despotism—political and ecclesiastical—have everywhere been closely united, and, as the vial was poured out upon the source of vitality, they would affect despotism, more or less, in all parts of the Christian world.

9.   But that they would not work the destruction of either, only tend to that result by greatly weakening both, reserving this grand result until after the outpouring of the seventh vial.

10.   We are not led to expect that they would make the chief parties, and, especially, those at Rome, where the vial was poured out, any better, for "they blasphemed the God of heaven, for their pains and their sores, and repented not of their deeds."

We will reserve the consideration of these remarks to our next lecture.

VI.

We have pursued this subject far enough to note several very important observations before proceeding directly to the subject in hand.

1. That the outpouring of the vials*—or, perhaps, we should better understand ourselves, if we should say, the bringing into active operation the causes symbolized by their outpouring, as historic forces, while they may, though possibly not necessarily, succeed each other, in the order in which they are named—need not be at regular intervals of time. The symbolism, while it does not forbid, does not require it. One may succeed another so quickly—the two may seem to be so nearly contemporaneous—that it may be difficult to determine their chronological order. This may be observed of the first and second vials; and, if we notice the first and the fifth, as associated together in our text, by the allusion in the fifth to the sores, we shall be almost at a loss where to put the fifth, after the first. But this may come from the fact, that we have scarcely passed the epoch of history marked by the fifth.

So, again, between others, there may be a marked interval of years, as, beyond doubt, there is between the sixth and seventh.

2. We may observe that the causes symbolized, which are to produce the fearful calamities, need not, necessarily, be instantaneous in their preparation. Some may be gradual, like the rise of a river, swollen by rains, which sweeps away cities on its banks, and inundates large tracts of country. Others may require years, yea, centuries, of preparation, as the long attrition of the waters of Niagara finally undermined Table Rock, and it fell, with a crash, into the chasm below.. The cause and the effect must not be confounded. The outpouring of the vials are causes; the

* Note 37, stanza 91.

calamities which follow, are the effects—both adequately symbolizing historic forces and events. Thus, the falling rains and the attrition of waters are causes; the destruction of cities and the falling of the rock are effects.

3. Again, the effects of the outpouring need not immediately appear, nor at the same intervals of time, in each case. The taking effect of various causes, in history, may be similar to their preparation. To illustrate: some poisons introduced into the animal system, take effect almost instantaneously, while others may be months and years in producing death. Thus, if seven different poisons, varying in their rapidity of operation, be given to seven different individuals, successively, the seventh may be first to die, because the poison given to him, might be the most active. So, if the effects of these vials should appear, in their fulfillment, to be somewhat mingled, one event coming before, which, according to the chronological order of the vials, should have come after another, this need not cast discredit upon the fulfillment of the symbols.

4. We may observe, again, that the time when the effects of each vial shall cease to be traceable in history, need not, necessarily, follow the order of the vials. Thus, if we find the sore of French atheistic republicanism still afflicting the bodies politic of the nations, long after the waves of the sea have lost their bloody tinge, the rivers and fountains have run clear, and the sun has ceased to scorch the nations, we need not feel that the symbolisms are at all impaired.

5. Neither need we be surprised, if the effects of one vial become the causes of another. This is the order of sequence in the natural world. Every cause is the effect of some other cause, running back, until we reach the great First Cause.

Feeling the force of the foregoing observations, we shall not wonder, if we find the events, which are the fulfillment of these prophetic symbols, somewhat involved, nor need it shake our faith, if we do.

We will now discuss the points named in our last lecture, as meeting the demands of this symbolism.

1. Our first remark was that the calamities foreshadowed should come, clearly in connection with the events of the fore-

going vials, and be a part of the chain of events tending to the same general result, *i. e.*, to the destruction of civil and ecclesiastical despotism.* The vials plainly foreshadowed a series of connected events, interdependent upon each other, all, undoubtedly, aimed at the destruction and removal of obstacles in the way of the progress of pure Christianity over the world. We have found that political and ecclesiastical despotism have been, pre-eminently, the two great hindering causes, and we shall expect that the events foreshadowed here must fall heavily upon them. This was the case, as we shall see, in the progress of our discussion.

2. Our second remark was, that these calamities must fall directly upon the source, common center, or seat of influence, of these powers.† On the hypothesis, that the beast, in its various forms and modes of administration, as seen by John, symbolized political and ecclesiastical despotism, in their bearing upon the progress of Christianity, can we find anything in the events which occurred in connection with those already mentioned, which will answer the demand? We think we can, and those clear enough to satisfy any reasonably candid inquirer, whose theories do not compel him to an opposite opinion, regardless of evidence. We have no hesitancy in endorsing the theory, that Rome, the city of the seven hills, is the place where this vial was poured out, as being in harmony with, and demanded by, our previous expositions. Here were the causes generated which have resulted in the solemn, interesting, and, to the enemies of God, the fearful events foreshadowed by the symbolism of the fifth vial. And a point that I have not seen noticed by any writer, is well worth mentioning here, and that is, that there must have been a nearer connection between the first and fifth vials, than between any of the others and the fifth. This is demonstrated by an allusion, in our text, to the sore which was the effect of the outpouring of the first vial. The wars of Napoleon, upon the Papal power, were, no doubt, largely assisted by the atheistic republicanism of France—the sore of the first vial. This had been working upon the masses of Europe, particularly

. * Note 38, Canto I, stanza 92. † Note 37, Canto I, stanza 92.

in Italy. We should, hence, expect, and we shall find, that French influence was largely instrumental in bringing about the calamities of this vial of wrath.

Before proceeding further, I cannot do better than to give place here to an interesting prediction of an old commentator, Mr. Fleming, in an exposition of these chapters, published about 1700, quoted by Barnes. I cannot quote it in full. He entered upon his calculation, that the fifth vial would be poured out in 1794, and last till 1848, when the Pope would be banished, and the Papacy greatly weakened, but not destroyed, as other vials were yet to be outpoured. It is worthy of remark, that this covers the period from the first Italian Republic to that which succeeded the French Revolution, in 1848, both of which were affected by the leaven of French republicanism. Also, that, in 1851, the Pope was restored by France, though greatly shorn of power.

For an extended account of the events which followed the outpouring of this vial, I refer you to Alison's History of Europe, Volume I, pp. 542–547—a passage which, as remarked by Albert Barnes, could hardly have been more fittingly worded, if it had been written out on purpose for the history of the fulfillment of this vial. No one, who has read Alison, will, I think, accuse him of writing in the interest of this interpretation, as his sympathies were, decidedly, with the Papal powers, though not a Papist himself. It is an entirely unconscious witness to the foresight of prophecy. I can only give a synopsis of the passage here. It was under the instigation, and by the help of the French Directory, that Rome was revolutionized.*   It had long been its object of ambition, to plant the tricolor in the city of Brutus. The situation of the Pope, since the wars in Italy, had been extremely precarious, as the northern provinces were under the dictation of the French Republic, thus cutting him off from the active sympathy of Austria, which was then his chief supporter. I pointed out the effects of these Italian campaigns upon the Papacy, in my exposition of the third vial. It was now a favorable time for the outpouring of the vial of wrath upon the seat of the beast. The Papacy, deprived of its military support, impoverished in its treasuries by pre-

* Note 40, Canto I, stanza 92.

vious conflicts, would be an easy victim to the plague of French republicanism, which had been working and spreading among the people of the Papal States, until the Papal throne was like a city on the heaving sides of Vesuvius, just before an eruption which breaks forth and sweeps all to destruction. The explosion came on the seventeenth of December, 1798. A great crowd was assembled at the French consulate. A collision occurred between the Papal troops and some of the insurgents, who, on that occasion, openly wore the provoking tricolored cockade, and several were killed, among whom was Duphot, a member of the French Legation. This aroused the insurgents to open hostilities. Being technically a violation of the law of nations, it called the armies of the French Republic to the gates of Rome. On the fifteenth of February, 1799, a great crowd was assembled in the Campo Vaccino—the ancient forum—and, amid the cries and tumultuous cheers of the populace, the venerable ensigns of ancient Rome—S. P. Q. R.—after a lapse of fourteen hundred years, were again displayed and floated to the winds. In the language of Alison: "The multitude tumultuously demanded the overthrow of the Papal authority; the French troops were invited to enter; the conquerors of Italy, with a haughty air, passed the gates of Aurelian, defiled through the Piazza del Popolo, gazed on the indestructible monuments of Roman grandeur, and, amid the shouts of the inhabitants, the tricolor flag was displayed from the summit of the Capitol." Thus the Papal government was subverted,* and the Roman Republic, as it was styled, was inaugurated as the first direct effects of the outpouring of the fifth vial. The revolution spread, and Papal authority was speedily extinguished in all the Papal States.

3. In the light of the above, it is easy to see the truth of our third remark, viz.: That, as the Pope is the head of despotic influences at Rome, he must, of necessity, be the chief victim of these calamities.† Whatever revolutionizes a kingdom, must, necessarily, involve its sovereign. He was ordered to retire into Tuscany, under French, instead of his

---

* Note 41 Canto I, stanza 92.   † Note 42, ibid.

Swiss, guards, and to dispossess himself of all temporal authority. He refused to comply. Force was soon called in; he was dragged from the altar in his palace; his repositories were ransacked—even his rings were taken from his fingers—the whole effects in the Vatican and Quirinal were seized and inventoried, and he was conducted, in great ignominy, with only a few domestics, into Tuscany. Thence he was dragged about in exile, until in the month of August. Then, from the hardships of travel in the mountainous regions of the Appenines and of the Alps, the old man expired. Thus ended the Pontificate of Pius VI. His lamp went out in darkness, amidst the tempests of civil and ecclesiastical revolution.

4. This brings us to our fourth remark: That the darkness which followed the outpouring of this vial, must symbolize something in these calamities, which, in some sense, resembles, or would suggest, natural darkness. That the friends of the Papacy must have been in great doubt and perplexity in the midst of such unpropitious events, is the most rational expectation in the world. The plague now invades the very *sanctum sanctorum* of the Papacy, already stunned and weakened by the effects of the former vials of wrath, and drives out the sovereign Pontiff. What greater and more humiliating disasters could fall upon the head of the Papacy? If there were no power to turn aside the fiery inundation from France, what power could now roll it back, repair its damages, and restore the treasures which French soldiers had taken fròm the world's repository? Surely, his kingdom was full of darkness. Even the people of Rome, after the Pope was driven from the chair of the Papacy, were in a state of the utmost confusion and foreboding. Berthier, who commanded the French troops when they took possession of Rome, writes to Napoleon: "I have been in Rome since this morning, and I have found nothing but the utmost consternation among its inhabitants." As events progressed, they did not realize what they hoped from a Roman Republic: for the greed of France soon absorbed the Papal States and Southern Italy, as it had already absorbed the Northern States, under the illusory professions of establishing freedom for the people, where blood had so stained the rivers and

the fountains, and the condition of the people, under French dictation and domination, was scarcely less tolerable than under that of the Pope. And what can better describe the condition of the Papal States under Napoleon, after he had become Chief Consul and Emperor, than to say that they were full of darkness? All efforts to stay his aggressions, abortive; every barrier they had erected, sinking under the weight of his iron hand, where was the visible hope of that power—from what point in the political heavens, now dark as hades, could they look for light to break forth?

5. We are prepared by the above, to consider our fifth remark, viz.: That revolution and war would constitute an important part of these calamities.

It is, however, worthy of remark, that the great battles which have involved the fate of the Papacy, have not been fought in the hearing of the seven hills. Thus, the first Italian revolution was a logical consequence of the battles of Northern Italy—of Lodi, Arcole, Rivoli, and many others. And that which kept the Papacy in a state of servile dependence upon the will of the Emperor Napoleon, and its kingdom full of darkness and doubt, was his astounding successes in the awful battles of the period when men were scorched, as it were, by the heat of the sun. Thus, during the seventy-five years of its subsequent history, up to the present time, which are supposed to be covered by the symbols of this vial, so far as they relate to the seat of the Papal domination, all the great battles which have weakened that power, and brought it where it is to-day, have been out of hearing of Rome, with few exceptions. Great upheavals in mid-ocean have sent their waves, thundering and crashing, against the walls of the Eternal City, until, at length, they have broken them down, and overflowed the seven hills. The disasters of 1848 were effects of the great tidal wave of revolution, heaved up in France and rolled over the city of the Cæsars. The battles under the leadership of Garibaldi, which shred away from the Pope a number of the States of the Church, were fought, principally, in Sicily and Southern Italy. The battles of Magenta and Solferino, which confirmed the Italian crown, including several more of the States of the Church, to Victor Emmanuel, were fought under

3*

the Alps, out of hearing of Rome.   The collision of great powers, compared to which the troops of the Papal States were but a small handful, brought about these results.   One of the most terrible blows which the Papacy has received in modern times, was struck at Sadowa, where one of the two strongest, and almost its only, supporters, was struck down by Protestant Prussia.   This fearful campaign separated Lombardy from the Austrian crown, and gave it to Victor Emmanuel—an excommunicated son of the Church.   And the last great blow, which culminated at Sedan, has stricken down the other power, whose bayonets held the Pope in his place, viz., the French Empire; and to-day his capital and kingdom are both in the hands of his rebellious son, Victor. The leniency of the Italian Parliament toward the Holy Father, which some deplore, will, doubtless, tend more to disarm reactionists, and secure to the Italian crown a permanent possession of Rome, than that severity which would again drive him into the hardships of exile.   Thus, while revolutions and wars have clamored around Rome, they, as from the nature of the symbolism we should not expect they would, have not proved as severe as those foreshadowed under other symbols.   Yet, it must not be forgotten that the Papal Government has repeatedly become so odious to its subjects, that it has been revolutionized by the sword, and driven from its capital at the point of insurgent bayonets.   That no great battles have been fought around the walls of Rome, to accomplish this, only shows how low that power had sunk under the repeated shocks of former reverses.   He who once could have called the armies of all Europe around the seven hills, if that had been necessary, to defend his prerogative, could now call to his support but a contemptibly small army, a mere squad, in comparison with the mighty armies which won or lost the great battles of Europe, during that unprecedentedly stormy period.   Poor, sickly Spain gave Napoleon more trouble than all the power which the Pope could call to his especial aid, though he was the so-styled Sovereign Pontiff of Christendom.   Yet, his overthrow, under Garibaldi, was still more humiliating.   In the revolution of '98, and for some time after, Spain and Austria were taxing all their powers for existence against the aggressions of France and Napoleon.   If they did not send him many troops, it was because they could not.   But now, France, Austria and Spain, and other minor powers, all professed friends of the Pope, were at liberty, and nothing but the will was wanting, to send more than enough troops to crush both the armies of Garibaldi, and of Victor Emmanuel, too, if he should oppose them in helping the Pope.   The fact that they did not do this, shows how little influence the Papal power had.   France afforded her tardy aid, just enough to keep the army of Garibaldi from entering the Eternal City; that was all; while she consented to see the Pope robbed of nearly all his kingdom, for the benefit of Victor Emmanuel.

6.   This prepares the way for our sixth remark, viz.: That while revolution and war must be expected to result from this outpouring, the calamities must consist, widely and deeply, in something else, and that this must proceed, not only from the fifth vial, but also from all the previous vials, especially from the first, as allusion is made to it in our text. We can allude to but one among many of these effects, and that is, to the progress of liberal ideas not so immediately dependent upon great civil convulsions, which is surely rob- bing the Papacy of its power and prestige in the world. Men are learning that this polity belongs to a former period of the world's history.   They might submit to it during the dark ages, but now they are rising above those superstitious fears with which the Papal power has held such unlimited sway over the world for fifteen hundred years.   Men begin to see that countries under Papal and Jesuitical influence do not keep abreast of the age.   In this view, then, every new railroad built, every steamboat that plows waters where such crafts have been comparative strangers, every printing press put in operation, every free school house built—the dread and abhorrence of Jesuits,—every advance of Protestant churches, every step towards liberalizing the constitutions of kingdoms, every limit set to kingly prerogative, is a loud tocsin in the ears of ecclesiastical prerogative.

And here, I may as well say, that whatever is symbolized by the contents of the vials, it need not be intrinsically evil. If its effects prove disastrous to the powers on which it is poured, the conditions of the symbolism will be satisfied. If we suppose, then, that the contents of the fifth vial symbolize the spirit of inquiry and independence of thought which distinguishes the present age, and, although subject to many abuses,—as all good things are, in this world,—is the impelling power of the age, we should not do violence to the symbol. It is surely a vial of wrath, a sore, a mortal enemy to all forms of despotism, poured right on its very throne of power, and will surely work its destruction. As men learn to think and act for themselves, they will cast off the trammels which despots of every class and grade would throw around them. The open Bible, which this spirit is giving to the world, which teaches the law of equality and love, is the greatest enemy, yea, I may say, the principles drawn from its inspired pages are the only enemies, of despotism. For, while it teaches submission to the powers that be, as ordained or permitted of God, it lays its most crushing interdicts upon political or spiritual lording it over God's people. The Jesuits are plotting, and they will continue to plot as long as they have an existence, and they will, no doubt, instigate reactions in favor of despotic prerogative, as they seem likely to succeed in doing in Austria, with the imbecile Francis Joseph, but the spirit of free inquiry, amid the increasing light of the age, will, in the end, prove more than a match for them, and they will go down before the armies of heaven, which come on the white steeds of liberty and virtue.

VII.

AMERICA IN PROPHECY.

REV. XVI., 10, 11.

MY seventh remark, regarding the fulfillment of this passage, was that the calamities following this outpouring, must be very severe, as the men having the mark of the beast "gnawed their tongues for pain." This indicates extreme suffering.* The Greek word, rendered *gnawed* here, is found nowhere else in the New Testament, and but once in the Greek version of the Old Testament by the Seventy. There can scarcely be any stronger symbolism of pain, than is found in this. Several special remarks regarding it may, perhaps, quicken our apprehensions of its force in the application.

1. We may regard this suffering, in an important sense, as the culminating result of all the previous vials. We have already alluded to this feature. This symbol is, probably, an allusion to extreme thirst—so extreme as to force men to gnaw their tongues for pain. Take all the symbols, thus far presented, in their bearing upon this anguish, and see if the prophet has not made out a strong case. Men are smitten with a noisome, grievous sore or plague. Such a disease must, of course, be cutaneous. All cutaneous diseases are more or less inflammatory, and will produce fever and thirst. With burning bodies, we may suppose they go to the seaside for the cool breezes which fan its coasts, to cool the smarting sore. But the angel's wings have been over the sea; its waters are red with blood, and its basin a vast, hideous sepulchre of the dead. They fly, in horror, from the great, surging hades, to escape further contagion. Their thirst impels them. They hasten to the cool, mountain

---

* Note 43, Canto I, stanza 43.

valleys, to assuage their thirst in those sweet rivers and fountains which flow perennial from their unfailing sources. But alas! the footsteps of the angel of death have been there, and changed their waters into blood, while the land reeks with the stench of the slain. Horrors! Blood to slake their burning, maddening thirst! While they are looking here and there for relief, and, it may be, are meditating flight to the mountain tops to find it amid their eternal snows, the angel smites the sun, and his flaming rays scorch their already smarting bodies, and intensify their horrible thirst.

> O where is there covert in this hour of trial?
>   What glen, or what cavern, can shelter afford?
> O how can they flee from the flames of that vial?
>   Say, how can they 'scape the fierce wrath of the Lord?
>
> Will they fly to the ocean, and hide in its billows?
>   Ah, no! for its waters are reeking with blood.
> Will they seek the cool streams, 'neath the sheltering willows?
>   No! no! for contagion fills fountain and flood.

Yet men, in their madness, repent not, but blaspheme the name of God, which hath power over these plagues. While cursing and casting about for relief in vain, the fifth vial is poured out, the sun, as if his rays had been consumed by the previous burning, is veiled in sackcloth, and a horrible darkness covers them with its pall. Is there wonder that by this time we find men gnawing their tongues in the mad agony of their pains?

2. Remark a little further on the actual severity of the calamities indicated by this symbolism. If we note that the rapacity and iconoclasm* of the revolutionists, assisted by the French soldiers, far outstripped the Goths, Vandals and Huns, which of old had subverted the Western Empire, and even the Saracens and Turks, who subverted the Eastern, we may increase the vividness of our impressions. They out-vandaled the Vandals. The clergy, and the nobles who were also generally supporters of the Papacy, were stripped of everything; and those who were not put to death, were driven into exile. Many of the venerable monuments of

---

* Note 44, Canto I, stanza 94.

antiquity, which the northern barbarians had spared, were ruthlessly torn down. The iconoclasts re-enacted the scenes of Antwerp in the seventeenth century; and even that wondrous structure, the Church of St. Peter, narrowly escaped destruction. Alison says: "The spoliation exceeded all that the Goths and Vandals had effected. Not only the palaces of the Vatican and the Monte Cavillo, and of the chief nobility of Rome, but those of Castel Gondolfo, on the margin of the Alban Lake, of Terracina, the Villa Albani, and others in the environs of Rome, were plundered of every article of value. The whole sacerdotal habits of the Pope and Cardinals were burned, to collect from the flames the gold with which they were adorned. The Vatican was stripped to its naked walls; the immortal frescoes of Raphael and Michael Angelo remained, in solitary beauty, amid the general desolation. A contribution of four millions [pounds] of money, two millions of provisions, and of three thousand horses, was imposed on a city already exhausted by the enormous exactions it had previously undergone. Under the direction of the infamous commissary, Haller, the domestic library, museum, furniture, jewels, and even the private clothes of the Pope, were sold." Amid this accumulation of disasters, the symbolism of gnawing their tongues for pain, does not appear too strong. Of course, we shall understand that this anguish was mental, and not, of necessity, wholly, or largely, physical.

3. Still more, if we cannot see enough in these calamities, to justify this strong symbolism, we may remember, that we have, probably, not seen all that is foreshadowed. All was not realized in the revolution of '98. Other revolutions have since succeeded. Thrice has the Pope been compelled to leave his capital; and all know his condition to-day. What may yet be in store for him, of course, we do not know; but of this we may be well assured, from what has already passed, that the full cup of this anguish must be drained by those men who have written the names of blasphemy so thickly upon the seven hills.

I will call attention now to my eighth remark on this symbolism, viz.: That, inasmuch as these two forms of despotism have been closely united during their joint existence, if this vial be poured upon their seat or source of life, it must affect both forms throughout the world.   This is self-evident, and needs no argument to prove it.   If the heart be touched, the whole body must, of course, suffer.   It remains for us to trace the subject further in history, and see if such has been the case.   Have great calamities fallen upon political and ecclesiastical despotism, since 1798, in other parts of the world?   I must remind you, again, that we do not trace all the calamities which we shall name, to the fifth vial, but to others, in connection.   It will be remembered, that some of the battles foreshadowed under the third vial, occurred after the above named year; and all the wars of Napoleon, as foreshadowed by the fourth vial, after that date.   I have alluded to, and shall speak again of, their fate in France, Italy and Austria, in the course of current events.   I call attention to Spain, where despotic government and religious intolerance have lately been overthrown; also, to England, where there has been a steady, and, for. staid Englishmen, a rapid advance towards the full recognition of the rights of the masses.   There have, also, been encouraging signs of progress in other and minor nations of Europe.   But one of the most cheering indications is the manumission of the serfs in Russia, without bloodshed.   When we heard of that great Exodus from Slavery, we felt like shouting across the seas:

> Imperial Russia, hail to thy great Czar,
> Who spake the word, and serfdom ceased to be,
> Without arousing the dread fiends of war;
> My native land extends the hand to thee.
> Thy forty million serfs, at once made free,
> With our enfranchised sons of toil, may raise
> Their psalms of Freedom, borne above the sea,
> To our predestinating God, and praise
> The goodness that foreshows his wondrous works and ways.

This was a great advance.   But a great work must yet be done in that extensive Empire before its Emperor shall become only the executive of the will of the people; and we will hope that all her advances may be as peaceful as this.   It would be interesting to trace, more minutely, this advance in Europe; but I must leave the subject here.

During the course of my preparation of the poem, to which these lectures are designed to be, mainly, introductory, a friend asked me: "Do you find America* in Prophecy?" I told him I had what seemed to me a plausible theory on that point. I purpose to present it here.† I have a good deal of confidence that it is true. But let me say, that I do not profess to be sustained by authority. My hypothesis must stand or fall on its own merits, as it is not bolstered up by any great names.

Let me refer the reader back to the twelfth chapter of Revelation : ‡

And there appeared a great wonder in heaven ; a woman clothed with the sun, and the moon under her feet, and upon her head a crown of twelve stars :

And she, being with child, cried, travailing in birth, and pained to be delivered.

And there appeared another wonder in heaven ; and behold, a great red dragon, having seven heads and ten horns, and seven crowns upon his heads.

And his tail drew the third part of the stars of heaven, and did cast them to the earth ; and the dragon stood before the woman which was ready to be delivered, for to devour her child as soon as it was born.

And she brought forth a man-child, who was to rule all nations with a rod of iron : and her child was caught up unto God, and to his throne.

And the woman fled into the wilderness, where she hath a place prepared of God, that they should feed her there a thousand two hundred and three score days.

And there was war in heaven: Michael and his angels fought against the dragon ; and the dragon fought and his angels,

And prevailed not ; neither was their place found any more in heaven.

And the great dragon was cast out, that old serpent, called the Devil, and Satan, which deceiveth the whole world : he was cast out into the earth, and his angels were cast out with him.

And I heard a loud voice, saying in heaven, Now is come salvation, and strength, and the kingdom of our God, and the power of his Christ : for the accusers of our brethren is cast down, which accused them before our God, day and night.

And they overcame him by the blood of the Lamb, and by the word of their testimony : and they loved not their lives unto the death.

Therefore, rejoice, ye heavens, and ye that dwell in them. Woe to the inhabitants of the earth, and of the sea ! for the devil is come down unto you, having great wrath, because he knoweth that he hath but a short time.

* Note 45, Canto I, stanza 100.　　　† Note 46, Canto I, stanza 100.
‡ Note 47, Canto I, stanza 102.

And when the dragon saw that he was cast unto the earth, he persecuted the woman which brought forth the man-child.

And to the woman were given two wings of a great eagle, that she might fly into the wilderness, into her place, where she is nourished for a time, and times, and half a time, from the face of the serpent.

And the serpent cast out of his mouth water as a flood, after the woman, that he might cause her to be carried away of the flood.

And the earth helped the woman, and the earth opened her mouth, and swallowed up the flood which the dragon cast out of his mouth.

And the dragon was wroth with the woman, and went to make war with the remnant of her seed, which keep the commandments of God, and have the testimony of Jesus Christ.

I have already called your attention to the dragon, as a symbol of civil despotism, as exercised in the persecutions of Pagan Rome,—such an awfully malicious and bloody power, that John further designates it as the Devil and Satan. I showed that it was the same power, under modified administrations, which is designated in the seventeenth chapter, as "the beast that was and is not, and yet is." I hinted at the fact that this beast, political despotism, as a hindrance to the progress of a pure Christianity, would be the last to go down under the shock of the armies of heaven, on white horses. We may call this dragon the symbol of that which has another name, and that is "KINGLY prerogative," as interpreted by absolutists. It means the same as that to which we have already called attention. In such a connection, a few notes on the symbolism will be interesting and profitable, though not coming directly under my subject. The prophet says, "there was war in heaven." Satan had, as of old, come up to present himself before God. ·Kingly prerogative claims that kings reign by divine right. Why not? God says in His Word, "By me kings reign." But if we had His own interpretation of this expression, we should, beyond a doubt, find it *destructive* of the claims of absolutism. The first king which the Bible tells us of being chosen by divine direction, was given to His people as a mark of His wrath. It would be pretty hard work to establish the divine right of kings from such examples, surely. This claim was contested in heaven.* Michael and his angels warring with the dragon, cast him down to earth,

---

* Note 49, Canto I, stanza 105.

though he had drawn after himself one-third of the stars, who became the fallen angels, always on the side of wrong and oppression. Heaven repudiated the claim, and earth must become the theatre of the contest. "They overcame him by the blood of the Lamb;" *i. e.*, by the power of a Christianity embodying the great work of atonement, despotism is to fall. A woe* is uttered against the inhabitants of the earth, because the devil is come down among them, filled with great wrath, because he knoweth his time is short; *i. e.*, heaven having solemnly repudiated the claim that one man may be born with the right to rule over the body and soul of another, and that being proclaimed to the inhabitants of the earth, they will soon repudiate it too.

Let us refer, here, to the woman,† clothed in the sun, with the moon under her feet, having upon her head a crown of twelve stars. All agree that this woman symbolizes the Church, or that body of men that receives and practices the doctrines of Christ and his Apostles,—a glorious woman, clear as the sun, fair as the moon, and terrible as an army with banners. "She was persecuted by the dragon." Despotism has instinctively recoiled from the pure religion of Jesus; and in the Roman Empire it was a matter of State policy with her most politic Emperors, to suppress it, if possible, and they sought to do it by bloody persecutions. They foresaw what it would do to the Empire. It was this instinct which led that power, when it found that Christianity could not be crushed, to corrupt it, and make it a Ganymede to pander to the lusts of kingly prerogative. So the great significancy of the conversion of the Roman Empire from Paganism to Christianity, consisted in the acknowledgment that it had become too strong to admit of a hope of its ever being crushed by violence. The symbols of the sun, moon and stars, must not be pressed too far. They simply show the great glory with which the Church is yet to be surrounded and crowned.

When the dragon began to persecute the woman, after he was cast down, she made her first‡ flight to the wilderness,

---

* Note 50, Canto I, stanza 106. † Note 51, ibid.

‡ Note 52, Canto I, stanza 106.

where she should be nourished a thousand two hundred and three score days. Go with the Church of Christ, after the Papacy was fully installed on the seven hills; follow her into the vales of Piedmont, tracking her by the blood of her martyrs; listen to her solemn prayers and praises among the fastnesses of the Alps, whither she was driven by persecution; hear her groans in the dismal dungeons of the Inquisition of Spain; see her flying to the glens of Scotland; behold the smoke of her torture rising from the blood-stained fields of Bohemia, where the martyr, Huss, was burned at the stake as a witness for Jesus; see her contending, with unparalleled bravery, for existence on the dykes of Holland; follow her, in later times, in her second flight across the stormy Atlantic, in the cabin of the Mayflower, to this then vast wilderness, and tell me if you could find a happier symbol of her than John has here furnished us.

I call your attention, before proceeding further in this line, to the period of the woman's exile.* The days are symbolic of years—twelve hundred and sixty years—at the expiration of which she and her offspring should cease to be exiles, and become the aggressors upon the persecuting powers of despotism. Of course, the only difficulty in knowing when this event shall come, consists in determining when the period began. The task of fixing the exact date of the full installation of the Papal power as a politico-religious despotism, as symbolized by the second beast, is difficult, if not impossible. Authorities differ by a number of years. But all Protestant expositors, so far as I know, place this event near the beginning of the seventh century, when ecclesiastical prerogative made exceedingly rapid advances. Some of the dates at which various authorities have fixed this, are as follows: 538, 588, 606, 610 and 629. Adding the 1260 years to each of these numbers, gives us the following remarkable dates: 1798, 1848, 1866, 1870 and 1889. It may be remarked that the dates for the beginning of this power, were fixed by the different authorities in years when, according to the same authorities, the Papacy had made some large advance. I cannot stop to point them

---

* Note 53, Canto I, stanza 106.

out here. The destruction of the Papacy has been predicted for all these years. It is worthy of profound attention, that the year 1798 saw the first Italian revolution, 1848
saw the second, 1866 saw Sadowa, 1870 saw Sedan, all of
which were tremendous blows upon the Papacy. What may
occur in 1889, just one hundred years after the outpouring
of the first vial, remains for the future to disclose. All see
what has been accomplished. Political and ecclesiastical
liberty have been installed in the Eternal City, and the Bible
is freely circulated under the shadow of the Vatican, from
which so many bulls of suppression have been thundered
forth in the name of religion. Has the Church yet fully
returned from her exile in the wilderness? Or have civil
and religious liberty yet to receive and repel other shocks?
I think they have. I do not pretend to predict, but I expect
that whoever of us may live twenty years, will see a desperate effort made to restore the Papacy, undoubtedly by
arms, as that is their usual resort. The Jesuits are preaching another crusade. The battle of Armageddon is yet to
be fought, and they may be the leaders on the side of the
Papacy. When, or how, this must occur, we may not know.
Perhaps a vast army of loyal Roman Catholics will be gathered together from all parts of the world, into Italy, around
the walls of Rome. "Where the carcass is, there will the
ravens be gathered together." Victor Emmanuel, or his
successor, would not stand alone in opposition to such a
gathering. Millions would be arrayed against each other.
The seventh vial will be outpoured, and the powers of despotism will go down in the shock, never to rise again in the
Christian world; and Rome, or that which answers to the
symbol, will be destroyed in the great earthquake, either of
nature, or civil strife. Then shall the Church come up from
the wilderness, leaning on the arm of her Beloved, Religious
Liberty leaning on the arm of Civil Liberty, her first born
child.

I ask the reader to contemplate, one moment longer, this
remarkable prophetic period. Think of these calculations
of men who lived years before these great events occurred.
Look over the whole civilized world, and see how it conforms
to their expectations. Witness the great revolutions that

are occurring. See ancient prerogatives destroyed, sceptres broken, crowns torn from kingly brows, and robbed of their jewels, the royal purple of kings stained, dishonored, covered with ignominy; hear the crash, as tottering thrones are falling, one by one; hear the thunder, as the political heavens of great and proud empires pass away; hear the roar of the waves, as they dash against the ancient bulwarks of despotism; see those bulwarks falling; see religious liberty unfurling her banners over the ruins of the fallen thrones of her despotic persecutors; see the Church hastening from her long exile, and where is the stark-mad scepticism that shakes the head, in doubt that those lightnings, and thunders, and voices are the same which John saw and heard on Patmos, almost two thousand years ago. Great God, we reverently bow before the march of Thine Omnipotence, and acknowledge the voice of Him

> "Who plants his footsteps on the sea,
> And rides upon the storm."

* Thus far I have been sustained in my exposition, on the chief points, by our standard authorities. The hypothesis I now advance, is quite a wide departure from all, so far as I know. It is with reference to the application of the man-child,* born of the woman. Some say that it foreshows the increase of the Church. Some say that this child was a symbol of Christ himself. The true hypothesis, probably, is, that it foreshows constitutional liberty, as embodied more perfectly in the government of the United States. Perhaps it will be allowable to call it constitutional government. I wish it clearly understood that I propose to prove, merely, that if it was the design of the prophet to foreshow this form of government, the symbolism is well adapted to that purpose.

It does not appear, to my satisfaction, that the birth of one child could be interpreted as symbolical of a great increase of the family of God in the world. While, if it should be made to symbolize the evolution of some potent principle in human affairs, the symbolism would seem more

* Note 54, Canto I, stanza 109.

appropriate. Besides, if this symbolize the mere increase of numbers, it will be difficult to explain the meaning of the child being caught up unto God and unto His throne. If it denote increase of the Church, then it is a part of the woman herself that was thus caught up, as the woman symbolizes the Church, which would be an incongruity hardly to be admitted.

Let us, then, briefly examine the symbols in connection with this, and see whether they will sustain the hypothesis, that the man-child represents a government of free institutions, as it finds its nearest embodiment in our own. We will take them in their order, as mentioned in their connection.

1. This would most satisfactorily explain why the dragon stood ready to devour the child as soon as ever it was born. Despotism, symbolized by the dragon, and such a government, where all the citizens are equal before the law, are mortal enemies. They cannot co-exist. One must destroy the other. All know that the instincts of despotism have ever been to destroy republicanism as soon as ever it has been born.

2. All know that our republican government, so far as it is purely republican, was mainly the offspring of the Church which came to these shores in the cabin of the Mayflower. And, as yet, no other government, so nearly answering to the ideal of a model republic, has been given to the world.

3. The child should rule the nations with a rod of iron, that is, his influence was finally to become strong and controlling over the world. This does not necessarily demand that this, or any other republic, or form of civil government, should extend its empire over the world by intrigue or arms. The symbol will be entirely fulfilled, if its influence should mould the destiny of other nations. What are the facts with reference to this point? Does not every school-boy know that the influence of the United States is revolutionizing the world? It is true that there have always been aspirations in the human heart after liberty, but not until the blessed doctrines of Jesus began to permeate the masses, were they after an equal liberty for all. The republics of

Greece were sustained upon a system of the abject slavery of large masses of the population. The republics of Carthage and of Rome had similar defects in their internal constitution, and only became powerful by ceaseless successful aggressions upon their neighbors. The Dutch Republic, so admirably set forth by Motley, came very much nearer a realization of the ideal, because it was so strongly leavened with the Christianity of the Bible. But it did not approximate the ideal so nearly, nor attain so commanding an influence, as our own republic.

We may see, from the above, that the symbolism of ruling the nations with a rod of iron (or with a wide and controlling influence) is fully satisfied by the Republic of North America. This subject might be indefinitely extended, but I must hasten.

4. This also better explains the child's being caught up to God and to His throne. The Church gave birth to the principle, but wandered in the wilderness a thousand years before any extensive attempt was made to form a Christian Republic. But the principle was preserved by the especial oversight of God, as if it had been protected by the shadow of His eternal throne, until the time of the exile of the Church should cease, when it should assert its sway in the world. I have already noticed the flight of the woman into the wilderness, and her stay. In due time her son should be restored to her, and she and he—religious liberty, as enjoyed in the true Church of Christ, and constitutional government, the offspring of Christianity—Mother and Son shall go forth, hand in hand, to rule the world, casting their sunlight over its shadows, or cheering its night with the mild radiance which shines from the stars which glitter in her crown. Is not the day coming? Is it not almost here?

5. We find that the dragon, after the conflict described in this chapter, which probably foreshadows the times of Luther, filled with wrath, renewed his aggressions in fearful persecutions of the woman. It was after this that the awful persecution of the Huguenots, in France, assumed its most atrocious form, terminating in the infamy and horror of St. Bartholomew's Day, enacting one of the most stupendous crimes in history. After this, too, Spain, in the meridian of

her glory and power, waged her atrocious wars against the Dutch Republic. And let it be remembered that it was from Holland that the Church, in the Mayflower, first started in her flight to this country, and from France that the Huguenots came, who settled in various parts of the Carolinas, and planted Christian institutions there, flying from the persecution of the dragon of despotism.

6. I ask attention to a still more striking symbolism. After the dragon had renewed his persecutions upon the woman, to her were given two wings of a great eagle,* that she might fly into the wilderness, into her place, where "she is nourished a time and times and a half time from the face of the serpent." This is the same period, under a different symbol, that is mentioned in the sixth verse. As interpreted, a year, two years, and a half year, which would be the forty and two months of Daniel. Thirty days to the month would give us the 1260 days already mentioned. This is called her second flight because it is different from anything heretofore recorded of her. We contend that this symbolizes her flight to this country. I find that I am sustained here by Andrew Fuller, who remarks on this passage, "If one place was more distinguished than another as affording shelter for the woman during this, her second flight, I suspect it was North America, where the Church of Christ has been nourished, and may continue to be nourished, during the remainder of the 1260 years." But the most striking feature of the symbolism seemed to escape him—the two wings of a great eagle. I demand of any who may be skeptical, if it can be rationally called a mere coincidence that the Church, thus flying into the wilderness, has given birth to a great Republic, whose national symbol is the king of the air. Not as it was perched upon the standards of old Rome and of some modern nations, but with his wide pinions spread in grand and rapid flight. *I* dare not call it a coincidence. And when I look at the device which I have often seen, of a great strong eagle, bearing on his back, between his wide-spread wings, the Goddess of Liberty, personated by a beautiful woman, wrapped in the starry splendors of our national banner, and wearing upon her sweet

* Note 55, Canto I, stanza III.

4

brow the escutcheon of the nation, on which appear the stars and stripes which glitter on the flag, I think of that beautiful woman of prophecy, " clothed with the sun, and the moon under her feet, and upon her head a crown of twelve stars," flying to the wilderness on " the two wings of a great eagle, where she is nourished for a time and times and a half time from the face of the serpent."

VIII.

AMERICA IN PROPHECY.—Continued.

REV. XVI. 10, 11.

I MAY as well ask here, if it was the design of Revelation to disclose, by appropriate symbols, the future history of the world, as it relates to the progress of Christianity and its final triumph, is it not highly probable, that a nation, that has had such an influence as ours, in breaking down the barriers to such progress, would be set forth by some important and striking symbolism?   I answer, unhesitatingly, it is, and I will give my reason.

I affirm, what must seem reasonable to all, that a country of such vast extent, such unbounded resources, such great population, as this is likely to sustain—which has already done more for the spread of a pure Christianity, and weakened the powers of despotism more than any other nation—could not have been overlooked by the All-seeing Eye, when he wrote that book which John saw in the hand of Him which sat upon the throne.   It, therefore, seems to me nearly certain that the symbolism we have been considering, has reference to this country.

It will appear still more plainly, as we proceed.

We find that, after the woman's second flight, "the serpent* cast out of his mouth water as a flood, after her, that he might cause her to be carried away of the flood."   This is a very interesting and important passage.   It contains a peculiar symbolism, and requires something unusual in the conduct of the powers of despotism, to explain it.   Barnes says: " The figure here would well represent the malice of the Papal body against the Church, in those dark ages when

* Note 56, Canto I, stanza 115.

it was sunk in obscurity, and, as it were, driven out into the desert. That malice never slumbered, but was continually manifested in some new form, as if it were the purpose of Papal Rome to sweep it entirely away." This exposition, though having great weight, is still unsatisfactory. I find nothing in the history of the Church, during the dark ages, which might not have been repeated a half score of times, at all calculated to satisfy the demand of the symbolism. There was no great movement of floods sent out from the bosom of despotism, to drown the Church, which would seem to me to justify this figure.

This chapter is a synopsis of all that comes after it; and the events shadowed in this symbolism, should not occur in the dark ages, but much later. In order to substantiate my views, I call attention to the general structure of the whole book. After five introductory chapters, containing epistles to the seven Churches of Asia, and other important matters, three sets of symbols, of seven each, run through the rest of the book: 1st. The opening of the seven seals, with which the book in the hand of Him who sat upon the throne, was sealed. 2d. The seven trumpets. 3d. The seven vials of the wrath of God. Each set of symbols ends with the final consummation of all things. For instance: the opening of six seals of the book, occupies the sixth and seventh chapters, and, together with the opening of the seventh seal, gives us a general glance of the whole history of the Church. In the eighth chapter, the prophet enlarges upon the events of the seventh seal, by the introduction of the seven trumpets. He does not repeat anything back of the seventh seal, but specifies, more particularly, what he has already, in a general manner, hinted at. The next three chapters are filled with a description of the sounding of these trumpets. The account of the sounding of the seventh, is found in the last part of the eleventh chapter, in the following language: "And the seventh angel sounded, and there were great voices in heaven, saying, The kingdoms of this world are become the kingdom of our Lord, and of his Christ, and He shall reign forever and ever." This brings us, also, to the close of the contest, which must, consequently, carry us forward over the events covered by the seven vials. Commencing with the twelfth chapter, a more minute delineation of events already hinted at, is given, and the fuller history of the Church disclosed in the seven vials. Thus, the opening of the seventh seal includes all that is comprehended in the sounding of the trumpets and the outpouring of the vials. The sounding of the seventh trumpet includes all that is comprehended in the seven vials.

You will observe that the twelfth chapter introduces a new series of visions, and, as Barnes says, is properly introductory to all that comes after,—as we have called it a synopsis of the whole. There is, therefore, no necessity of looking for the fulfillment of the passage we are considering, in the dark ages of the Church. I think it comes more naturally towards the close of the period, largely, as I am contending, during the period covered by the fifth vial. After coming to this conclusion, I was very happy to find the following in the writings of Andrew Fuller: "The flood of waters cast after the woman by the dragon, and the war upon the remnant of her seed, referring, as it appears, to the latter end of the twelve hundred and sixty years, may be something yet to come."

With reference to the flood of waters, you find that the abandoned woman of the seventeenth chapter is represented as seated upon many waters. The angel himself, in that chapter, interprets this symbolism to John: "The waters which thou sawest are peoples, and multitudes, and nations, and tongues." If the floods of waters there means multitudes of peoples, it must mean the same here. The power which persecuted the woman, sent after her a multitude of men, of nations, and peoples, and tongues, to overbear her, live her down, sweep her away as with a flood. Note, narrowly:

1. That these waters were cast out of the dragon's mouth, or from the midst of the power which overspread so large a portion of Europe. The multitudes went, at the instigation or command from his mouth. They were separated from the place where he had his seat, as if—the woman having fled beyond where he could go after her in person—he should send his emissaries after her, in great multitudes, to destroy her.

2. That there was no country in Europe into which this power had sent its emissaries to suppress the true Church, in sufficient numbers to justify this figure. Hence, it does not relate to anything that has yet occurred there.

Let the hypothesis be kept in mind, that the dragon represents the persecuting powers of despotism, which see in the true Church a mortal enemy, and are striving to destroy both her and her offspring, and we will see if there is anything in the history of our own country which justifies such a symbolism.

1. The vanguard of the floods, which came to this country at the behest of despotism,* were the negroes—the victims of American slavery. It was the minions of despotism from over the sea that planted slavery here. No matter if it was Protestant England. She was under the curse of the dragon's power, and had not yet been emancipated from ecclesiastical despotism, for she persecuted. Besides, let us remember that it was not so much ecclesiastical as political despotism, which was active against the liberties of mankind in those days, here, which will justify the use of the dragon as a symbol, instead of the beast which is afterwards introduced. So despotism sent here its multitudes of blacks, as essential to the system of slavery that was to blight our name, blacken our annals, and threaten our existence. That this came from the heart of the dragon, no one can doubt.

2. Then, after the Church had been nourished here in this wilderness for one hundred and fifty years, and God was about to restore her offspring, constitutional liberty, to her, English and Hessian armies, sent here in the service of despotism, swarmed our lands and darkened our waters, to swallow up the man-child that was about to commence his career in the world. It was England's purpose to sweep away the woman's offspring as with a flood.

No one can fail to see that these events very plausibly satisfy the demands of this symbolism, yet not in full. We ought to find something which has a more direct aim at the destruction of the woman than either of these. England's

* Note 57, Canto I, stanza 121.

aim was not at the Church, but to the end of keeping the colonies in a state of vassalage, under the foot of the dragon. The devil saw that political despotism would serve his end here, and he used it. But to meet the demands of the case more fully, we should expect that he would bring some other agencies into operation.

3. We find these in what is transpiring among us—in the multitudes of Papists which pour a ceaseless flood upon our shores every year, and in the wily designs* and far-seeing policy of the Papacy, with reference to our country. Their designs will be futile and their policy will be balked, I fully believe; but who does not know that Jesuitism aims at the control of this country, through the waters which the dragon has thus cast forth, to cause the woman to be carried away of the flood? Who does not know that they are making their boasts that it is only a question of time when their minions shall be installed in the high places of trust in our land? Who does not know that they look to the swelling of these waters by more rapid multiplication among us, for the flood which shall sweep our Protestant religion from the high vantage ground it has hitherto occupied? Who does not know that the physical deterioration of American women, from following the wretched fashions and modes of life adopted here, and from the unnatural aversion to the burdens of maternity, inducing, in some cases, a crime at which the unperverted heart revolts with horror, and should make every true mother turn pale at the thought of it—prevailing among those who lead society—enters as a large element into their calculation of this result? And what man, with his eyes open, does not see that there is danger in this direction?

This subject is of such vital importance to Americans,† that I feel constrained to enlarge somewhat more upon it. But first I must be allowed to say that I do not claim that these symbols have an entire reference to our country. The utmost I would claim is that they have a more striking resemblance to the events of our history than to any others that have occurred. There is no other nation on the pages

---

* Note 58, Canto I, stanza 150.　　　　　　† Note 59, Canto I, stanza 150.

of history, since the flight of Israel from Egypt, which originated from a body of men flying from religious persecution. The resemblance is too striking to pass unnoticed. But the Church belongs to the whole world. As the theatre of her conflicts, foreshadowed in the first part of this chapter, was the whole Christian world, so I believe that the theatre of the war waged by the dragon upon the woman and her seed, mentioned in the last part of the chapter, will be the whole Christian world greatly enlarged. My principal aim has been to show that America was one of the chief objects which passed before the prophet's vision in these peculiar symbols.

Let us look a little more closely at the designs of Rome* upon our Protestant religion. The intelligent student need not be reminded that the Papal hierarchy are, and have always been, enemies of republican institutions. The controlling power of a great Church, which acknowledges a head who claims infallibility, cannot be otherwise than an unmitigated despotism in itself. No subject has a right to think, or speak, or act for himself, if he thinks, speaks, or acts contrary to the will of the Pope. All must bend in abject obeisance to him. They are bound by their oath to the Church to believe whatever he tells them is the will of Heaven. Now, the very essence of republican institutions is the right to think, speak, and act for one's self, upon individual responsibility, only restrained from actions which would come in conflict with some of the natural rights of others. This is the pre-eminent distinction of such institutions. This right opens the Bible to all, secures to all a right to read and interpret it for themselves, secures free speech to all, eventuates in free schools for the masses, and of course covers the whole, and makes them all available to each citizen by guaranteeing to him his own personal liberty, when not forfeited by crime. To be sure, the Jesuits, who so largely control the Papacy, being cutters and trimmers, can manage to live under all forms of human government, and yield an external obedience to the powers that be. So they live, and profess to be loyal under our form of govern-

* Note.60, Canto I, stanza 150.

ment.   But who cannot see that they are enemies to free institutions.*   Their aversion to an open Bible is unmistakably declared by their efforts to banish it from our public schools.   Their plea that our version is a sectarian book is glaringly insincere, since they refuse to allow their own version a place there.   That they are the declared enemies of our free schools is also notorious.   That they would destroy them if they could, needs no better proof than we have already.   They know very well that an educated constituency are not always going to be held in their leading strings.   They know as well that if the educated classes of Catholic countries are attached to the Papacy, it is because, being privileged classes, they would use that Church to keep their vassals ignorant of their rights to secure a continuance of their vassalage.   That they deny the right of free discussion is notorious, and that they would rob men of it if they could needs no argument to show.

Now every schoolboy must know that if an open Bible,† free schools and free speech be taken from our people, republican institutions will be impossible.   Let it be understood that every attempt upon these things in this country is made by the enemies of the Republic, whatever their professions may be.   Put it down as one of the swellings and ebullitions of the waters with which the dragon would carry away the woman.   I have very little doubt of the significancy of these symbols in this direction.

These symbols properly suggest the methods with which they hope to accomplish their work.   A flood symbolizes a vast number of people.   If they hope to carry away our Protestant religion, it is by vastly preponderating numbers.‡ In a country where all have a right to the ballot-box, this can be done as soon as they have a majority, unless the minority resist by force, which would be revolutionary. They already have that majority in some of our largest cities, which are as much under Papal rule as Madrid or Paris ever was.   If the dragon could flood our ballot-boxes, he would undoubtedly accomplish his purposes in this direction.   That he is pouring his floods upon our shores for this

* Note 61, Canto I, stanza 151.   † Note 62, Canto I. stanza 152.
‡ Note 63, Caton I. stanza 155.

4*

purpose no sensible man, Roman Catholic or Protestant, doubts for a moment.

The propriety of this interpretation is also suggested by the vigor of the institutions and the persistency of the appliances with which the Papacy seeks to outweigh us. To see the churches,* monasteries, colleges, and other public buildings they are erecting all over the land, and especially in our Western States, a stranger would almost conclude that he had sat down in a Roman Catholic country. The manner of their building and the permanency of their structures show conclusively that they hope to possess the land. But I predict from these prophecies that these very structures will be used by the children of these zealous Papists for the promotion of a purer and better religion,— the religion of Jesus purged from the abuses with which the Papacy has loaded it.

I invite attention for a moment to the next verse: "And the earth helped the woman; and the earth opened her mouth and swallowed up the flood which the dragon cast out of his mouth." Earthquakes, as symbols in the Word of God, mean civil commotions, convulsions, revolutions and wars. These things should help the Church, though not made in her behalf, but for ambitious purposes. We have seen that the revolutions and wars foreshadowed by the outpouring of the vials, thus far, though for the most part not undertaken in behalf of civil and religious liberty, have invariably resulted in disaster to despotism.

How has it been in the crises of our own history? How was it in the Revolutionary War? Much as we revere and praise the valor and glory of our revolutionary fathers, if we are good students of history, we shall have to admit that our cause must have failed, if the earth, in the sense of this passage, had not helped the cause of religion and liberty. It was the rivalry of England and France which, under God, delivered us. If it had not been for French aid and sympathy, after the successful battle of Saratoga—which afforded them an excuse for interfering in our behalf—the cloud of despotism, humanly speaking, would not have lifted off our land.

* Note 64, Canto I, stanza 155.

So in our second struggle with England, she had Napoleon Bonaparte on her hands, or the result might have been different then.

So also the earth helped the cause of Freedom in our great Rebellion.   Neither party was fighting directly for Emancipation.   Doubtless, if the few friends of such a measure had taken the sword to promote it, they would all have perished by the sword.   It was the rivalry of great political parties, which precipitated the fearful war.   Defending the institution of Slavery, was, for the most part, only a pretext with Southern leaders, their real object being personal ambition, while the armies of the Union were mainly fighting for its integrity.   Every one knows that there were thousands among the latter, who would not have struck a blow, if that had been the distinct issue in the beginning, unless it had been on the other side—enough, doubtless, to have turned the scale against us.   But the earth helped the seed of the woman, and Slavery sunk under the fifth vial of Almighty wrath.   So, doubtless, it will be in all future conflicts with the Papacy.

IX.

PARIS UNDER THE FIFTH VIAL.

REV. XVI. 10, 11.

BEFORE proceeding with this subject, we will remark a little further with reference to the earth's helping the woman. We reverted to several particular instances of this, in our last, and hinted that, by some such interpretation, it might be expected that the cause of truth would be helped in all the future conflicts with the Papacy. We have a remarkable record of the kind now to make. The same political earthquake which swallowed up those who defended domestic Slavery among us, threw into our body politic a counteracting flood, to balance at the polls the floods with which the Papacy would seek to carry our Protestant religion away. I allude to the four million blacks, whose volume before, in point of numbers, was cast by their masters into the flood which was seeking to engulf Freedom, in the increased suffrage their slaves gave to them. And as in the case of Emancipation, no one thought of protecting the Protestant religion by this movement. It was still the rivalry of parties seeking to gain, or hold, the seats of power. Yet such has, undoubtedly, been the result. The Irish and African elements (I speak without disrespect to either) will not for many years, if ever, be ranged under the same party banners—such is the antagonism between them. Pat—"*niver a bit of it*"—is going to the polls to vote on the same side with Sambo. The political party which would have one, must inevitably do that which will cut it off from sympathy with the other. And this state of things must continue until Pat rises above the narrow prejudices which persuade him that he has a right to monopolize all the labor in the country, and he is taught that other races have a right to our broad land as well as the Celtic. Until then, Protestant Sambo, who can now count about as many fingers in the political pie as Papistical Pat, will serve as a strong check upon any designs which Jesuits have upon this country, through Pat's help at the polls. Then we may confidently expect that Pat will pass his minority and conclude to set up for himself—*i. e.*, think, act and vote for himself, and not as designing Jesuitism secretly points out.

Mark how the malice of Satan overreached itself in this instance—how Satan cast out Satan. We have seen how political and ecclesiastical despotism have been twin sisters during their joint existence; how they have supported each other; how that which has helped one has always helped the other, and how that which has hurt one has hurt the other. Satan instigated greedy despotism to plant Slavery here, so as to doom this country to the most odious form of tyranny that ever existed, and, to human view, he came near succeeding, for it dominated this country for more than a half century. But this political earthquake which swallowed up Slavery, by enfranchising its victims, struck the first great and stunning blow upon the Papacy in this country, *i. e.*, provided Protestants take care of these forming elements of political power.

This same blind prejudice may be preparing another stunning blow upon this intriguing power, in the case of John Chinaman, who may yet become a lad of some importance, toward whom Pat is showing the same hostility which he has manifested toward the negro. At any rate, if our interpretation of this symbolism be correct, we may rest entirely assured that the earth will help the woman and her seed, and open her mouth and swallow up the flood which the dragon cast out of his mouth, so that neither she nor her offspring will be carried away of the flood.

We now return to notice more directly the symbolism of the fifth vial.

I call attention to my ninth remark on this, viz.: *That we should not expect that it would work the entire destruction of the anti-Christian powers, those hindrances which have been in the way of Christianity. It would only greatly weaken them.* They were still alive amid the darkness—they gnawed their tongues for pain, they could still blaspheme the name of God, because of their pains and their sores, and they repented not of their deeds. The beast which has lived so long must die a hard death. Even when the spear of Saint George (to use one of their own legends as an illustration) has transfixed the heart of the dragon, his dying agonies will shake the world, cast down the stars of heaven, (thrones and empires,) and cause the earth to open her mouth and swallow up the city of the seven hills, whereon he has had his seat. He may now have received his mortal wound, and the future great struggles foreshadowed in the next vials may be his dying agonies. What they may be we cannot predict. But we may judge of their general character from what has already occurred. If former symbols foreshadow civil convulsions, we must, of course, look for something similar in the future. Neither can we tell when they will occur. But one thing we know certainly, and that is, they will work the utter destruction of all anti-Christian powers.

I now call attention to my tenth, and last, remark upon the symbolism of the fifth vial, viz.: That the calamities would not make the persons affected by them any better. In their agony they blasphemed the God of heaven, and repented not of their deeds.

I call attention to the fact that the Papacy is still blaspheming the name of God—writing its names of blasphemy upon the seven heads of the monster on which the scarlet woman is seated. Take the decree of the Ecumenical Council, at Rome, in the year of grace, 1870—a year not to be forgotten by the Church, through eternity. THE INFALLIBILITY OF THE POPE!* much as its supporters and apologists may endeavor to gloss it over to cover its glaring impiety from Protestant eyes, much as they may endeavor to sugar-coat the pill, to make it go down smoothly into stomachs which already begin to nauseate with their absurd doses, that decree is a glaring blasphemy, hurled into the face of Deity, to support the consciously sinking cause of the Papacy. If they can make their adherents believe that the so-called Holy Father is infallible, they can easily make them do whatever, in their opinion, may restore or strengthen

---

* See Poem, Canto I, stanzas 142-148.

the cause of the hierarchy. Provided the two hundred millions of Roman Catholics should endorse the monstrous assumption, it would place a still frightful power in the hands of the Pope. It might restore again his pristine control over the nations, and make kings again obedient to his nod. In the desperation of his circumstances, the experiment is worth trying. If it succeed, he can preach another crusade to restore the States of the Church to his kingdom, and millions of Roman Catholics will rush to his standards. He can lay aside his Shepherd's crook, take the sword, and lead his own armies to great achievement.

So the great lights of the hierarchy swarm to Rome, bow at the feet of the Pope, perform the highly dignified operation of kissing his toe, and, in solemn mockery, ascribe to him an attribute belonging only to Deity. Perhaps two hundred million Roman Catholics will follow the example of these great lights in what they have done. But it surpasses my own belief. Many will do it, no doubt, and, it may be, make it possible for the Papacy to preach another crusade. But it will be its expiring struggle. The mass of the Roman Catholic world, I do believe, are too sensible, long to follow such leaders. Germany, under the leadership of Dr. Dollinger, refuses to endorse it, and seems swinging away from her moorings to the Eternal City. Other peoples will follow. When the idea of an infallible Church and an infallible Pope is exploded, the power of the Papacy is hopelessly gone. The Catholic Churches will thenceforward begin to fall into line with the Protestant, and they will vie with each other in spreading the knowledge of Jesus. That the powers which have controlled that Church will foment wars, is morally certain. That many will perish in them, will be a necessary consequence, but it will be a comparatively small proportion of the two hundred millions, no doubt. The rest will join the parties of progress, when the beast is overthrown.

That the Papacy has not repented of its deeds is equally clear. None of its edicts in former times, justifying persecution, have been revoked. None of its claims to the right of penal inflictions have been abated. Not even the slaughter of St. Bartholomew's Day has ever been publicly repudiated.

That these leaders will not repent, until they are overthrown in the civil convulsions they themselves foment, is a point about which there can be no doubt.

To close up our remarks upon the symbolism of the fifth vial, let us now revert to France,* and especially to Paris. There can be no doubt that the capital of the most influential kingdom that has for ages upheld the pretensions of the Papacy, and, at its bidding, bathed the secular sword in the blood of millions to exterminate heretics, is comprehended, if not expressly pointed out, in the symbols which foreshadow the present period of history. I call attention to a hypothesis which I do not pretend to defend, because we do not yet know what the fate of Paris will be, viz., that she is the Babylon† mentioned in the 18th chapter. That she is feeling the effect of this vial of wrath, in the midst of her darkness and madness, cannot be doubted by any who receive the interpretation of these symbols as endorsed by our best expositors.

We may remark, regarding the 17th, 18th and 19th chapters, that they are a more detailed account of what is described in the 16th, under the seven vials. They also contain the sequel of the outpouring of the seventh vial, the final destruction of all anti-Christian powers before the rider on the white horse. The 17th chapter introduces a variation of the symbols used to designate the Papal power in its different stages of development. It is an abandoned woman, seated upon a scarlet-colored beast, having seven heads and ten horns. This symbolism must certainly cover things, persons and events already noticed to some extent, but for the purpose of bringing out to a more striking view the Papal power in its last development. It would not, therefore, be straining the prophecy to suppose that the 18th chapter covers in part the identical ground which is occupied by the fifth vial. I will introduce it here:

And after these things I saw another angel come down from heaven, having great power; and the earth was lightened with his glory.

And he cried mightily with a strong voice, saying, Babylon the great is fallen, is fallen, and has become the habitation of devils, and the hold of every foul spirit, and a cage of every unclean and hateful bird.

* Note 65, Canto I, stanza 102.   † See Poem, Canto II, stanza 116.

For all nations have drunk of the wine of the wrath of her fornication, and the kings of the earth have committed fornication with her, and the merchants of the earth are waxed rich through the abundance of her delicacies.

And I heard another voice from heaven, saying, Come out of her, my people, that ye be not partakers of her sins, and that ye receive not of her plagues.

For her sins have reached unto heaven, and God hath remembered her iniquities.

Reward her even as she rewarded you, and double unto her double according to her works: in the cup which she hath filled, fill to her double.

How much she hath glorified herself, and lived deliciously, so much torment and sorrow give her: for she saith in her heart, I sit a queen, and am no widow, and shall see no sorrow.

Therefore shall her plagues come in one day, death, and mourning, and famine; and she shall be utterly burned with fire: for strong is the Lord God who judgeth her.

And the kings of the earth, who have committed fornication and lived deliciously with her, shall bewail her, and lament for her, when they shall see the smoke of her burning,

Standing afar off for the fear of her torment, saying, Alas, alas! that great city Babylon, that mighty city! for in one hour is thy judgment come.

And the merchants of the earth shall weep and mourn over her; for no man buyeth their merchandise any more:

The merchandise of gold, and silver, and precious stones, and of pearls, and fine linen, and purple, and silk, and scarlet, and all thyine-wood, and all manner of vessels of ivory, and all manner of vessels of most precious wood, and of brass, and iron, and marble,

And cinnamon, and odors, and ointments, and frankincense, and wine, and oil, and fine flour, and wheat, and beasts, and sheep, and horses, and chariots, and slaves, and souls of men.

And the fruits that thy soul lusted after are departed from thee, and all things which were dainty and goodly are departed from thee, and thou shalt find them no more at all.

The merchants of these things which were made rich by her, shall stand afar off, for the fear of her torment, weaping and wailing.

And saying, Alas, alas! that great city, that was clothed in fine linen, and purple, and scarlet, and decked with gold, and precious stones, and pearls!

For in one hour so great riches is come to nought. And every ship-master, and all the company in ships, and sailors, and as many as trade by sea, stood afar off,

And cried when they saw the smoke of her burning, saying, What city is like unto this great city!

And they cast dust on their heads, and cried, weeping and wailing, saying, Alas, alas! that great city, wherein were made rich all that had ships in the sea by reason of her costliness! for in one hour is she made desolate.

Rejoice over her, thou heaven, and ye holy apostles and prophets; for God hath avenged you on her.

And a mighty angel took up a stone like a great mill-stone, and cast it into the sea, saying, Thus with violence shall that great city Babylon be thrown down, and shall be found no more at all.

And the voice of harpers, and musicians, and of pipers, and trumpeters, shall be heard no more at all in thee; and no craftsmen, of whatsoever craft he be, shall be found any more in thee; and the sound of a mill-stone shall be heard no more at all in thee;

And the light of a candle shall shine no more at all in thee; and the voice of the bridegroom and of the bride shall be heard no more at all in thee: for thy merchants were the great men of the earth; for by thy sorceries were all nations deceived.

And in her was found the blood of prophets, and of saints, and of all that were slain upon the earth.

We may say that if this means a literal city, none has ever existed that answers the description better than Paris; and if that city should be destroyed, wholly or largely, in the revolution which is now deluging its streets with blood, it would lend plausibility to the theory which some minds could scarcely resist. Paris is a gay, gaudy, godless and licentious city. That is most emphatically true of her, which John says of the symbolic Babylon: "All nations have drunk of the wine of the wrath of her fornication, and the kings of the earth have committed fornication with her, and the merchants of the earth have waxed rich through the abundance of her delicacies." We have seen what millions have been slain, what rivers of blood have deluged the world in wars fomented or decreed in this licentious city. Not a city on the globe furnishes a parallel to it in this respect.

What nations have not thronged her gay boulevards and her brilliant haunts of licentious pleasure? Into what parts of the known world have not the delicacies of the French capital been carried for merchandise? What article of man's wear, from the hat on his head to the boots on his feet, is not considered better for having the epithet French prefixed to it?—even if it has never seen France, which is often true. What article of woman's wear, what style of dress, what habit of etiquette, must not first receive its sanction in Paris? Look at the articles of merchandise of symbolic Babylon, and compare them with the articles found principally in Appleton's list for modern Paris:

Of Babylon.	Of Paris.	Of Babylon.	Of Paris.
Gold, Silver, Precious stones,	Gold in bars and leaf; gold and silver ware; jewelry.	Wine, Oil,	Wine; cider; beer; alcohol.
Pearls,	Buttons.	Fine flour, Wheat,	Solid food.
Fine linen, Purple, Silk,	Haberdashery. Clothing; linen drapery; silks; woolens; cotton fabrics.	Beasts, Sheep, Horses,	Butchers' meat; prepared skins, and articles fabricated of them.
Scarlet,	Cudbear and carmine.	Chariots,	Mitrailleuses; steam engines: cars.
Thyine-wood,	Wood for building and for musical instruments.	Slaves, Souls of men.	Votaries of vice. Sold for her delicacies.
Vessels of ivory, Vessels of wood, Vessels of brass, Vessels of iron, Vessels of marble, Cinnamon, Odors, Ointments, Frankincense,	Goldsmiths' and jewelers' work; clocks; watches. Perfumery.		Fancy articles; pasteboard; paper; books; engravings.

That she traffics in the souls of men,—who does not know that thousands are yearly immolated upon her shrines of pleasure? But it is in her gay and voluptuous character, and in her crimes, that she answers this description best. How much she hath glorified herself and lived deliciously! How proudly has she sat like a queen at the head of the nations! How have her streets and public places of execution streamed with the blood of martyrs, and of her citizens, slain in civil strife and in her reigns of terror! How have her sins reached up to heaven! Now how are her sober, law-abiding citizens,—she has a few,—coming out of her, flying before the scowling face of mad sedition, that they may not be partakers of her sins nor receive of her plagues? What may yet come the future must be left to disclose But in view of the awful state of the French capital, the words of the prophet may almost be literally applied to her, "Babylon the great is fallen,* is fallen, and become the habitation of devils, and the hold of every foul spirit, and

* Note 66, Canto I, stanza 171.

the cage of every unclean and hateful bird." How do the devils of sedition, robbery and murder rage in her streets! Behold her petroleuses, like incarnate fiends, spreading conflagration over the devoted city! How do her dens and gilded haunts of vice reek with the foul spirits of the pit! How do the unclean and hateful birds of communism, socialism, infidelity and stark atheism, throng in her public gatherings, and haunt her secret conclaves!

Smarting under the vial of wrath, they blaspheme the name of God and repent not of their deeds. It has been thought, by historians and moralists, that the awful experiment of France in 1793,—that of conducting the affairs of a nation without a God,—would be sufficient for all time; that no nation, with the horror and crime that were enacted during the Reign of Terror before them, would ever dare repeat the experiment. But scarcely three-quarters of a century have passed before France would try it again. The Commune, which have been elevated by the mob to misrule Paris, have again, it is said, enacted the blasphemy. Truly they do not repent of their deeds. That all these things are the legitimate consequences of long ages of political and ecclesiastical maladministration is plain enough, and clearly enough demonstrates their relationship to the dragon and the beast. Their own legitimate offspring, like that of Milton's personation of Sin, have turned upon the parents to rend and devour them. And the earth is opening to swallow them all up; and thus will religion and liberty be helped.

I know of no sadder picture in the history of modern nations than France presents to-day. Scourged by a more powerful foe, whom her ambition had raised against her, until the blood has flown in streams from her lacerated body, and reddened half the kingdom, with a half million new-made graves covering her fallen sons, with her frightful battle-fields still reeking with myriads of unburied dead, her homes draped in sackcloth of mourning, darkened by the presence of death's angel, whole provinces desolated, many cities, towns and villages in ruins, her unhappy children, in the madness of their agony and amid the thick darkness which broods over her, are tearing and destroying each other. Over the black cloud which covers her, we see naught but the flaming sword of the cherubim, proclaiming that God and his angels are at war with a wicked nation. Amid the storm a solemn voice peals above the turmoil, coming down from the distant past, uttered in awful warning and verified by fallen empires and ruined cities, "The wicked shall be turned into hell with all the nations that forget God." Is there no hope for prostrate France? None whatever in any course she has heretofore pursued. None, unless on that dark tempest-cloud the falling tears of repentance shall light up the splendors of the rainbow of hope from light reflected from the sun of righteousness, which then would rise in her sky and scatter the uneasy spirits of the storm. She is rapidly going down to the hades of nations. Soon the abyss will engulf her, and over the spot will belong the epitaph which the traveler reads on the ruins of fallen Nineveh, Babylon, Thebes and Carthage, and among the mouldering archives of dead empires, "PERISHED AMONG THE NATIONS THAT HAVE FORGOTTEN GOD." Will not France take warning from these solemn monitions? Will not the nations which stand afar off for fear of her plagues, and lament her sad fall, take warning? Will not America take warning? I appeal to all who would erect temples to strange gods among us, to science, philosophy, or reason, or offer unholy incense upon the altars of Bacchus and the pleasures of sense, take warning. Seek not to banish or destroy the influence of the Bible among us. Do not secularize our Sabbath. France has done these, and you see whither she is tending. Dissolution and death will surely follow if you succeed.

X.

THE SICK MAN OF CONSTANTINOPLE.

From Araby, the land of rocks and sands,
 There flowed a wondrous river long ago.—CANTO II, STANZA I.

And the sixth angel poured out his vial upon the great river Euphrates; and the water thereof was dried up, that the way of the kings of the east might be prepared.

And I saw three unclean spirits like frogs come out of the mouth of the dragon, and out of the mouth of the beast, and out of the mouth of the false prophet.

For they are the spirits of devils, working miracles, which go forth unto the kings of the earth, and of the whole world, to gather them to the battle of that great day of God Almighty.

Behold, I come as a thief. Blessed is he that watcheth, and keepeth his garments, lest he walk naked, and they see his shame.

And he gathered them together into a place called in the Hebrew tongue Armageddon.—REV. XVI. 12-16.

WE now proceed upon ground on which we must tread softly. We are undoubtedly somewhere near the line which divides the past from the future. We may feel tolerably sure as to the application of those symbols which plainly refer to past events, but as to those which refer to the future we cannot be certain, except, perhaps, as to their general character. The peculiar character of specific events can only be determined by the events themselves. Yet there is much that is instructive in those symbols which plainly refer to future events, and they invite our attention and scrutiny. All the expositors to whom I have access express the opinion that the events indicated by this symbolism are yet in the future. Barnes, the most recent, who wrote his exposition twenty years ago, hints that the outpouring might have already passed, and the events following it might have been passing in his day.

From careful study of the subject, I am inclined to the opinion that the outpouring followed not long after the fifth vial, that events indicated in the twelfth verse are nearly passed, and those indicated by the rest of the passage are in the near coming future.

I will first call attention to several observations on the demands of these symbols, and then see if we can find anything in recent and passing history that will meet the demands.

1. The great river Euphrates must, of course, symbolize some great anti-Christian power which has been arrayed against Christianity, and has stood in the way of the kings of the East in some movement which must have a bearing upon it, perhaps embracing it. Moreover, as it was a great river, and consequently made up from the gathering together of many waters, we should expect that this power would be composed of many peoples or nationalities.

2. The outpouring of the vial must symbolize letting loose upon this power some influence that would cause it to decay like the gradual drying up of a river after its sources are cut off by the failure of rains upon the hills and mountains which supply them. It would require not a sudden and violent, but a gradual decay.

3. The power must be associated in some manner with the dragon and the beast in their opposition to civil and religious liberty.

4. The three unclean spirits must be an outgrowth of these anti-Christian and anti-progressive powers, or at least must proceed from the same source.

5. The unclean spirits must do, or make men believe that they do, some great and wondrous things in order to gain an influence over the kings which they are said to gather together to the "great day of God Almighty."

6. This great day must symbolize some great conflict in which these malign spirits will be engaged, that will result in their overthrow. It may be a conflict among themselves, in which they will mutually destroy each other. Christianity has been helped by such conflicts, as we have already seen, more than in those where their adherents have been directly assailed and driven to take the sword in self-defense.

7. The Lord's coming as a thief, may symbolize his hand in the conflict, his enemies, and possibly his friends, not knowing it.

8. Their gathering the kings together into a place called Armageddon, must be regarded as only preparatory to the awful events of the seventh vial.

We may remark generally, before proceeding to a consideration of the application of these symbols, that, as the fifth and sixth trumpets, relating to the same powers, occupied a very long time, even centuries in their fulfillment, it would not be unreasonable to expect that the fifth and sixth vials would require a much longer time for their fulfillment than the preceding.

Do we find anything in current history answering the demands of these symbols?

1. As to the power indicated by the great river Euphrates, we may have little doubt as to its referring to the Mohammedan power, as now more particularly embodied in the Turkish Empire. The same symbol is used in the sixth trumpet, which is believed to refer to the rise of that power. The Mohammedan religion, as is well known, was first proclaimed by Mohammed, in the early part of the seventh century.* Its rise and progress are set forth in the fifth and sixth trumpets, showing God's method of visiting the corrupt Churches which had overspread Northern Africa, Southern Europe, and Asia Minor. The signs of corruption had begun to manifest themselves in the Seven Churches, as recorded by John. Five centuries after this, these portions of the earth were ripe for the inundation of God's wrath. This began to be revealed to John under the symbol of locusts released in vast numbers from the bottomless pit, at the sounding of the fifth trumpet. Mohammed began his career in Arabia; with the Saracen armies which he called around his standard, he spread his religion and power with amazing rapidity. Nearly the whole of Arabia soon submitted to his sway. Two centuries had not passed, before his successors had overrun Egypt, Syria, Asia Minor, twice besieged Constantinople, overrun all of Northern Africa, broke over the barriers of the straits of Gibraltar, subdued Spain, crossed the Pyrenees, and carried the triumphant crescent up to the walls of Potiers, when the tide of conquest was checked at

---

* Note 2, Canto II, stanza 1.

Tours, by Charles Martel, at the head of a great army, chiefly from France and Germany. A vast number—some say as many as two hundred and fifty thousand—were slain, and they were driven back beyond the Pyrenees, never to return. But the Moors remained in Spain for several centuries.

The Mohammedan power thus almost completely blotted out the nominal religion of Jesus, over more than half the Christian world. The ruin was sweeping; thousands of magnificent churches were transformed into mosques—many of them remaining unto this day. This power, after an existence of almost a thousand years, culminated in the siege and capture of Constantinople, and the establishment of the Turkish Empire, with that city for its capital. The Turks had been known as a people in the North of Asia, for fifteen hundred years. They had embraced the religion of Mohammed but a short time previous to this event. This completed the overthrow of the Eastern Empire, in judgment upon the corruptions of an idolatrous Church. In the application which our expositors make of the prophetic symbols of Revelation, it is regarded as the culmination of the second woe, or sixth trumpet, which ended in placing the sun of the Turkish Empire at its meridian, where it is called the great river Euphrates.* (See Barnes, in loco.) The propriety of choosing that river† as a symbol of this power is seen, when we remember that it is a great river, and on its banks, on the fertile plain of Shinar, stood the renowned city of Babylon, the capital of one of earth's greatest and oldest empires.

The allusion to the kings of the East would seem to strengthen the position that the Turkish Empire is here intended. Kings must, of course, be taken here as representative of nationalities or races. We may, perhaps, understand the meaning of this to be, that the way of Eastern races may be prepared—opened to the reception of Christianity; *i. e.*, some hindrance removed that has hitherto been in the way. Appleton's Cyclopedia says: "Perhaps no country in the world is inhabited by so great a variety of races as the Turkish Empire. The Turks are divided into

---

* See Poem, Canto II, stanzas 1-27.   † Note 3, Canto II, stanza 28.

two races :   The Osmanlis, or Turks proper, whose numbers are estimated at about three millions in European, and ten million five hundred thousand in Asiatic Turkey; and the Turkomans, who are principally found in Northern Mesopotamia and adjoining districts, and do not, probably, exceed an hundred thousand.   The Greeks are about equally divided between the European and Asiatic divisions, and number somewhat more than two millions.   The Armenians are about five hundred thousand in European, and two millions in Asiatic Turkey.   The Sclavic nations, under which term are principally included Bulgarians. Servians, Bosnians, Herzegovinians, and Montenegrins, number about six millions, and are all in European Turkey.   The Roumans, or Wallachs, a Daco-Roman race, inhabiting, chiefly, the Danubian Principalities, number about four hundred thousand. Besides these, there are upwards of one million Arnauts, or Albanians proper, inhabiting a province called after them; not far from one million Arabs in Asiatic Turkey, and four millions in the African Turkish possessions; about two hundred and forty thousand Syrians, all in Asiatic Turkey; about two hundred thousand Jews, ninety thousand Franks, or Western Christians, one million or more Koords, twenty thousand Gypsies, thirty to fifty thousand Druses, about the same number of Tartars, and a large number of Circassians and other Caucasians, and in Africa, Copts, Nubians, Berbers, &c." The whole population, according to the larger estimate, is somewhat over forty millions.   All these are held in subjection to the Turks, numbering, as we have seen, only thirteen millions—less than one-third of the entire population.   That Turkish rule has been unfriendly to Christianity, every student of history knows.   It has certainly been in the way of these races; and when taken away, there will be no political hindrances to the spread of Christianity. And through them, doubtless, will be prepared a way for still other kindred races of the East, not under Turkish rule.

2.   Our second remark was to the effect that the outpouring of the vial upon that power must symbolize letting loose upon it some influences that would cause it to decay, like the gradual drying up of a great river.   The gradual decay of the Turkish Empire during the present century,

satisfies the demand of this symbolism, and at the same time furnishes one of the strongest proofs that it is the power foreshadowed in the symbol. We ought not, of course, to be very positive until we see more of the ways of God in current events. There are those who suppose that the sixth vial has not yet been poured out, and they look for some great war on the Eastern question. I have followed such a line of thought in my Poem. But if this gradual decay has any significance, it shows that the vial has already been poured out, and is at work upon it. At the same time this does not render future wars of great magnitude improbable. We do not know what form of power that Empire may yet put on, nor what attitude it may assume towards its subjects who do or may profess Christianity. The labors of Christian missionaries are spreading a purer Christianity very rapidly there, and from such résults it would seem that the Empire, as a hindrance, has almost ceased from the way already. But this increase of Christians may yet be the very cause of another outbreak of Moslem fanaticism, and persecution may again rage against them, until its atrocities shall provoke other nations to interfere, as they did when Greece was delivered at Navarino, when this vial may reach its grandest consummation, and the river be dried up. The history of Turkey during this century favors my second remark in the main. I refer the reader to the sketch of Turkish history in Appleton's Cyclopedia, too long to insert here. Near the beginning of this century, we find Egypt conquered by Bonaparte. This led to a war with France on a more extended scale, which weakened the Empire considerably. Then wars with Russia and England, together with the rebellion of Janizaries, made the condition of the Empire exceedingly perilous. They involved the Sultan in considerable loss of territory, and resulted in a great slaughter of the Janizaries. He had scarcely concluded peace with England and Russia, when Greece revolted, and Mehemet Ali raised the standard of insurrection in Egypt, which involved him in still graver difficulties. Greece achieved her independence in 1821, at an almost fatal cost to Turkey. Egypt, too, would have been utterly lost, and the Empire itself would, doubtless, have sunk under the accumulated weight of its disasters, but for the interposition of France and other powers, who deemed the adherence of Egypt to the Empire, and the existence of the Empire itself, necessary to preserve the balance of power. These and other minor causes, super-added to the *effects* of internal decay, have so weakened the Sultan, that he has been designated the " *Sick man of Constantinople*." The Crimean war resulted in strengthening Turkey somewhat, by enlarging her territory; but recent troubles in Europe have nearly neutralized all she gained then.

But even this war, apparently to the advantage of Turkey, went far towards removing the Empire as a hindrance out of the way of Christianity, and thus contributed to the general result contemplated in the outpouring of the sixth vial. Doctor Dwight, a missionary of Constantinople, under the appointment of the American Board, with whom I conversed on this subject but a short time before the fearful accident on the Rutland Railroad, which caused his death, informed me that this war had a powerful effect in breaking down the barriers to Christianity there. The intercourse of Turks with other nations sharing common dangers, being engaged in a common cause against the designs of Russia, made great inroads upon Moslem exclusiveness, and greatly soft-ened fanaticism. The confirmation of the Hatti-sheriff, revoking the death penalty upon Mohammedans for forsaking their religion, was a very important public act resulting from this war, and bears in the same direction. We therefore conclude that, if our exposition be correct, the results of the outpouring, so far as they relate to the Turkish Empire, are, doubtless, nearly all realized; for the removal of civil and political hindrances to the spread of Christianity, is all, I suppose, that is contemplated in any of these symbols.

But there are other things indicated in our text, which fol-low the outpouring of the sixth vial chronologically, and, doubtless, as the logical consequence, fraught with startling interest, which may extend over the world, and quite far into the future, before the seventh vial is outpoured. They are indicated in what the unclean spirits* shall do. We remark on this passage :

* Note 4, Canto II, stanza 61.

The dragon must here be still considered the spirit of Paganism, in its opposition to the pure religion of Jesus; the beast, the Papacy, and the false prophet as the Mohammedan religion, in its wider existence, embracing, as it does now, nearly one hundred and sixty million adherents.

With reference to the special meaning and application of this passage, we cannot speak positively, but we may be permitted to make the following suggestions:

The Pagan power, as a metaphysical hindrance to Christianity, was a religion of rationalism* in its more refined culture, or at least a religion in which the rationalistic element largely predominated. You find this among the old philosophers. You find marked traces of it in the system of Julian, the Apostate. It has always attracted minds of a philosophical turn. The unclean spirit which proceeded out of the mouth of the dragon, may symbolize modern rationalism embodied in the various schools of infidelity, prominent among which, for numbers, is spiritism, which has received an immense impulse during the present century. I have been struck more than once with the Paganistic elements which largely pervade the systems of modern free-thinkers. They have attempted, in philosophy, what it is said a Roman Emperor attempted in the Pantheon at Rome; *i. e.*, to put the God of the Bible into a niche by the side of Jupiter, Zeus, and other deities of the ancients, and of Vishnu, Brahma, and Jos, of more modern times. We may say that if this was the design of this symbol, it was well chosen. There are more of the spirits of old Paganism among us, croaking like unclean frogs, than we are aware of. A great portion of our secular press seem to lean that way.

The religion symbolized by the beast has ever been one of blind, groping ignorance and superstition—that of a Church which has, to no small extent, cherished and taught the idea that "ignorance is the mother of devotion," and countenances a superstition that can believe anything which a designing Jesuitism may promulgate, as calculated to strengthen the Church in its hold, upon its illegitimate

---

* Note 5, Canto II, stanza 63.

powers. The spirit which came out of the mouth of the beast may symbolize that recent exhibition of credulity which blindly subscribes to the infallibility of the Pope, the immaculate conception of the Virgin, and other absurdities *ad finem.*

It is well known that the religion of the false prophet is one of grossest sensualism.* The spiritual element is almost entirely wanting in it. Materialism composes it almost exclusively. For instance, the ideal summit of heavenly bliss, to a mussulman, is a farm, in heaven, of seventy thousand square miles extent, with proper appurtenances; a vast diamond palace, with the moderate allowance of seventy thousand of the blue-eyed nymphs of heaven as his wives. This reward has been actually promised to the most faithful.

Would not the spirit which proceeded out of the mouth of the false prophet properly symbolize the sensualism which begins to be so prevalent in the world, the indulgence of which has, even now, been claimed as a religious right? It comes from the same source as when proclaimed by the prophet to his followers—a corrupt human heart. It seems to me that there has been no time, for many years, when sensualism interposed stronger barriers to religion than it does to-day, and in our own country. The motto with vast numbers is, " Let us eat and drink, for to-morrow we die." How is it with a vast mass of foreign immigrants? How is it with the vast influence wielded by strong drink among us? How few of our popular elections are not carried by lager or whisky? They begin to be proscriptive, and it needs no great stretch of the imagination to suppose that they may, by and by, resort to general and open violence.

Let me say in reference to this whole subject, that rationalism, superstition (especially in our own country), and sensualism, are *the* three great powers arrayed against the Church and opposing the progress of Christianity, Satan's last great triumvirate with which he would suppress the religion of Jesus in all Christian lands. They talk great things, and profess to do great things, to lead men to embrace their tenets.

* Note 6, Canto II, stanza 69.

With regard to these powers being closely associated, the dragon, the beast and the false prophet have their votaries everywhere. But in a remarkable degree have these different hindrances to Christianity prevailed in Turkey. There you find Roman Catholics, Mohammedans and Pagans, elements ready to assume some new form, like the three unclean spirits, as soon as the symbolical Euphrates is dried up. In this country we find Papist, skeptic and sensualist combining to thrust the Bible out of our public schools, and manifesting a close affinity for all forms of opposition to the religion of an open Bible.

It would not conflict with the record of past history, nor do violence to these symbols, nor be in disharmony with the spirit of hatred manifested by these opposing powers, to anticipate their coalescing for more extensive aggressions.* Indeed, there may be a general league among them, as there is now ramified all over this country a liquor league, for the purpose of getting possession of the places of power, by fair means or foul. To suppose that proscription and persecution would be foreign to their spirit or policy under such circumstances, would be ignoring all their precedents and instincts. For some such purposes of aggression, such as reinstating the Pope as a temporal power over his unwilling subjects and suppressing free speech, or it may be to revolutionize everything in the present order of things, these unclean spirits will gather their adherents together to the battle of the great day of God Almighty.† Then let the warning be sounded in every ear, "Behold I come as a thief. Blessed is he that walketh and keepeth his garments, lest he walk naked and they see his shame." Thus the world is prepared for the last dread outpouring of wrath before the glorious dawn of the millennial Sabbath. (See Poem, Canto II, stanzas 82–95.)

---

* Note 7, Canto II, stanza 82.　　　　　† Note 8, Canto II, stanza 83.

XI.

THE SEVENTH VIAL.

The angel commissioned the vial to bear,
Pours out its contents into the air.—Canto II, Stanza 96

And the seventh angel poured out his vial into the air ; and there came a great voice out of the temple of heaven, from the throne, saying, It is done.

And there were voices, and thunders, and lightnings ; and there was a great earthquake, such as was not since men were upon the earth, so mighty an earthquake, and so great.

And the great city was divided into three parts, and the cities of the nations fell: and great Babylon came in remembrance before God, to give unto her the cup of the wine of the fierceness of his wrath.

And every island fled away, and the mountains were not found.

And there fell upon men a great hail out of heaven, every stone about the weight of a talent: and men blasphemed God because of the plague of the hail: for the plague thereof was exceeding great.—Rev. xvi. 17-21.

This passage describes the results of the outpouring of the seventh vial. The seventeenth and eighteenth chapters seem to be a more detailed history of the same great events that are here foreshadowed. That these chapters foretell the destruction of ecclesiastical despotism—in other words, the utter overthrow of Papal Rome, as well as every ecclesiastical power to oppress the masses by a resort to the civil arm—has, to my own mind, the force of absolute conviction: though I would by no means presume to show just how it is to be .done. We read in the sixth vial, at the close of its fearful delineations, that there was a gathering together for "the great day of God Almighty." The kings of the earth and of the whole world were gathered together into a place called in the Hebrew tongue Armageddon. This was but a preparation for a great battle. The hosts stand opposed to each other, ready for the strife, when the vial is poured out into the air as a signal for the conflict to commence. Barnes says, with reference to this: "Why the vial was poured into the air is not stated. The most probable supposition as to the idea intended to be represented is, that as storms and tempests seem to be engendered in the air, so this destruction would come from some supernatural cause, as if the whole atmosphere should be filled with wind and storm, and a furious and desolating whirlwind should be aroused by some invisible power."* I do not know that it is necessary to expect any supernatural power, but merely that this indicates an exceedingly stormy period in human affairs. The symbolism would seem to describe great political and ecclesiastical revolutions and commotions. The description is awfully sublime. The angel hovers in the clouds, with pinions far outstretched, and as the warring nations stand expectant on the brink of a most tremendous battle, he lets loose from his vial—their prison—the giants of the storm, as the winds were wont to be loosed from the cave of Æolus. Just as the whirlwind and thundergust are about to dash their ruin over the world, "a great voice† is heard out of the temple of heaven, from the throne, saying, IT IS DONE." The pending conflict shall be decided in favor of the powers of righteousness. Political and ecclesiastical tyranny shall go down in the crash of battle, and civil and religious liberty, twin daughters of a pure Christianity, shall be enthroned, henceforth to rule the Christian world. And now the battle begins. Earth and sky join in the tumult of arms. There are voices,‡ and thunders, and lightnings, first as the distant murmurs§ of the coming storm which is gathering over the world, its pealings and mutterings growing louder, the winds hissing and roaring more fearfully, the clouds increasing in volume and gathering blackness as they approach, until the earthquake and the thundergust shake and cleave the solid earth, the mountains sink in the convulsions, the islands are swallowed up by the greedy ocean, and terrified nature trembles and turns pale lest her doom should be utter destruction. The account says: "There was a great earthquake, such as was not since men were upon earth, so mighty an earthquake, and so great." This may portend a literal

---

* See his Notes, in loco.
‡ Note 11, Canto II, stanza 99.

† Note 10, Canto II, stanza 97.
§ Note 12, Canto II, stanza 100,

5*

earthquake, along with the conflicts which distinguish this stormy period,—for the earth seems to sympathize with her children in their struggles,—which may result in great physical changes, though the symbolism does not absolutely require it.

Appleton's Cyclopedia says: "The approach of earthquakes is heralded by premonitory symptoms of unmistakable character. The air seems to be affected in some respect, perhaps in its electric condition, and the brute animals show a sensitiveness to this, by uttering cries of distress and running wildly about. Men are sometimes affected by dizziness and a sensation like sea-sickness. The atmosphere is often hazy for months, and the sun, seen through it, is often red and fiery. The weather suddenly changes from fierce gusts of wind to dead calms, and rains pour down in torrents, at times or in places where they are of rare occurrence. Immediately before the shocks occur, the air is generally very still, while the surface of the ocean or lake is usually disturbed. A sound* then breaks from the stillness, like distant thunder, or like a carriage rumbling afar upon a rough pavement; or it may break at once with an awful explosion, as when the peal and the flash come together from every part of a cloud in which one is enveloped; at the same time the ground is shaken, or lifted upward, or thrown forward, as by the passage of an irresistible wave beneath it. The shocks may be repeated several times in quick succession, or recur after long intervals; the movements may be so great as to rend the surface into chasms, and these may open and shut again, or remain in fissures the width of a few feet or yards, and extending to unknown depths—smoke and flames are occasionally sent forth from them during the continuance of the earthquake, even if the region be not volcanic. Torrents of water are ejected from these chasms, and springs of water are often forced by the convulsions into new directions. Objects on the surface, as dwellings, trees, and animals, are engulfed in the chasms, and by subsidence of the surface, large trees. mountains even, and whole cities are swallowed up."

There was an awful exhibition of this power in the earth-

* Note 13. Canto II, stanza 101.

quake at Lisbon. The city was shaking and falling. Fifteen thousand people rushed out upon the quay which had just been built, to get away from the falling houses; an awful crash of the earthquake, and the quay, harbor, ships, people, all sank into the tremendous chasm, and caught fast in the adamant jaws of the earth, not a spar, not a shred came back to the surface to tell what had been there. This terrible power was also fearfully illustrated by the earthquake in Peru in 1868, in which whole provinces were devastated, and cities and mountains sunk. "Occurring also, as they most frequently do, along the seaboard,* the water is observed commonly to retire for some distance, leaving the harbors dry, and then to return in a great wave of many feet in height, which sweeps everything before it." This was peculiarly the case in the last named earthquake. The tidal wave was frightfully destructive. "Of all calamities† to which men are exposed, there is none of so fearful a character as earthquakes; none involve such terrible and devastating destruction to life and property. There is none of the approach of which he is less forewarned, and none against which he can take as few precautions. The very mysteriousness of the danger oppresses him with terror. He is ignorant in what form it is most imminent, or in what direction to seek a way of escape."

There can be little reasonable doubt ‡ that the earthquake and hailstorm of our text symbolize the commotions of the great battle of Armageddon. Yet, if this war is to occur in Italy, around Rome, the possibility of which has already been hinted, it being a country subject to terrible volcanic influences, an awful earthquake, with some frightful eruption of Vesuvius, or of some other volcano, scattering volcanic stones for miles around, may not be among the impossible incidents of those stormy days; though the symbolism will be satisfied by the fearful civil commotions which are undoubtedly here intended. A coincidence of the kind is furnished by the battle of Lake Trasymenus, during which there was a severe earthquake, which destroyed one city and many smaller towns.

* Note 14, Canto II, stanza 102.   † Note 15, Canto II, stanza 102.
‡ Note 16, Canto II, stanza 103.

The further effects of this great earthquake are noted: "And the great city was divided into three parts,* and the cities of the nations fell." This effect may be accomplished on Rome by a literal earthquake, as some believe. Scientific men tell us that there is a subterranean current or vein of volcanic material or influence—whatever is the cause of volcanoes and earthquakes—running from Vesuvius out under the sea along the coast, and again under the land, directly beneath the city. So, when Jehovah sees fit to light the train, Rome may be overthrown without a miracle. Or, this may describe the divided state of the city, when the war of Armageddon is thundering around its walls, as Jerusalem was divided into three hostile factions during the siege which resulted in its destruction. Or, again, it may describe the Roman power; the Roman Catholic world may be divided into three discordant factions, by these political and ecclesiastical convulsions, and thus Papal domination will be destroyed. And those cities of the nations which have upheld it shall fall in the same convulsions as Paris has fallen; or they may fall away from supporting the Papacy, as Munich has under the lead of Doctor Dollinger. Barnes remarks upon this: "All that it seems to me can be said on the point now is, (*a*) that it refers to Papal Rome, or the Papal power; (*b*) that it relates to something yet future, and that it may not be possible to determine, with precise accuracy, what will occur; (*c*) that it probably means that, in the time of the final ruin of that power, there will be a three-fold judgment; either a different judgment in regard to some three-fold manifestation of that power, or a succession of judgments, as if one part were smitten at a time. The certain and entire ruin of the power is predicted by this, but still it is not improbable that it will be by such divisions, or successions of judgments, that it is proper to represent the city as divided into three parts."

We read, further on, that "Great Babylon came in remembrance before God."† As this is a common symbol of the Papal power, the mention of it in connection with the oregoing, would seem to preclude the idea that the city there

<hr>

* Note 17, Canto II, stanza 105.　　　† Note 18, Canto II, stanza 107.

symbolizes that power. It would rather favor the idea that some literal city is there meant. But, however this may be, we may be sure of one thing, and that is, the ultimate end of these calamities is "to give unto" Papal Rome "the cup of the wine of the fierceness of God's wrath."

The next clause in our text seems still further to favor the idea that these convulsions may be in part physical, as well as political. It informs us that "every island fled away,* and the mountains were not found." Islands are often temporarily covered by the tidal wave during the continuance of earthquakes, and sometimes permanently sunk under the waves. And, as we have seen, mountains are sometimes sunk out of sight. This may be the case in Italy and along the coast. The great earthquake may cause her beautiful islands to disappear, and even Vesuvius itself, with other mountains around, may be sunk into the bowels of the earth, in the awful convulsion. Some look for some such events. Thus the hailstorm† would be explained. Amid the wrack of continents, and the terrific eruptions of volcanic fires from the convulsed earth, such a hailstorm as never before was known might be a natural accompaniment of the great earthquake. Stones might fall for miles around, flung out of the bowels of the earth by the Titanic powers of subterranean tempests, even larger than those mentioned in the text. When we see the winds and the flames destroying such a city as Chicago;‡ the very "elements" in the mighty furnace "melting with fervent heat;" the most enduring structures prostrated before the fiery blast, we are, in a measure, prepared to expect the possibility of these predicted convulsions. We can more easily imagine how the tremendous powers of the earthquake, the flaming vomit of the volcano, heaved from its burning entrails, the winds carrying the devouring fires along the parched surface of the earth, the heavens black with the wrathful tempest, pealing their thunders in answer to the voice of the earthquake, and launching their thunderbolts like hailstones upon the works of men, all combined, should produce a

* Note 19, Canto II, stanza 109.   † Note 20, Canto II, stanza 110.
‡ This lecture was rewritten after that great fire.

scene of indescribable terror, when the very mountains, having their foundations battered away by the warring Titans beneath, should sink in the limbos of the tempest, the islands, overwhelmed by the waves, should disappear, and the Eternal City, with its environs, its mighty walls, its lofty domes, and its enduring structures, which have withstood the impinging elements for more than two thousand years, should sink beneath the storm, like frail reeds before the tornado. At any rate, these tremendous agencies, used merely as symbols, must shadow forth terrific political convulsions. What they may be, or when they may occur, remains yet to be seen.

Before proceeding to my final inquiry with reference to this great war of Armageddon, I will notice briefly the next two chapters. Mr. Barnes says of the seventeenth: "This chapter properly commences a more detailed description of the judgment inflicted upon the formidable anti-Christian power referred to in the last chapter, though under a new image. It contains an account of the sequel of the pouring out of the last vial, etc." As we have remarked before, it contains the symbol of the abandoned woman clothed in purple and scarlet color, and decked with gold and precious stones and pearls, "seated upon the scarlet-colored beast having seven heads and ten horns."* This represents the Papal power as it existed some time before and during the continuance of the plagues we have been contemplating. (See my lecture on the symbols of Despotism. See also Barnes' Notes on this passage.)

The 18th chapter contains a lament for Babylon, portraying by its striking symbolism the condition of all despotic powers after the awful battle or war of Armageddon. (See Poem, Canto II, stanza 116; also, Barnes' Notes on this chapter.)

The 19th chapter, to the 10th verse, speaks of the triumphant songs† of God's people over Papal domination hopelessly overthrown in this war. Henceforth there is to be no hindrance in the way of the gospel, from this power

---

* Note 21, Canto II, stanza 114.
† Note 22, Canto II, stanza 118. See also stanzas 119 122.

uplifting the civil arm in the Christian world against the truth. All such opposing powers go down in the shock of Armageddon. But the work is not all done, for the heathen world still remains. What shall be done in that, as shadowed forth in the remaining symbols, shall be the subject of my last lecture. Our next question here is—

"When shall these things be?" In the light of the events of the sixth vial, may we look for any of them in passing events? Has the seventh vial yet been poured out? We will not dare to affirm our conviction very positively that it has. But we may say,

1. The supposition that it has been poured out does not come in collision with Mr. Barnes' opinion that it was, when he wrote, a future event. He wrote his Notes on Revelation more than twenty years ago. That period has been crowded with some of the most momentous, fearful and portentous events in the history of the world, especially in their bearing upon despotic power. In the rapid march of events it may be considered probable that room would be made for this last outpouring during that period.

2. It would not clash with my own exposition of the sixth vial as symbolizing events that may yet be far in the future. For we have seen that the effects of some vials have not ceased even until after the outpouring of several subsequent ones. Those things symbolized by the three unclean spirits may yet be far in the future, and yet this vial may have been poured out. There are difficulties, I know, in the way, but not, I think, insuperable. The natural connection of the passage would lead us to suppose that the three unclean spirits of the former vial led or inspired the evil powers that were marshaled against the Church in the war of Armageddon. If so, according to the interpretation which we have defended, the seventh vial could not have been poured out until after the gathering together of these powers. We cannot be certain in this matter until time brings the consummation of the great impending events of this momentous age; and if we find those which pretty clearly point to the seventh vial as their symbol we need not be stumbled in receiving them as such, fully confident that all will, in the end, harmonize with each other, and with the

symbols which foreshadow them. So, if the student of prophecy should conclude that the seventh vial has already been poured out, it may be that coming events will prove that he is correct. It may be that we are hearing the voices and the thunders, and seeing the lightnings of the fearful war of Armageddon. Undoubtedly the seventh vial will reach every influence opposing Christianity. Papal Domination and Political Despotism are not the only forms of opposition which must go down in the Christian world under this outpouring. Mammon, Intemperance, Infidelity and Licentiousness must be scorched and consumed in the fires of wrath. I confess that my search among the symbols of prophecy for the great war in Europe and the horrors of Paris; for the recent folly of the Ecumenical Council of Rome and the destruction of the temporal power of the Pope; for the swinging away of Germany from Rome, under the lead of Dollinger, and even for Sadowa, has not been, and cannot be, entirely satisfactory, without supposing that the seventh vial has been already outpoured, and that these events are the voices and thunders and lightnings of the stormy period foreshadowed by this aerial outpouring. The earthquake, the falling cities, the fleeing islands, the sinking mountains, and the great hailstorm, may yet be future events, which the uneasy elements are preparing for the offending powers of evil. Their outburst may be nearer than we think. It may be that the fearful destruction of property by recent fires, unparalleled in the history of the world, is the effect of this vial upon the power of Mammon, designed to rebuke his greed and prepare a better state of things for the spread of a purer and nobler type of Christianity. Undoubtedly such will be the effect of them. If such be the case, we may look for other fearful visitations which shall more directly touch the other forms of evil mentioned.

Whether the above be true or not, we may be sure that the time of the seventh vial is close upon us. No doubt the next twenty-five years will be crowded as thickly with great events as the past. In an age of steam and lightning the forces of history, evil as well as good, are generated and matured with astonishing rapidity. The harvest and the vintage of the earth are both rapidly ripening, and the angels, with their sharp sickles, stand ready to reap. The harvest shall be gathered into the garner of Jehovah; the clusters of the vine of the earth shall be cast into the wine-press of the wrath of God. A voice in current events seems to sound from the heights of Revelation: "Be ye also ready"—"Blessed is he that watcheth and keepeth his garments, lest he walk naked and they see his shame."*

* See Poem, Canto II, stanza 87.

XII.

THE DARKNESS AND TEMPEST BEFORE THE DAWN.

But yonder rises a black cloud of wrath.—CANTO III, STANZA 17.

And I saw heaven* opened, and behold, a white horse ; and he that sat upon him was called Faithful and True, and in righteousness he doth judge and make war.

His eyes were as a flame of fire, and on his head were many crowns ; and he had a name written, that no man knew, but he himself.

And he was clothed with a vesture dipped in blood : and his name is called The Word of God.

And the armies which were in heaven followed him upon white horses, clothed in fine linen, white and clean.

And out of his mouth goeth a sharp sword, that with it he should smite the nations : and he shall rule them with a rod of iron : and he treadeth the wine-press of the fierceness and wrath of Almighty God.

And he hath on his vesture and on his thigh a name written, KING OF KINGS, AND LORD OF LORDS.

And I saw an angel standing in the sun ; and he cried with a loud voice, saying to all the fowls that fly in the midst of heaven, Come, and gather yourselves together unto the supper of the great God ;

That ye may eat the flesh of kings, and the flesh of captains, and the flesh of mighty men, and the flesh of horses, and of them that sit on them, and the flesh of all men, both free and bond, both small and great.

And I saw the beast, and the kings of the earth, and their armies, gathered together to make war against him that sat on the horse, and against his army.

And the beast was taken, and with him the false prophet that wrought miracles before him, with which he deceived them that had received the mark of the beast, and them that worshiped his image. These both were cast alive into a lake of fire burning with brimstone.

And the remnant were slain with the sword of him that sat upon the horse, which sword proceeded out of his mouth : and all the fowls were filled with their flesh.—REV. XIX. 11–21.

WHILE I fully believe that these prophetic symbols are receiving a rapid fulfillment in our day, I am not, in any proper sense, a Millerite nor a Second Adventist, as a certain

* Note 1, Canto III, stanza 1.

sect of modern origin is styled. Mr. Miller, and others who have followed in his steps, have undoubtedly done great service in calling attention to these startling prophecies, and inducing a great deal of study of prophetic symbols. But there are several serious defects in their methods of interpretation.

1. One is, they often assume to forecast future specific events from these symbols, whereas, such is their nature that nothing but of a general character can be, or, indeed, ever was intended to be known of them until the events themselves shall furnish the correct interpretation of them. The reason for this is obvious: men are to be the unconscious agents in the fulfillment of very many of the most important of them.

2. They have mistaken the method of interpreting the prophetic period of the "one thousand two hundred and sixty days." They proceed as if the rise of the anti-Christian powers, whose term of existence is here foreshadowed, had been instantaneous, whereas it was by gradual steps. We have hinted before, that if this period, added to the date of any considerable advance of Papal Prerogative, should mark the date of any considerable loss of the same, and the process be repeated until the date of the final destruction is reached, the symbolism will be satisfied. Suppose the student of history and prophecy should find that in, or near, the year 529 the Papal Prerogative made considerable advance, and should add the period in question to that date, and find the date of the French Revolution, which was a heavy blow upon the Papacy; suppose he should find another advance in the year 538, and by the same process should obtain 1798, the year of the Italian Revolution, which drove the Pope from Rome. Again, suppose he should find still another advance of Papal Prerogative in 588, and from that should find the date of the second Italian Revolution, 1848, when the Pope was again driven from Rome; and another advance in 606, and find the date of Sadowa, 1866, by the same process; and still again another advance in 610, by which he would reach the date of the great war of 1870, and the destruction of the temporal power of the Pope,— would he not find a key to the meaning and application of

this prophetic period?   Most of these several dates have, on some such data, been fixed by different authorities for the destruction of the Papal Domination.   That they have all marked a great loss to the Pope's prerogative is a fact which must be put down as something more than a mere coincidence.   This may explain the mistakes that have been made in calculating the time of the destruction of this power.   It will doubtless be seen that when the last blow is struck, if from its date the period in question be deducted, we shall find the date of another important advance of that prerogative.   It is very plain that the student could not, from this data, predict the time of the utter downfall of this power, only, at best, some disaster which would, it is true, tend to its destruction.

3.   They have made another mistake in supposing that this period indicates the time of the second advent of Christ; whereas, it was, evidently, only designed to mark the date of the destruction of anti-Christian powers.   If a long period should elapse before the commencement of the millennium, after these powers shall be put out of the way of the progress of Christianity, it would in no degree impair the truthfulness of these prophetic symbols.   We shall endeavor to show that the Church is only just prepared by these events for her great aggressive work in subduing the world to the power of Christ, preparatory to his second coming.   This must require time, though how long is not indicated in these symbols.

I.   We have already remarked that the first ten verses of this chapter are descriptive of the songs* of triumph over the powers of evil, sung by the people of heaven.   The eleventh verse introduces a new set of symbols, and, as it seems to me, a new epoch in the history of the Church.   The vision has hitherto been confined to the Christian world.   Little reference has been had, if our exposition is correct, to the vast portions of the earth which are covered with the darkness of heathenism.   We cannot suppose that in a book of the future history of the Church so many peoples would be left out.   The great struggles, up to this point, have been for

* See.Poem, Canto II, stanzas 118-122.

the purpose of putting the obstacles which have opposed themselves in Christian lands, out of the way of the spread of the religion of the Bible. Now the piercing eye of prophecy is directed, for a moment, to the great work of evangelizing heathen countries. The grandest achievements of the Church are yet to come. It was for these that she endured long ages of the severest discipline. The terrible scenes through which she has passed during the outpouring of the seven vials, have prepared her for abounding in the work. The destruction of life and property in the wars, floods, and flames, has taught her to put a proper estimate upon these things. Now heaven is opened,* and the man who is called "Faithful and True," and also "The Word of God," as well as other significant names, comes upon a white horse, and the armies of heaven follow him on white horses, clothed in fine linen, white and clean; and out of his mouth goeth a sharp sword, that with it he should smite the nations. These symbols indicate some triumphant demonstrations from heaven, of unusual power. That one of the names of this rider is, "The Word of God," and that a sword *proceedeth out of his mouth*, instead of being held in his hand, would seem to point to the preaching of the gospel with an unparalleled power and success. I have no doubt but it has reference to the same event that is referred to in Rev. xiv. 6, where John says: "And I saw another angel fly in the midst of heaven, having the everlasting gospel to preach to them that dwell on the earth, and to every nation, and kindred, and tongue, and people." The sword is to "smite the nations;" in other words, to subjugate them. The gospel is to be preached, and gain a stronghold among all the nations of the earth.† We remark, with reference to this:

1. The Christian world will have been so thoroughly prepared by the conflicts that are just past, that it will go to work with a zeal and energy it has never before shown. Skepticism will have been so rebuked and shamed by the displays of God's hand in these things, that it will no more interpose obstacles in the way of the aggressive work of the

---

* See Poem, Canto I, stanza 1.　　　　　† Note 2, Canto III, stanza 3.

Church; but will rather join hands with the people of God, and help on the glorious cause. The Church will be baptized anew with the mission spirit;* she will give her wealth a hundred-fold more liberally into the treasuries of the Lord; missionaries will go by thousands,† instead of by twos; they will preach Christ with unwonted faith and fervor; the Holy Spirit will carry the preached word to the heart and conscience with unwonted power, and "the mountain of the Lord's house shall be exalted above the tops of the hills, and all nations‡ shall flow unto it."

2.   We should expect, from the unwonted display of the heavenly powers in these symbols, and from other circumstances already hinted at, that the conquests of the gospel would now be exceedingly rapid.

(*a.*)   The unanimity of Christians in the work would conduce to this end.   If all the Church could, at any time, feel the pressing importance of laboring for the salvation of the heathen at all commensurate with the greatness of the work, there would be such an impetus in this direction as the world has never seen.   But in this epoch of the Christian world, men will see better the mighty meaning of redemption, and they will labor, pray, and give with a more commensurate zeal and liberality.

(*b.*)   The tremendous scenes through which the men of the world will have passed, will also prepare their hearts for the reception of the truth.   The plowshare of Jehovah will have been so fearfully and thoroughly driven through the soil of humanity, that the fallow ground will be broken up, and the seed of the gospel will have abundant chance to germinate and bear fruit.

(*c.*)   The appliances of art, the facilities of communication by steam and electricity, the amenities of commerce, and the sympathy thus engendered and nourished between the nations of the earth, will facilitate immensely the work of the Church.   So rapid shall this work be, that "a nation will be born in a day."   Hundreds of millions will embrace Christ, the world over.

---

* Note 4, Canto III, stanza 33.   † Note 5, Canto III, stanza 34.
‡ Note 6, Canto III, stanza 35.

3. Smiting with a sword, and ruling the nations with a rod of iron,* implies the great influence which Christ will acquire by the successful preaching of the gospel. That it will be very great, cannot, for a moment, be doubted.

II. But the rider on the white horse bears a two-fold character. That which is implied by the sharp sword proceeding out of his mouth, is his prerogative in the preached gospel. But "he treadeth the wine-press of the fierceness of the wrath of Almighty God." This indicates something more than a spiritual warfare. Again, the angel standing in the sun† and calling to the fowls of heaven to gather themselves together to the supper of the great God, is an undeniable symbol of carnal warfare on a tremendous and sanguinary scale. There can be no doubt of the meaning of the symbol.

The nineteenth verse is a declaration of the same thing. The beast and the kings of the earth and their armies are gathered together to make war against him that sat on the horse and against his army. I have no doubt but this is the beast on which the woman sat, as represented in the 17th chapter, which I have called the symbol of Political Despotism. The woman, or the Papacy, was destroyed in the war of Armageddon. But "the beast which was and is not and yet is,"‡ still lives, and is now rallying the kings of the earth and their armies against the Church. How this may be, of course, we cannot speak positively, as this symbolism undoubtedly points to still future events. But we may suppose that the Church of Christ will have multiplied so extensively, in all heathen countries, as to threaten, not only the hitherto prevailing religions, but even the despotic prerogative of the kings of those countries. Paganism will feel its throne crumbling, as of old in the Roman Empire, before the advance of truth and righteousness, and will be aroused to a final conflict for existence. Under the symbol of the beast it will call the kings§ of the earth to a combined effort to crush the Church. This may be by a simultaneous attack upon it throughout their realms,—by the torch of the incendiary, the dagger of the assassin, and by the sword of

* Note 7, Canto III, stanza 51.   † See Poem, Canto III, stanza 7.
‡ Ibid, stanza 19.   § Note 8, Canto III, stanza 74.

persecution, now let loose again and flaming over the world. The Church will prove too strong to be crushed in this manner, for it will rally armies to defend its hearthstones and altars. It will have millions of friends throughout the now Christian world who would not stand idle and see the horrors of Pagan Rome re-enacted on a more tremendous scale than even under that Empire. The facilities for communication will soon send vast armies to threatened points, and the same agencies may draw the kings and their armies together into one or a few vast camps of Mars. We may well imagine that in the populous districts of Asia,—China, Hindustan and Burmah,—millions, and it may be tens of millions, would be gathered into those camps. Perhaps Europe and America may also send their millions of volunteers to help the cause of right; and such a war may be waged as has never before shook the world,—as the Last great conflict before the Dawn.* The imagery of this passage justifies such an expectation. The mighty angel whose brightness eclipsed the sun, his call to the fowls of heaven; the supper of the great God, or that which he will give to the fowls of heaven; the armies of heaven on white horses, and the fate of the beast and false prophet and of their armies, all lead us to expect the most tremendous and sanguinary struggle that has ever occurred on the globe.† But the result of the battle will be a glorious triumph for the Church. It prepares the way for the binding of Satan for the thousand years, and for the reign of Christ on earth.

We may remark on this:

1. This view shows the mistake of those who are looking for the speedy coming of Christ and the beginning of the Millennium. It is, to my own mind, folly to be looking for the immediate personal reign of Jesus, with the heathen world in its present state, unless we are to expect that all heathen nations are to be swept off by the besom of one fearful destruction. My mind revolts at any such thought as this. I look for the evangelization of the heathen by the ordinary appliances of the gospel, extraordinarily blessed. And if this be so, this expecting the immediate coming of

* Note 9, Canto III, stanza 86.   † Note 10, Canto III, stanza 89.

Christ may be pernicious by tempting the Church to relax her efforts for the evangelization of the world. This work must require time in the ordinary methods of God's Providence. Even though the great events of the world march on with the accelerated velocity of steam and electricity, still it must require time, and it may be centuries.

2. If our scripture chronology is correct, the morning of the blessed Millennium may be when the great dial of time indicates that the world is six thousand years old, which will be some over a hundred years hence. It may be much longer; it may be shorter. Children may now have been born who will see that propitious day, in the flesh. But it is hardly worth while to speculate on the subject.

3. One thing is certain: we know the day is coming. These signs of its coming cannot lie, and we are almost as sure that, compared with the long pilgrimage of the Church thus far through the wilderness, the event is in the near coming future. Then let us lift up our heads and take courage, and battle valiantly for the Lord,* "forasmuch as we see the day approaching."

* See Poem, Canto 3.

6

BEFORE THE DAWN.

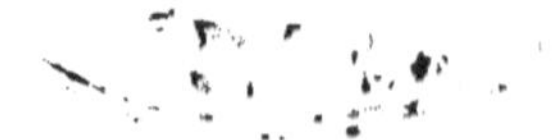

BEFORE THE DAWN.

CANTO I.

NIGHT AND STORM.

I.

NIGHT, gloomy queen, upon thy dusky throne,
Night of the world beneath the power of sin,
Night, when the race the reign of death must own,
Midst thy deep shadows must my song begin.
Thy clouds and tempests, with their fearful din,
Must now the rapture of my muse inspire,
As from her stormy harp some strains she'd win,
To kindle with its tones poetic fire,
That, roused by music, she may gain ambition's hire.

II

Night is the time when good men are asleep,
Seeking, from toil and tumult, balmy rest;
When wicked men their secret vigils keep,
To watch for mischief; when, in stealthy quest,
The assassin creeps to pierce his victim's breast
With murderous knife; when prowling thieves
    abroad
Search, with unholy hands, their neighbor's chest,
To steal his honest gains; when hags, outlawed,
Pursue their wretched trade, by nothing overawed.

III.

Night is a season when tempestuous wrath
More metely conjures up its boisterous storms,
When, glancing fiercely on the thunderer's path,
The lightning, with its leaping fires, transforms
Stark midnight into noon ; when, in swift swarms,
The legions of the tempest rush and thunder,
Peal from the shaking sky their dread alarms,
As if to rend the heavens and earth asunder,
And, with their tumult, fill all hearts with fear and
    wonder.

IV.

But night has calms, when wrangling storms are
    hushed,
When, from the clouds, the torrents cease to fall,
When, off the sky, the murky mists are brushed
By blandest winds, when, sparkling over all,
Rears the blue, spangled dome ethereal ;
When moon and stars their glittering hosts array,
And all to one another grandly call,
Each emulous heaven's mandates to obey,
Far as their orbits run out on the milky way.

V.

Night hath its voices, harsh, discordant, some,—
The owl's weird cry, the howls of beasts of prey,
As they, for food, out from their coverts come :—
Yet on the city's wall, in each highway,
Is heard the watchman's call, till coming day,
Assuring safety : then are trilled the songs

Of nightingale, which sweetly die away,
And whip-poor-will her plaintive notes prolongs,
In lonely groves, retired from daylight's bustling
throngs.

VI.

There is a night that ne'er shall have a day,
When ceaseless storms their fearful conflicts wage,
Which fill the soul with trembling and dismay,
When moon nor stars the darkness can assuage,
Nor joy the wretched, hopeless heart engage;
But nature's night, though stormy, hath an end,
The tempest's sharpest turmoils cease to rage,
When, o'er the sleepy hills, the sun shall send
His kindly rays, and all the darkened world befriend.

VII.

A night there is, of sorrow, when the soul
Bows low in grief, and shakes with pallid fear,
When waves on waves of anguish o'er her roll,
And earthward turned, she finds no helper near;
But when to heaven she looks, with listening ear,
Comes from the bending sky, a message sweet—
" But for a night, shall sorrow drop the tear
On ruined hope, for, when day's heralds greet
Thine eyes, then shall return bright joy on bounding
feet."

VIII.

Night of the grave! thy symbol nature's night,
How dark and dismal is thy rayless gloom!

When sets life's sun, or quenched its joyous light
Amid the darksome mists that shroud the tomb,
In which all men may read their final doom.
Yet for the Christian this dread night shall end,
For on his grave sweet flowers immortal bloom,
Assuring that the trump of God shall rend
Its bars, and bid the prisoned saint the skies ascend.

IX.

But likest nature's night, the night which shrouds
The world with sin's long, lasting, fearful gloom,
When heaven's sweet sky is covered thick with
    clouds,
Dark as the shadows which at midnight come;
When desert winds have blasted Eden's bloom,
And night's damp shades the fruits of Eden killed;
Darker the pall thrown o'er Religion's tomb,
Than that, when souls are with deep anguish filled,
When warm and loving hearts, with death's cold touch,
    are chilled.

X.

Ah! what a night of revel, sin and shame,
When o'er the earth, from hell, an endless flood
Of fiends came trooping, legion is their name,
Whose work is robbery, violence and blood;
To fill with poison what is sweet and good,
Kill peace and joy, and bathe the world in tears,
To mix with bitterness man's earthly food,
And chase his weary soul with gloomy fears,
When, last, he sinks in death to end his toilsome years.

XI.

And oh! this night brings tempests in its train,[1]
When warring, groaning giants of the storm,
Their long, fierce, fearful fights, with hate maintain,
When thunder doth unbare his mighty arm,
As o'er the sky his fiery coursers swarm,
And war's tornadoes, sweeping land and sea,
Dash ruin o'er the world;—when dread alarm
Of earthquake's voice, makes men in terror flee
From shaking cities, to avoid the dread catastrophe.

XII.

And yet this night hath calms, when conflicts cease,
At times, their wrathful din and fearful roar,
When weary earth doth hear the hymns of peace,
As purged, awhile, her fields from human gore,
While stars from the blue heavens their radiance
    pour—
A brightness caught from him whose face is veiled
Behind a world which now, from shore to shore,
Is filled with darkness; men the light have hailed,
And wait a morn, when his bright face shall be unveiled.

XIII.

Once a sweet star rose o'er this darksome night,
And glowed in beauty o'er Judea's plains,
On Bethlehem it cast its cheering light,
Where shepherds heard those high angelic strains,
When angels came in trailing glorious trains.
That star, to Eastern sages, points the way
6*

To where the joys of birth, maternal pains
But lately have succeeded, where he lay,
The Lord and " King of glory," veiled in mortal clay.

XIV.

That star hath sweetly blent its guiding light
With the bright, blissful beacon, flaming forth
Through nature's midnight gloom, from Calvary's
    height,
Where stands the cross, and east, west, south and
    north,
Flings its bright, gladdening beams o'er all the
    earth ;
The wandering steps of pilgrim feet to guide
To rest and safety, and where holy mirth
Doth spread her feasts of joy, in arbor wide,
Where all, 'neath stormy skies, may see their storms
    subside.

XV.

O, glorious cross ! upraised amid the gloom,
Where trembling nature feels the tempest's shock,
And Eden's glory molders in the tomb,
Which sin hath dug.   Upon the eternal rock
Forever stand, and though the tempests mock,
Their Titan blasts can ne'er put out thy light ;
Nor hell's dark powers thy waxing triumphs block :
Beam on the grave, and death shall take its flight,
And Eden's bloom revived shall make earth's deserts
    bright.

XVI.

O blessed Christ, I see thee sit beneath
That cross whereon in anguish thou didst die,
And out where tempests scatter wreck and death,
Where wrangling billows lift their heads on high,
'Midst roaring rocks, direct thy pitying eye,
To watch for shipwrecked souls in anguished strife
With choking waves, to hear their piteous cry,
And then command a peace, where storms are rife,
To draw them to the rock and give them joy and life.

XVII.

That cross, dear Jesus, is my joy and song:
To it I'll cling 'mid wrecks by tempests blown;
Light of the ages, beaming clear and strong,
It stands, though wicked men and devils frown,
It stands, though thrones and kingdoms topple
down;
It stands above the wrecks of ages past,
It stands, though floods of wrath the world shall
drown;
Yea, and shall stand, while earth and time shall last,
Till crowns and kingdoms, all, shall at thy feet be cast.

XVIII.

Amidst the sounds, discordant, of this night,
Sweet voices, too, are heard, the gloom to cheer;
Sounds from the heavens, which fill with sweet
delight
The soul that listens; music full and clear,

Like what o'er Judah's plains, to upturned ear,
Poured its deep rapture through the shepherds'
     souls,
Proclaiming peace to nations far and near;
A joy that thrills in hearts which love controls,
While from the heavenly hosts the glorious anthem rolls.

XIX.

This night of earth, too, hath upon the walls,
And in the streets, to give the warning cry,
Its watchmen, by whose faithful, night-long calls,
Men are admonished when their foes are nigh,
And taught amid the tempest where to fly.
How oft we hear, " O watchman, what of the
     night ?"
Sound 'mid the gloom, and then the quick reply:
" The morning comes, and soon methinks the light
Will dawn, and all the earth's dark shadows take their
     flight."

XX.

Sweet are the words of invitation given
To men, to flee from dread impending wrath,—
Sweet words of Jesus drop, like dews, from heaven,
Benighted souls to turn from danger's path,
To find in him relief from sin and death.
Heard his sweet words: " Come unto me and rest,
Ye weary, heavy laden, and beneath
Your burdens groan no more; come and be blest,
For I have healing balm for all by sins distressed."

XXI.

Sweet are the songs of joy for sins forgiven,
When new-born souls first sing redeeming love;
When saints bid welcome to the joys of heaven,
Begun on earth, for aye to thrill above.
And when to Zion's hill in crowds they move,
To throng her courts to wait, and sing, and pray,
All God's abundant promises to prove,
Through Him who died and washed their sins away,
This night of earth is vocal with the sounds of day.

XXII.

And so, like nature's night, this night shall end;
It hath its day-star pointing to the dawn;
Forth through the orient gates the Lord shall send
Bright heralds of the morning long foreshown,
That shall proclaim him coming on his throne,
To pour his glories from the bending skies,
While on the clouds, by milk-white coursers drawn,
His chariot rolls; and joyous shouts shall rise
From the dark scenes of earth now changed to Paradise.

XXIII.

Of that dim night, but just before the dawn,
The poet tunes his harp, prepares to sing,
Ere its deep shades are from the earth withdrawn;
And though his theme but little rapture bring,
And his wild harp with war's harsh notes must ring,
He hopes, before his stormy song shall cease,

To bear his reader up, on faith's strong wing,
Where, coming in his power, earth to release,
He may behold, from mountain heights, the PRINCE OF
    PEACE.

XXIV.

The scene begins upon the heavenly hills,*
Where round the throne, in snow-white garments
    dressed,
Those angels, by whom vengeance now fulfills
The wrath of God, stand waiting his behest,
Upon the quailing earth prepared to cast
The contents of those vials in their hands,—
The seven plagues, most dreadful, and the last,
Which scatter burning fires o'er many lands,
Rebellion to consume where'er it Heaven withstands.

XXV.

There is in heaven a sea of beauty rare,
Of pure transparent glass and mingled fire,
Of holiness, the symbol bright and fair,
And justice, too, which reddens with hot ire.
Ye who despise the oft proclaimed desire
Of pardoning love as tenderly it speaks

---

* And I saw another sign in heaven, great and marvellous, seven angels having the seven last plagues; for in them is filled up the wrath of God. And I saw as it were a sea of glass mingled with fire: and them that had gotten the victory over the beast, and over his image, and over his mark, and over the number of his name, stand on the sea of glass, having the harps of God. And they sing the song of Moses the servant of God, and the song of the Lamb, saying, Great and marvellous are thy works, Lord God Almighty; just and true are thy ways, thou king of saints. Who shall not fear thee, O Lord, and glorify thy name? for thou only art holy: for all nations shall come and worship before thee; for thy judgments are made manifest.—REV. XV. 1-4

Of God when clad in mercy's sweet attire,
See! pardon scorned, his glittering sword he shakes,
And on the startled ear his wrathful thunder breaks.

XXVI.

On the green banks of that wide-spreading sea
The saints are standing, clad in robes of white;
They wave their palms of blood-bought victory,
And trill their golden harps with sweet delight
To a new anthem, sung with all their might,—
The song of Moses and the Lamb once slain,—
Whilst God and angels listen from the height.
Moses, who did the law of God ordain,
Commissioned by high heaven, bears not the sword in
    vain.

XXVII.

But he holds back the swift descending blow,
While Jesus pleads, who for each sinner bled,
And cries, while he his wounded hands doth show,
Stay, *stay* destruction from the guilty head.
Nor is the sinner's cause thus vainly plead,
For as the storm sleeps on yon glassy sea,
Where waves are hushed to rest and winds have fled,
So sleeps the sword, dear child of God, for thee
Dispersed the clouds of wrath and dread calamity.

XXVIII.

As saints, with joy, in that unnumbered throng,
Stand on that sea, and wave their victor palms,

As to Eternal Mercy, loud and long,
They shake the hills with their high-sounding
　　psalms,
So they rejoice when Justice overwhelms
The unrepenting enemies of God,
Who by disloyal deeds have marred his realms,
Because rebellion sinks beneath her nod,
Blasted and crushed for aye by the Almighty's rod.

XXIX.

Justice they love, she makes them safely dwell,
Because upheld by an unchanging power,—
And Mercy, too, she saved their souls from hell,
When o'er their pathway vengeance stern did lower;
Moses and Christ, in that triumphant hour,
Stand side by side, uniting heaven's poles;
No wonder music waits, 'tis heaven's dower.
List to their song as up to God it rolls,
Triumphant pæon sung by thousand thousand souls.

XXX.

Of God's great marvels in his works and ways,
Of truth and stainless righteousness displayed,
Of love and mercy, highest psalms of praise
They sang.　Who on his terrors undismayed
Can look?　Or gaze, and never be afraid
Of his dread sword?　Nor glorify his name?
Yea, to his name be ceaseless homage paid.
All lands shall come and his great power proclaim,
Who now displays his wrath to men in flood and flame.

XXXI.

Now die away, amid the heavenly hills,
The echos of that wide-resounding song;
While glory heaven's high sanctuary fills,
Which bursts from open portals,* clear and strong;
And, where those splendors roll their floods along,
Those angels clad in white, begirt with gold,
Walk forth before that vast angelic throng:
Let sinful mortals quake as they behold,
For they the secrets of Jehovah's wrath unfold.

XXXII.

Behold! before that throne of power they stand,
And, from the living creature's hand they take
The seven last plagues of God.   His high com-
    mand
They wait, to bid their scorching wrath to break
Upon the trembling world.   Now terrors shake
The earth and sky, and glory crowns the height;
While men, at the dread vision, fear and quake:
No man can, living, stand before his sight,
Until those plagues have wrought on earth their death
    and blight.

* And after that I looked, and behold, the temple of the tabernacle of the testimony in heaven was opened : And the seven angels came out of the temple, having the seven plagues, clothed in pure and white linen, and having their breasts girded with golden girdles. And one of the four beasts gave unto the seven angels seven golden vials full of the wrath of God, who liveth for ever and ever. And the temple was filled with smoke from the glory of God, and from his power; and no man was able to enter into the temple, till the seven plagues of the seven angels were fulfilled.— REV. XV. 5-8.

XXXIII.

THE WARNING.

Listen, O earth, to the voice of dread warning,
  For Justice aroused in her armor is clad,
And Mercy retires, who the sword hath been turning
  Away from its fall on the sinner's proud head.

Thy valleys and plains, and thy hills and thy mountains,
  Shall shake with the footsteps of God in his wrath;
Thy seas and thy rivers, and cool, bubbling fountains,
  Shall blush with the blood of thy sons laid in death.

The portents of heaven shall fill thee with trembling,
  The sun's flaming rays shall proclaim his dread ire;
While, in every land, his avengers assembling,
  Shall shake thee with earthquakes, and scorch thee
    with fire.

Repent, O repent, ere the day dawns in fury,
  Before the dread vials upon thee are poured;
Take warning! take warning! kind angels adjure thee,
  While Mercy's white hand yet may succor afford.

XXXIV.

A solemn voice* comes from yon temple gate,
And, rolling down, it shakes the sea and land.
Hark! hark! it speaks, in clamor loud and great,
And utters forth Jehovah's dread command,
As there enthroned he shakes his red right hand:
"Go, *go* your ways, ye messengers of wrath,

* And I heard a great voice out of the temple, saying to the seven angels, Go
your ways, and pour out the vials of the wrath of God upon the earth.—REV. xvi. 1.

On land and sea your blistering footprints brand;
Pour out my plagues on every rebel's path,
Nor stop till all the earth shall reek in gory death."

XXXV.

Wide o'er the astonished world an angel soars, [2]
His pinions shadow men with cloud and storm;
Out from his vial, on the land he pours
Contagions dire, which o'er the nations swarm,
And fall, in blight, and sore, and mortal harm,
On them who have received the beast's vile name,
And those who seek protection from his arm;—
His image worship, doing deeds of shame:—
In noisome, grievous sores the visitation came.

XXXVI.

If thou my muse to exposition turn,
To find this scene on the historic page,
I point thee to that impious land where burn [3]
The fires of civil war with fiendish rage,—
To France, the warning cry of every age.
She was the pillar of the despot's throne,
Both civil and religious; she'd engage
To make his odious, heaven-cursed cause her own;
With bayonets pin to his brows his fading crown.

XXXVII.

Religious Despotism yclept her king
Her eldest son, and she rejoiced to own
The flattering title; she would gladly bring
Her choicest treasures, and, before the throne,

Would lay them down supine in service prone,
To prop the Holy Father's sinking cause ;—
Though in his realms light nor religion shone ;—
To bind unwilling hands by crushing laws,
To tear the brows of Liberty with eagle's claws.

XXXVIII.

To strike from Rome this nation's strong support, [4]
The angel pours his fearful vial out ;
Its subtle influence shall not cease to hurt
Till her supporting armies, put to rout,
Shall cower before fair Freedom's hosts, and shout
Of disenthralled nations shall arise
To God, who brings deliverance about ;—
Until, from every land beneath the skies,
The Papal power cast down, in desperation flies.

XXXIX.

Dark atheism, with all its withering blight, [5]
And liberty, to starkest license grown,
Veiled that fair land in anarchy's deep night,
And myriads in streaming blood did drown.
If she no earthly king nor crown might own,
Why should she not, into the face of God,
Fling her defiance ?   With him overthrown
In hearts of men, no power above the nod
Of Freedom, she would spread her empire all abroad.

XL.

And so, in maddened conclave once convened [6]
Their sages great, blasphemously resolved—

There is no God (for they on Reason leaned),—
Declared allegiance to Heaven dissolved,—
Death an eternal sleep, from which evolved
Nor life, nor light.   Now nothing should restrain
Their votaries, thus from all law exolved,
From doing as they pleased, such right was plain,
Though by unlicensed power whole hecatombs are
   slain. [7]

XLI.

France had run mad, but, in her maddened mood, [8]
There was a fearful method; she arrayed
Her mighty armies, and, with deeds of blood,
She shook surrounding nations; on them preyed;
By thunder of her arms kings were dismayed;—
O'er Alpine heights her conquering armies poured,
Through Piedmont's sunny vales her trumpets
   brayed,
Among the Appenines her cannons roared,
Till, o'er the seven hills, her wrathful tempests lowered.

XLII.

Nor did she stay the impulse of her arms
Till, o'er the Pyrenees, she rolled on Spain
Tempestuous wrath, full fraught with war's alarms;
And on the Rhine her myriads she had slain
And, with audacious front, on many a plain,
The allied kingdoms she had faced in fight;
And, at the end of many a dread campaign,
Their gathering legions she had put to flight,
Till kings lay at her feet in conquered, ruined plight.

XLIII.

But every blow dealt by her frenzied hand
In ruin fell on despotism's foul head,
And superstition's chains, in many a land,
Were rent asunder, and its minions fled ;—
The same when 'neath the guillotine she bled,
As when the pandoors and the fierce hussars
Of Austria, she trampled 'mong the dead ;—
The same, when victor in her mighty wars,
As when o'erthrown, she felt the crushing heel of Mars.

XLIV.

Ere this first wrath is spent another comes, [9]
Over the sea the second angel flies,
And pours his vial on the waves, then looms
A tempest, mingling seas and cloudy skies,
Till in the deep each living creature dies,
And ocean's seething billows turn to blood
Amid the shrieks and wild despairing cries
Of victims, in the turmoil of the flood,
And desolation rules o'er many a briny rood.

XLV.

See ! how the furies of the battle rage, [10]
Where navies of the world arrayed in fight,
And earth's great kingdoms all their powers engage.
What is yon flash that blazes on the sight ? [11]
That thunder-peal that fills stout hearts with fright?
It is the dreadful broadside's blinding flash,

'Neath reeling rack, black as the clouds of night,
Whose thunderbolts to swift destruction dash
Great ships, whose quivering sides are shattered in the
    crash.

XLVI.

Hark! 'mid that horrid din a thunder stroke [12]
Resounds more fearful far, as if high heaven
Were falling, ocean vomits flame and smoke
Like a volcano, and the clouds are riven
Which veil the scene by battle's whirlwinds driven.
Behold the noble ship flung to the clouds,
In broken fragments to destruction given,
Masts, spars and rigging, stranded shrouds,
With all her crew, lie scattered on the gory floods.

XLVII.

Thus from the Nile, and far-famed Trafalgar, [13]
And, from a hundred battles on the sea
Are heard the thunders of a naval war,
Which sets the glittering stars of victory
On brows of fair Religious Liberty,
And breaks the power of Rome upon the flood,— [14]
The naval power of them that bend knee
To her,—and tinges many a rood with blood,
Wherever on the sea her ships have proudly rode.

XLVIII.

But ere that storm has swept from ocean's main [15]
The navies that uphold the seven hills,
Which sail in clouds from ports of France and Spain,
The sound of other woes the welkin fills,—

With fear the trembling hearts of nations thrills,—
Calamity crowds on calamity.
God, in his anger, heaps the earth with ills,
Hurls his dread thunder on the land and sea,
Till from despotic power the nations shall be free.

XLIX.

ADDRESS TO THE RIVERS AND FOUNTAINS.

O now, ye bubbling fountains,
  Ye rivers, broad and free,
Now singing down the mountains,
  Now surging to the sea ;
Where'er your waters glisten,
  On mount or lonely vale,
Unto your sentence listen,
  And your sad fate bewail.

Ye brooklets, speak your sorrow
  To the lilies of the field ;
Ye floods, the accents borrow,
  In notes o'er mountain pealed ;
Ye cataracts, sound your thunder
  Adown the dizzy steep,
And tell the tale of wonder,
  As on your waters sweep.

L.

Behold ! now swoops from Alpine heights sublime, [16]
On fair Italia's floods and fountains rare,

The angel who avenges every crime
Committed by the scarlet women there.
Thy mountains, Piedmont, and thy valleys fair,
Which blushed with martyr blood, in days of yore,
Shall see her minions smitten with despair ;
Shall see thy rivers crimsoned with their gore,
Where God doth now on them his burning plagues
    outpour.

LI.

Hark ! a dread voice sounds o'er those streams of
    blood,
Thrilling with terror hearts not cold in death.
The angel who presides o'er stream and flood
Now speaks ; the saints attend, and, with hushed
    breath,
Hear those dread accents of avenging wrath
Pealing o'er mountains, piercing valleys far,
And casting trembling in the despot's path,
O'er that doomed land, to feel the shock of war,
In fearful thunders, when Jehovah mounts his car.

LII.

THE ANGEL OF THE WATERS.

Righteous art thou, O Lord, Most High,
    Which art, and wast, and art to be ;
For Thou didst hear thy people's cry,
    And all their cruel wrongs didst see

7

These wicked shed the blood, for naught,
　Of prophets, saints, and martyrs, too;
And now the gory draught is brought
　For them to drink—it is their due.

LIII.

Now hushed, o'er every river, hill, and plain,
That dreadful sound which fills the earth with fear.
Hark! hark! a sound the stillness breaks again
In wilder accents, echoing far and near,—
From heaven it comes, and men the voice may
　　hear;—
It comes from 'neath that altar, where those souls
Which have been slain for Jesus now appear,
And cry for vengeance; each his blood condoles,
As from the awful height the clamorous utterance rolls.

LIV.

RESPONSE OF THE ANGEL OF WATERS.

Even so, God Almighty, let vengeance full sore
Be poured down the necks of these men stained in gore;
Of thy murdered saints, who for Jesus were slain,
With rack and with torture, in sorrow and pain.
Full long their strong cries for redress have been made,
Full long have the footsteps of vengeance delayed;
It is just thou shouldst press to their blistering lips
The festering cup, from which gory death drips.
With the fearful infection let thousands be slain,
Till, in heaps, their dead bodies shall cover the plain;
And the death-scenting vultures shall darken the air,
As they swarm to their blood-reeking feasts from afar.

LV.

The time has come for that prophetic voice,
Uttered on Patmos' Isle, to be fulfilled ;
Among the mountains hear portentous noise
Of busy preparation ; hearts are thrilled,
And cowered blood, with curdling fear, is chilled.
But, while the Gallic eagles rear their brood
Among the crags, the sounds of war are stilled.
At length, on war's black cloud, to fields of blood,
With screech and whirlwind's swoop, they rush a mighty
    flood.

LVI.

Fair Italy, the avalanche descends
From Alpine heights, a deluge red, on thee ;
The power that rules thee 'fore the tempest bends,
And, in the shock, its cowering minions flee ;
Sardinia, conquered, bends the suppliant knee ;
And, after Lodi thunders far and wide,
Tinging the Adda's tide, fair Lombardy
Becomes the conqueror's prey ; yet still, in pride,
He presses on to conquest with a giant's stride.

LVII.

Nor stay his footsteps in his march of wrath :
The fiery tempest o'er Arcole breaks,
And on he strides upon his bloody path,
Till Italy lies low, and Rome bespeaks
Her fulminating power in vain ; she shrieks
With rage and horror, as in clamor loud

The cannon of Napoleon rudely shakes
The seven hills, and round her ramparts crowd
His conquering legions, soon her glory to becloud.

LVIII.

Peace comes.   But soon the Austrian calls to arms,
To crush the proud Republic's spreading power;
At Rivoli he meets the Gallic swarms,
And low in dust his 'numerous legions cower;
Then over Rome again war's tempests lower.
The Senio blushes with the flowing blood;
Faenza, too, falls in her fatal hour;
And then Ancona sinks beneath the flood,—
She who the peer of Venice long hath proudly stood.

LIX.

And thou Loretto, canst thou tell me why,
With Casa Santa in thy sacred gates,
Thou couldst not the great conqueror defy,
But wast, in the dread conflict, put to straits?
They say a band of angels round thee waits,
Who brought the house of Mary, through the air,
From Palestine—for so the myth relates—
And placed within thy walls the treasure, where
It might be safely kept, beneath thy patron's care.

LX.

Why did thy patron thus thy walls forsake
When, with the siege which boded thy quick fall,
Thy towers and ramparts did so rudely shake?
Say, was she deaf, that thou shouldst vainly call?

And when thy foes poured o'er thy prostrate wall,
Why was that house to Paris borne away,
The prey of the great robber, in whose thrall
Were held art's treasures, for a time? We pray,
Let truthful Priests the story tell us, if they may.

LXI.

Oh, Italy! though now thy streams are red,—
Though God hath given thy children blood to
    drink,—
Though in the conflict thou hast fought and bled,
And made thy sunny vales with slain to stink,—
Still myriads more must in thy conflicts sink,
On dread Marengo's trampled field of blood,
Where thousands, driven o'er the awful brink
Of battle, died; Magenta, too, where stood,
In after years, another would-be scourge of God :—

LXII.

And Solferino, crimson fount and stream,
With awful carnage, while their heavy shocks
Fall on the Papal power, and break its dream
Of long endurance; fate its thunder mocks,
And with the earthquake Rome's foundation rocks.
O Great Avenger, just and true thou art,
And naught the wheels of thy dread chariot blocks.
Thy martyred saints are ever near thy heart,
And earth and hell can never thy just vengeance thwart.

LXIII.

APOSTROPHE TO THE SUN.

Thou orb of day, serenely throned
  Upon thy chariot high,
Whose flying coursers, glory crowned,
  Sweep grandly through the sky:
We look upon thy friendly rays
  Dispersing gloomy night,
And for thy benison we praise
  The God who made the light.

Round thee, in widening circles grand,
  The ponderous planets roll;
And, as if held in giant's hand,
  They own thy strong control.
No matter whether near or far,
  Each thy attraction feels:—
The comet, on its bickering car,
  Round its aphelion wheels,

Bends its obedient neck to thee,
  And hastens to return
From space's unfathomable sea
  To where thy splendors burn.
Far, far, thy arrowy beams of light
  Fly through the realms of space,—
No comet, in most distant flight,
  Has ever found a place,

Where is not seen thy radiance bright,
  Sent forth by hand divine,
To banish chaos and old night,
  Wherever thou dost shine.
Thy ministries are numberless,
  Above, below, around,—
Whatever realms thy beams may bless,
  There life and joy abound.

By thee the stormy billows rise,
  That beat on every shore,
To thee the evening zephyr sighs,
  And wild tornadoes roar.
The misty waters fill the clouds
  Raised by thy wondrous power,
And at thy beck come on, in crowds,
  The legions of the shower.

The melody of singing rill,
  The torrent's sturdy roar,
As tumbling down the steepy hill,
  Sing to thee evermore.
And when the tempest rolls away,
  Revealing the blue sky,
The rainbow, painted by thy ray,
  Rears its bright arch on high

Thy rays omnific bring to life
  The plants and trees of earth,—
But for thee naught, in nature's strife,
  Had ever come to birth.

LXIV.

LAMENTATION.

'Tis sad! O 'tis sad! that the sunlight so cheerful
　Should be made the dread agent of death and despair,
That from his bright orb should throng messengers
　　　fearful,
　To smite suffering men with their scourges of fire.
Yet over the sun the dread angel arises,[17]
　And spreads forth his pinions to shadow the world,
And while the eclipse trembling mortals surprises,
　Into his flaming disc the dread vial is hurled.

A great conflagration springs up in commotion,
　Enwrapping the heavens in its wide, fearful glare,
And as waters would flow were the bounds swept from
　　　ocean,
　There pours upon earth flaming cataracts of fire.
The green herb is withered, the blasted tree raises
　Its bare, leafless boughs, in the hot blistering breeze.
The earth, made a desert, its dwellers amazes,
　While torment and terror their trembling hearts seize.

O where is their covert in this hour of trial?
　What glen or what cavern can shelter afford?
O how shall they flee from the flames of the vial?
　Say, how can they brave the fierce wrath of the Lord?
Will they fly to the ocean and hide in its billows?
　Ah, no! for its waters are crimsoned with blood.
Will they seek the cool streams 'neath the shadowing
　　　willows?
　No, no! for contagion fills fountain and flood.

Or will they repent, to the Lord humbly turning,
  Confess his just judgments and own his great power?
Or will they still brave his dread wrath in that burning,
  And never beneath his hot thunderbolts cower?
O hark! 'midst that awful confusion and anguish,
  What sounds of dread import now break on the ear!
Although in their torment and terror they languish,
  Their blasphemous curses resound through the air.

They will not repent, though they feel the fierce burning,
  And glorify God, their Creator and Lord,
But they blaspheme his name, from obedience still
      turning ;—
  O they must sink down, of high heaven abhorred.
O think not, vain man, that the Lord's arm is shortened,
  That these dreadful plagues have exhausted his power,
That his vials are spent, and his counsels are straight-
      ened,
  To discover new methods his wrath to outpour.

Take warning, take warning, four vials outpouring,
  By the hands of avengers of his broken law ;
O do not, by longer his judgments ignoring,
  His uttermost wrath on your helpless heads draw.
Is it not enough that your bodies are writhing
  With sores,—that the ocean is changed into gore,—
That the rivers and fountains with slaughter is seething?
  Must the sun's scorching fires on your bare bodies
      pour?

7*

LXV.

Behold a universal flame of war [18]
Breaks on the plains of Europe, trampled o'er,
As if the sun infected, from his car
Should scatter fires on every trembling shore.
At Austerlitz, 'midst awful din and roar,
The flame breaks forth, and in its fearful glare [19]
Myriads lie scorched and reeking in their gore,
While far abroad, upon the startled air,
Howl war's hot furies, wakened from their sulphurous
    lair.

LXVI.

Jena and Auerstadt blaze next on the sight,
Twin furies of the same tremendous day
In which the sun of Prussia sinks in night,—
The nation crushed in the red battle's fray.
But from the German heart ne'er pass away
The blistering memories of that fearful time,—
Now France, the day of vengeance spreads dismay
O'er thee, and thou dost expiate thy crime,
As German foes besoil thy robes with blood and grime.

LXVII.

O! dreadful Eylau, 'midst thy din and noise, [20]
What horrid visions do thy flames reveal!
Where, in the battle's almost equal poise,
Two giants struggle with their frenzied zeal,
But Friedland comes and sets the bloody seal
Of victory on Bonaparte's proud head,

Though four score thousands in these conflicts reel
And fall, the wounded, dying, and the dead,
While far the trampled fields and flowing streams are red.

LXVIII.

And Spain must feel the great invader's feet, [21]
As o'er the Pyrenees his legions pour ;
She in her sunny vales the Gaul must meet,
And feel his heel press on her bosom sore,
And drink her cup of wrath long kept in store.
See, as his legions swarm from yonder height
Around old Saragossa, famed of yore, [22]
He summons to surrender or to fight,—
Hear her reply, hurled back with grim indignant might.

LXIX.

WAR EVEN TO THE KNIFE.

THE SPANIARD'S DEFIANCE.

Hispania, Hispania, prepare for the fight,
For down roll the war-clouds with darkness of night ;
Thy children are bleeding on fields of red strife,
Yet send back defiance, " War e'en to the knife."

Lo ! down from the mountains the eagles of Gaul
Are swooping, your children as serfs to enthrall ;
Dishonor to sister, to daughter, to wife,
They bring ; then, brave boys, give them " War to the
knife."

Their bugles are sounding, prepare for the storm,
Round their death-shotted guns their artillery-men form,
The loud tocsin ring, beat the drum, blow the fife,
Let your war-cry forever be, " *War to the knife.*"

Though their pinions for springing be poised on the air,
And from their hot eye-balls the red lightnings glare;
Though the rush of their legions with slaughter be rife,
We will breast the tornado with " WAR TO THE KNIFE."

Proud birds from the mountains, your plumes shall be
      soiled,
With the bolts of the Spaniards your flight shall be
      spoiled,
Your pinions be smeared with the streams of red life,
And Spain shall be freed with her " War to the knife."

LXX.

But, Saragossa, valor bleeds in vain,
To crush thee down thy Gallic foes aspire;
Fate to the invader gives thy sunny Spain,
And clothes her valleys with a robe of fire.
Long years shall pass before thy foes retire,
For Reynosa, Burgos, Tudela,
Must see the Gallic banners rising higher;
Corunna, too, must have its bloody day,
Where gallant Moore falls wounded, dying in the fray.

LXXI.

Till Talevera sees the flying Gaul,
And Albnera glances back the flash

Of cannon, and Badajos hears the call
Of England's bugles, and in battle's crash
Sees, o'er its prostrate walls, her squadrons dash,
Till Salamanca shakes his waning power,—
Yea! till Vittoria, with war's gory lash,
Drives the invader from her trampled shore,
And shouts her VIVA EL REY in that triumphant hour.

LXXII.

VIVA EL REY.

THE SPANIARD'S SONG OF TRIUMPH.

Lo! thy deliverer comes,
Peal thy loud Te Deums,
  HISPANIA.
Long, over hill and vale,
Did the proud Gaul prevail;
Now to thy king all hail!
  "VIVA EL REY."

Thy field, Vittoria,
Covered with gloria,
  In the red fray,
Where thine oppressors die,
Whence bloody tyrants fly,
Rolls the loud anthem high,—
  "VIVA EL REY."

Dire was the din and rack,
Red was the siege and sack,
  Of Gaul's dread sway.

Now flies war's tempest cloud,
Falls the oppressor proud ;
Shout forth the welcome loud,
  " VIVA EL REY."

Long live King Ferdinand !
Long may our rescued land
  Thy rule obey.
Hail to great WELLINGTON !
England's victorious son ;
But thee, our King, we crown,—
  " VIVA EL REY."

LXXIII.

Doomed Austria, prepare thy hosts again, [23]
For lo ! the giant and his legions come ;
The Gallic bugles sound the martial strain,
Thy mountains echo to his thunder-drum ;—
Arouse, ye brave ! defend each hearth and home
Now Eckmuhl sees thy shattered ranks go down [24]
Beneath the tempest's shock ; but, midst thy gloom,
Aspern and Essling's battle sets the crown [25]
Of victory on thy head—the giant overthrown.

LXXIV.

But O, alas ! on Wagram's fatal field, [26]
His host's recuperated, dash on thee ;
Thy sons, though brave, borne down by numbers,
    yield
Before the charge tremendous ; see, they flee !

But in their track what myriads, ah! me!
Fall bleeding, dying, dead, upon the plain,
And thy fair, weeping daughters there must see
Their lovers, brothers, husbands, fathers slain,
While the great conqueror's feet thy sacred shrines
    profane.

LXXV.

Bear of the North, thy hibernating lair [27]
Bestir; for in the South a gathering cloud
Of Gallic eagles, darkening earth and air,
Glooms o'er thy forests; hear their screechings
    loud!
They come upon the whirlwind; see them crowd
Thy great highways, thy cubs from thee to tear.
Russians, arouse! and meet the invaders proud;
Upon your sacred shrines and hearthstones swear,
Rather than they should rule, destruction shall reign
    there.

LXXVI.

Ah! how shall I describe that march of death?
Now crossing marshy fens, now barren moors,
Now half a million men war's clouds enwreath,
Where thunder breaks on grim Smolensko's towers,
And then in wrath o'er Borodino lowers,
Till burning Moscow sends its blaze afar,
In whose dread light e'en great Napoleon cowers,
With cold and famine, makes unequal war,
As flies his scattered troops and sinks his glory's star.

LXXVII.

But not yet sated with the nations' blood, [28]
Though hecatombs have fall'n beneath her ire,
Gaul quickly rears another vulture brood
To bathe the world again in blood and fire.
On Lutzen, Bautzen, Dresden, ruin dire
Soon falls.   But Leipsic marshals Europe's power,
To crush. the giant burns a strong desire ;
And in the wrack of that tremendous hour,
His shattered armies fly, and Freedom claims her dower.

LXXVIII.

To exile gone, another takes his throne,
And Elba owns alone the conqueror's sway; [29]
" How has the mighty fallen !" dimmed his crown !
How sets the sun of his triumphal day !
His empire o'er the nations passed away.
But yet not long, as Elba's island king, [30]
The terror of the nations deigns to stay ;
Again on Gallia's shores his footsteps ring,
The eagles of his hosts again have spread the wing.

LXXIX.

How, at his magic call, the hosts of France [31]
Swarm forth, obedient to his high command !
His clarion sounds, those hosts, in swift advance,
Haste from the furthest corners of the land
To place the empire once more in his hand.
The reigning king, without one manly blow,

Flies from his throne, his armies quick disband,
Or, rallying, on the breeze their banners throw,
And cries of " Vive Napoleon " forebode the nation's
    woe.

LXXX.

To crush his power the allied kings again
Send forth their armies in their veteran might,
And war resounds again o'er land and main,
Its glittering pageantries bedaze the sight,
Till, Waterloo, thy thundering furies fright [32]
The world, and pour on France the burning hail,
Till allied armies, clamoring in the fight,
At length o'er the great conqueror prevail,
And chase his shattered legions on their bloody trail.

LXXXI.

That sun is set which, with its burning rays, [33]
The nations scorched, quenched in red seas of blood.
On that lone isle, where ocean flings its sprays
On rocky shores, o'er his great fall to brood,
The conqueror stays, and there he dies.   The flood
In heaving billows sings his funeral dirge
While thundering on the rocks in angry mood,
Instead of booming cannon, 'midst the surge
Of waving plumes, where marshaled armies wield the
    scourge.

LXXXII.

Of gory war.   Great man is this thine end ?
Thou, whose ambitious genius thought to weave

A crown from many crowns, and to extend
Thine empire o'er the world, and didst believe
Thyself the man of destiny, to give
The law to nations?　Thou, whose soul
Burned like a blazing comet to achieve
Unthought-of battles; thus o'er earth to roll
A flood of tears and blood.　Great man, is this thy goal?

LXXXIII.

Art thou the man who, like the Thunder King,
Glared on the startled nations through the smoke
Of battle?　On kingly crests, with deathly ring,
Rained thy hot bolts, and, with thy thunder-stroke,
Didst lay them low, their ancient sceptres broke?
Thy once bejeweled head now lies as low,
Thy grave as humble as was e'er bespoke
For meanest soldier, who, in overthrow,
From thine exterminating sword received the blow.

LXXXIV.

Now turn, my muse, to that old throne of power [33]
Upon the seven hills so long upreared:
Behold the man before whom millions cower,
Who, as a God, in former times was feared.
Well wears he robes with crimson hue besmeared,
Fit symbols to his numerous minions given,
Who on the world through blood-red clouds have
　　leered,
And with their works the hearts of millions riven,
Who sought with fire and sword to win the world to
　　heaven.

LXXXV.

Behold the man who, in the place of God,
Has claimed the homage due to Him alone ;
The man who smote the world with iron rod,
And made its kings obedient to his throne,
That all their realms his sovereign power should
    own ;
Beneath whose interdict no king could stand,
But, outlawed by his subjects, and undone,
Must leave his throne and fly his native land.
Hear the old man of sin assert his high command.

LXXXVI.

What name than mine can greater be,
Though earth be searched from sea to sea ?
Yea, though the search reach up to heaven,
And down to hell with lightnings riven ?
For lo ! the sceptre of my power
Is owned by all.   My thunders lower
In every sky, and, o'er the world,
My blood-red banners are unfurled.

On land they wave most gloriously,
Where legions charge victoriously,
And on the sea, where navies ride,
Their glory crowns the heaving tide.
The kings of earth my sceptre own,
And pay allegiance to my throne.
All should be mine, the gold and gems,
And earth's resplendent diadems ;

The merchandise upon the seas,
With hoisted sails to every breeze;
The cattle on a thousand hills,
Whose lowing every valley fills;
And horses which to battle dash
Where'er their riders' helmets flash;
My sovereign power, all, *all* controls,
Even men's bodies and their souls.

Then with this power it well accords
    That I, by men and angels crowned
The King of Kings and Lord of Lords,
    Should in Jehovah's seat be throned.
And furthermore, I do proclaim,
By the dread sanction of my name,
That every tribe and people come,
Wherever they may rest or roam,
And me, their Lord and master, greet,
And pour their offerings at my feet;—
Or, with my thunder-shaking hand,
I'll scatter them o'er sea and land,
And break their armies o'er the world,
Their navies to destruction hurled,
Their souls to hell's hot furies given,
By lightnings scorched and thunders riven.

Curst be the man that will not raise,
    In honor of my mighty name,
Loud Te Deums of lofty praise,
    And wide my sovereign power proclaim;

Curst in his hands,—curst in his feet,—
  Curst in his head,—curst in his heart,—
Curst in his house,—curst in the street,—
  Curst in his fields,—curst in the mart,—
Curst when he roams,—curst when he rests,—
Curst be his friends,—curst be his guests,—
With fears and terrors let him start,
With burnings let his body smart,—
With rack and torture break his bones,
And fill his mouth with woeful groans;
Let thirst and famine pinch his flesh,
And pincers tear his wounds afresh;—
Let wild beasts rend him in the den,
  Till death shall seize him as its prey;
His name be outcast with all men,
  Nor in their recollection stay.
LET DEEP DAMNATION SEIZE HIS SOUL
WHO WILL NOT OWN MY STRONG CONTROL.

LXXXVII.

Ah! such were once his loud, blasphemous boasts,
When, at his beck, all nations vilely cowered,
Then he received the worship of the hosts,
And o'er all lands his potent thunders lowered,
And on each rebel's head his bolts were showered.
Into his hand the saints of God were given,
Beneath his heel, a season, overpowered,
Until the time shall come, decreed of heaven,
When he, by 'venging wrath, shall from his throne be
  driven.

LXXXVIII.

Old man, the hour of destiny has come,–
God's high decrees must be fulfilled in thee;
Not long o'er earth shall thy red legions roam;—
They shall be overthrown on land and sea,
And naught, from pain and scath, shall set them
　　free.
Down from the frowning heavens the angel stoops,[35]
Ye hear his wings now rushing frightfully,
As swiftly through the whirling air he swoops,
On Rome the plagues of God he brings in countless
　　troops.

LXXXIX.

Now stand in awe! upon his seat of power [36]
He pours the fearful vial of dread wrath;
Ah! the deep darkness of that awful hour
Foretells defeat, and direful rout and death;
And, like a pall of doom, hangs o'er his path,—
O'ercasts his cowering hosts with deathful gloom..
Ah! how they raise despairing cries, from scath
To be set free; but vain;—the reeking tomb
Is gorged with myriads, till for more there scarce is
　　room.

XC.

Vexed with the heat, the blight, the blain, the
　　smart,
They gnaw their tongues, bemaddened with the
　　pain

Of sore, and thirst, and piercing, fiery dart,
Groping in darkness, here and there; in vain
They of their dreadful sufferings complain,
And on the name of God their curses pour.
Deep, *deep* the avengers' swords with crimson stain
Are smeared; see, midst dire revolution's roar,
Their shattered kingdom falls, and falls forevermore.

XCI.

'Tis thus five woes, each other following [37]
In quick succession, from the first to last,
So quickly that the dread events they bring,
O'erlapping, crowd each other, till they're past.
While at the first the nations stand aghast,
A fearful war is raging on the sea,
And, ere 'tis o'er, Italia feels the blast,
And Europe flames with war most fearfully;
Woes heaped on woes, and deaths on bloody butchery

XCII.

Ere these are past, the fifth woe comes in wrath, [38]
And rolls upon disabled, sinking Rome [39]
Dire revolutions in war's gory path; [40]
The Papal power sinks prostrate. overcome, [41]
Robbed of its riches, filled with odium.
To pillage doomed, she drinks the bitter cup
Which she to other lips, so burdensome,
Full oft hath pressed; forced even to yield up
The sacred person of her trembling, senile Pope. [42]

XCIII.

A helpless prisoner, he is dragged away,
To die alone in foreign, hostile lands;
Helpless to hold his puny royal sway
From falling into some more kingly hands.
Say, sons of Italy, by whose commands
Do ye award old Rome a doom so rough? [43]
Why take the spoil once spared by Gothic bands?
Why from her gorgeous temples carry off
· Her choicest treasures, while at her ye gibe and scoff?

XCIV.

We blame not Italy that she thus casts
Rome's yoke of bondage from her children's necks.
But why, Italians, as iconoclasts [44]
Disgrace your noble cause? Why scatter wrecks
Of art's great triumphs in the glorious tracks
Which mark fair Freedom's progress o'er the world?
She art preserves, the soul of genius wakes,
And not destroys; her banner once unfurled,
The foes of art, not art, to ruin should be hurled.

XCV.

But foreign power installs another Pope
Within the walls of that old capital;
The friends of freedom strive in vain to cope
With brutal ignorance, and despot's thrall.
They yield; again, in Church and senate hall,
The minions of the harlot hold their sway.

And yet, not long, for he whom millions call
Head of the Church, again is borne away
By France, and lives in exile many a weary day.

XCVI.

And yet, again in Rome is reinstalled
The Holy Father, and, for fifty years,
His lessening realms are 'neath his sway enthralled,
And he to alternating hopes and fears
Is left a prey.   Again Nemesis rears
O'er him her fearful form, and rolls on Rome
Another revolution, which besmears
The seven hills with blood, drives him from home
An exile, all his boasting legions overcome.

XCVII.

In vain on Garibaldi's impious head
The worsted Pope invokes the curse of heaven,
And on his armies hurls his thunders dread,
By which, in former times, whole realms were riven.
Emancipated Italy is given
To fair Sardinia's king, who holds,
O'er North and South, a lenient scepter even,
And wide the flag of liberty unfolds,
While pure Religion sings for joy as she beholds.

XCVIII.

From exile he would never have returned
To occupy again the Papal chair,
Had not the bigot zeal of Frenchmen burned
With bayonets, to restore and hold him there.

8

The outrage done, how little was his share
Of what was his.   In senile helplessness,
Not half his realms for him did spoilers spare,—
· A patch round Rome is all he may possess,
Too feeble and forsaken to obtain redress.

XCIX.

But still his high pretensions he proclaims,
Is Christ's vicegerent o'er the earth alone;
He writes his name above all kingly names,
And, while he sits upon his ancient throne,
He stoutly hurls his Papal thunders down
Upon the daring head of heresy
Whose loud hosannas all his clamors drown,
It will not heed the Holy Father's cry,
And at his curses impotent will never die.

C.

In looking through the gloom before the dawn, [45]
My guide, the prophet on lone Patmos' Isle
My muse to thee, my native land, is drawn.
Did not the prophet gaze on thee awhile, [46]
When on his vision rose that wondrous pile,—
The temple of the future, reared of God,—
In which his saints should worship, weep and smile,
Whose long, dark aisles their bloody feet have trod?
Dost thou not form a part within that fane fore-
    shewed?

CI.

Wast thou not written in that wondrous book,
Held in His hand, who sat upon the throne,

Which none could open, none thereon could look,
Though challenged by the angel to make known
Whatever in the book might be foreshown?
Innumerous events do crowd its pages,
On both sides written; can there not be one
Which speaks of thee,—thy poets, heroes, sages,—
Where garnered are the choicest fruits of struggling
    ages?

CII.

Adown the dusky track of centuries,
Where shadowy wonders crowd upon the view,
Where wrangling storms and murky tempests rise,
Bestreamed with fire and war's ensanguined hue,
The prophet saw a woman, pure and true, [47]
In sunlight clad, while, under her white feet,
The full moon rolled upon her path of blue;
Her snowy brow and flowing ringlets sweet,
Were crowned with a coronal where the stars should
    meet.

CIII.

Blest mother soon to be, almost as dear
As Mary, who to Christ our Lord gave birth,
She loudly cried* in labor pangs severe,
To give a precious offspring to the earth,
Whose birth should cause the songs of holy mirth
To sound almost as loud as those of old,

* Rev. xii. 1, 2.

When angels rang their loud hosannas forth
To listening shepherds round the sleeping fold,
When from the highest heavens the answering anthems
    rolled.

CIV.

Then rose before his vision, huge, misformed, [48]
A seven-headed dragon,* red with blood,
Each head becrowned, and with ten horns full
    armed.
His monstrous tail, as he through ether rowed
Himself along, of stars a countless crowd
Drew after him, and cast them down from heaven.
Before the woman's face the dragon stood,
With greedy eyes, while she to pangs was given,
Her offspring to devour soon as her womb was riven.

CV.

The child was born, a man-child, hale and strong,
Who was to rule all nations with a rod
Of iron,†—he should rule so firm and long,—
And was caught up unto the throne of God.
The woman fled.   Then Michael sent abroad
The summons to his angels to make war, [49]
To crush the beast beneath Jehovah's rod.
They fought ; the battle clamored near and far,
The wrathful beast fell earthward like a blazing star.

CVI.

Dread was his wrath, he knew his time was short,
Woe ! woe to dwellers on the land and sea ; [50]

* Rev. xii. 3, 4.   † Rev. xii. 5-13.

With furious rage he sought the woman's hurt, [51]
That he on heaven avenged might surely be.
She fled his presence for security, [52]
On wings of eagle to the wilderness,
To wait the wonders of futurity,
A time and times and half time in duress, [53]
By hand of God sustained amidst her loneliness.

CVII.

The dragon war upon the woman waged,
And sent his armies after like a flood,
To drown her sons ; and fierce the conflict raged,
Till lo ! his minions, weltering in their blood,
Were swallowed by the earth, who pitying stood,
To help the woman in the fearful fight ;
She only gave the world the purest good,
And sought to bless all lands with truth and light,
Earth's sorrows lessen, and make glad her darksome
    night.

CVIII.

The battles which the dragon fought against
The woman and her seed for ages lasted,
While all his missiles from her ægis glanced,
Until the monster and his hosts were blasted
By heaven's increasing fire, and he, detested,
Into the horrid deeps of hell was hurled,
Of all his guile and mighty power divested,
No more to blacken, curse, or scorch the world ;—
Before the dawn his blood-red banners shall be furled.

CIX.

How like the Church may this fair woman be,
True to the Lord, clad in his righteousness;
Her wondrous son, like civil Liberty, [54]
Born of her pangs, decreed the world to bless;
And likest despotism's vile ugliness,
The seven-headed monster, horned and red,
Upon whose back she sat, in wantonness,
The woman for whose gain the nations bled,
Far from whose gloomy realms both light and peace
    had fled.

CX.

Dark ages o'er the world have cast their gloom,
And nations clanked their chains in slavery's
    night,—
Has Freedom with Religion found a tomb?
No, no! the first to heaven has ta'en her flight,
Until the time appointed for the right
To triumph in the world, and then descend.
And sweet Religion finds her heart's delight
In the lone desert, with her husband, friend,
Half exiled from the world until the night shall end.

CXI.

Far down the shadowy vista peers the eye
Prophetic, 'midst the turmoil of the storm,
Where Superstition, Tyranny, full high
Have raised their banners, nerved the murderou
    arm,

Around whose standards servile millions swarm.
From rift in yonder tempest cloud behold ! 55
A white-winged, graceful-gliding, beauteous form,
Rides proudly o'er the waves,* with aspect bold,
By wrangling demons of the tempest uncontrolled.

CXII.

See ! where she flies the tempest legions cower,
The clouds uplift and scatter from her path,
Nor does Old Ocean claim her for his dower,
So wont to swallow all that mocks his wrath ;
But o'er her way are hovering Hope and Faith
And Love, whose glorious trains her journey lighten,
Whilst on her head is set a starry wreath,
A turban blue, on which her glories brighten,—
Those stars which from their work the despot's minions
    frighten.

CXIII.

On, *on* she holds her way, the billows cleaving,
By angel hands conducted in her course ;
Sink down her native mountains she is leaving,—
From mother land she seeks a long divorce ;
Ring out the ocean's anthems loud and hoarse,
While endless wastes of waters round her roll.
Hark ! hear that music, set to sounding verse,
Which from her deck rings out the distant tocsin's
    knoll,
Loud hallelujahs pealed from Freedom's lofty soul.

* Rev. xii. 14.

CXIV.

O God of nations, speed her on her flight,
Conduct her to some harbor safe and large,
Cause her bright stars to cast their hallowed light
O'er all the world ; throw over her thy targe,
To shield her head when envious storms discharge
Their bolts to stop her flight, and in the deep
O'erwhelm her; stay the mountain floods that surge
Against her prow, and hush the winds to sleep ;—
All o'er her long and dangerous way thy vigils keep.

CXV.

Behold ! behold ! ye nations near and far,
The brave ship's pilgrimage across the sea,
Her mast-head lifts a second Bethlehem's star
To point the people where the child should be
Who is to rule the world, fair Liberty ;
Her home is far beyond the heaving wave
A land outspread in virgin purity,—
There is an empire for the free and brave,
Where shall not clank the chain of serf or cringing slave.

CXVI.

Far o'er the main a thousand leagues she's fled,
A boundless sea her lessening rudder laves.
What is yon object glimmering far ahead?
There 'mid the roaring rocks the ocean raves,
See how they break in spray the giant waves.
The land, *the land*, a rocky coast uprears

Across her path ; the way she boldly braves,—
Lo! yonder 'twixt the rocks a way she clears,
Into a broad haven the Mayflower safely steers.

CXVII.

High dash the waves along the rock-bound shore,
Shrill shrieks the wind as she approaches land,
But yet in accents heard above the roar,
Rolls the high anthem of that pilgrim band.
The vessel anchors near the stormy strand ;
They man her boats, and lo! on Plymouth Rock
They moor them fast, and soon upon it stand,
And make it a defense to break the shock
Of Titan tempest, all oppression's wrath to mock.

CXVIII.

Lo! there the woman, seen by prophet's eye,
To howling wilderness for safety fled,
To rear her offspring, raise her banners high,
And gather constellations round her head.
The Church of Christ, ere many years have sped,
Hath fixed her tendrils strongly in that soil,
And wide o'er rugged hill and vale hath spread
Her tabernacles, far from brunt or broil,
Or shock of hostile arms her heritage to spoil.

CXIX.

But, when to millions they have multiplied,
The greedy monster sends across the main [56]
The mercenary hordes to him allied,*
To bind the woman with the tyrant's chain.

* Rev. xii. 15-17.

8*

They wage a murderous war on her in vain ;
She tramples them in dust, and lo ! the earth
Doth drink their blood and cover up their slain.
Hark ! hear the pæons of triumphant mirth,
As from the throes of war a nation has its birth.

CXX.

What wondrous growth, my native land, is thine,
Thy ten-fold people throng thy hills and vales ;
Upon two oceans 'does thy baldric shine,
Seas, lakes, and rivers, whiten with thy sails ;
Across a continent are stretched thy rails,
Thy thundering cars shake mountain, valley, plain ;
Thy wealth in fields of commerce never fails,
And heaven's swift fires thy messages contain,
Though o'er thy broad expanse no king may ever reign.

CXXI.

But yet that dragon, cunning in his schemes, [57]
Did plant a germ in thy productive soil,—
While thy great statesmen reveled in their dreams
Of future good,—thy heritage to spoil,
Which laid in bonds three million sons of toil.
It grew a dreadful monster like its sire,
And circled half thy land within its coil ;
To seize the rest it burned with fierce desire,
And whelmed the anguished nation in a sea of fire.

CXXII.

Dark was the time when on that throne of power
The angel poured the fearful vial out ;*

* Rev. xvi. 10, 11.

And black the tempest which in heaven did lower,
And long it raged amidst the mingled shout
Of wrangling foes, until disastrous rout
Poured its hot bolts on Slavery's hydra head,—
Until his grizzly front was turned about,
And from the field he and his minions fled ;
Yea, till the sword of God had smote the monster dead.

CXXIII.

Thus this dread vial reached across the seas,
And thus its lightnings shattered slavery's throne.
So, o'er a mighty nation, on the breeze,
Far to the North, its subtle influence blown,
On forty million men in serfdom prone
It fell, and quickly all their bonds were riven ;
And when the glorious work abroad was known,
To every feeling heart great joy was given,
And Freedom's anthem rang exultingly to heaven.

CXXIV.

Imperial Russia, hail to thy great Czar !
Who spake the word, and Serfdom ceased to be,
Without arousing the dread fiends of war ;
My native land extends the hand to thee.
Thy forty million serfs at once made free,
With our enfranchised sons of toil may raise
Their psalms of Freedom, borne above the sea,
To our predestinating God, and praise
The wisdom that foreshows His wondrous works and
ways.

CXXV.

The solemn shadows of the coming time
Begin to cast their thickening gloom, before
The last night watch peals out its closing chime;
The earth prepares for conflict, fierce and sore,
And darkness deepens, but 'twill soon be o'er.
Around we hear the notes of preparation,
Full soon will break the battle's fearful roar,
To fill the foe with woeful lamentation,
And for the laboring Church complete a full salvation.

CXXVI.

Rome's hierarchy feels the heavy blows
That shake her power in Austria, France and Spain,
Redoubling on her head the dreadful woes
Which she received before, on land and main.
See! where she, wounded, writhes in deathful pain,
On dread Sadowa's fearful field of blood.
Ah! what a blow to weaken her long reign
By Nemesis, avenger of the good,
Where once the martyr, Huss, mid burning faggots
    stood.

CXXVII.

Ah! yes, Bohemia, from thy sprinkled ground
The blood of martyrs long to heaven has cried;
Four hundred years it hears the woeful sound,
And knows how many sons and daughters died
To sate the Roman's hatred, lust and pride.
But long delays the sure, descending blow,

That, when upon his chariot he should ride
For fullest vengeance, all the world might know—
THE MILL OF GOD GRINDS FINE, THOUGH IT GRIND
SLOW.

CXXVIII.

How was thy scepter broken, scarlet Rome,
In that great Empire, by that fearful fray,
When Austria was by Prussia overcome!
What millions ransomed from thy hateful sway!
See, as the smoke of battle rolls away,
So passes thy dominion from that land.
Its king enfranchised shall no more obey
Thy laws supreme, nor fear thy puny hand,
Though feebly grasping thunders to uphold command.

CXXIX.

Now Italy, fair land, thy Venice take,
In this affray wrenched from the tyrant's hand ;
With Lombardy she hastens now to make
Thine ancient realm o'er all thy sunny land
Complete ; and States torn from the Pope's com-
mand,
Still more enlarge thy fast increasing sway.
The time will come when, from the Tiber's strand,
United Italy shall drive away
All foes, with Rome her capital. GOD SPEED THE DAY.

CXXX.

Spain, bloody mother of a bloodier son,*
How supple was thy king to Rome of yore !

* Philip Second.

What horrors hath thy Inquisition known!
How swam thy dungeons dark with martyr gore!
How hast thou slain thy thousands many score,
And desolated kingdoms with the scourge
With which red Rome has lashed the nations sore,
Upon unwilling necks her yoke to urge,
The world from so-called fatal heresy to purge!

CXXXI.

On thee, in his full time, the avenger came,*
When endless thousands swarmed thy land from
    Gaul,
And lit thy towns and cities in the flame
Of war, and made thy sons by myriads fall,
And draped thy beauteous land in death's black
    pall;
When every breeze was laden with the wail
Of thy fair daughters, who could ne'er recall
Their lovers, slain amidst the battle's hail,
And widows' woeful moans arose without avail.

CXXXII.

Yet, though thy pride was humbled in the dust,
And glory faded from thy martial wreath,
Thy greatness gone, still thou didst put thy trust
In bloody Rome, and blindly sit beneath
Her upas shadow breeding naught but death;
And in thy folly impotently swear
Her monstrous claims, until thy latest breath,
With all thy might t' uphold, no force should tear
Thee from her bosom—yea, for aye thou wouldst be
    there.

* Napoleon's campaigns in Spain.

CXXXIII.

And there thou *didst* remain, as if entombed
In some dark crypt beyond all mortal ken,
Dead to the living world, forever doomed
To superstition's chains, and ne'er again
To wake to glory with thy fellow-men,
With them all emulous in high emprise.
Awake, O Spain, and from thy sleepy den
Come forth to-day, and ope thy wondering eyes,
And see what costly guerdon bids thy sons arise.

CXXXIV.

Where are thy works of art? pray tell me, Spain;
Where is thy wealth that whitened on the wave?
Thy golden galleons that plowed the main?
And where thy gallant soldiers, once so brave?
Search for these treasures at Religion's grave.
Where are thy railroads, with their engine's roar?
And where thy knowledge, industry to save
Thy people?   Go ask him who laid thy shore
Beneath stern interdiction's blasting, crushing power.

CXXXV.

Go, lay on Rome this fearful charge of guilt,
That she has barred thy sons from heaven's blest
    light,
While they for her their choicest blood have spilt,
She shuts them in with adamantine night,
And with her grasping, grim and ghostly might,
Has strangled all their highest aspirations,

Till from thy land Religion takes her flight,
And leaves thy sons to her stale incantations.
O pray, then, " RISE AND BLAST HER POWER, GREAT
    GOD OF NATIONS."

CXXXVI.

HARK! HARK! an echo borne across the sea,
Of revolution sweeping o'er that land;
Her sons arise, and swear she shall be free,
They tear the scepter from her tyrant's hand,—
The vile corrupter flies at their command.
They strike for liberty from Papal Rome,
And on religious freedom take their stand,
To give to all the land the sacred tome,
And ope the fount of life on every hearth and home.

CXXXVII.

HISPANIA, HAIL THE MORNING OF NEW LIFE!
Hail to the throes that give thee a new birth!
God save thee from a long continued strife,
And set thee in high places of the earth.
Thou turnst thy back upon the blight and dearth
Which Rome has fastened on thy hungry soul;
Turn now thy heart to pure Religion's worth,
Thy name beneath her banner now enrol,
And dread as much the atheist's as the Pope's control.

CXXXVIII.

Thou Rip Van Winkle of a thousand years,
Dost hear the train of progress thundering on?

Dost hear the kingdoms shake about thine ears?
Dost feel beneath thee now thy tottering throne?
Dost know thy thunder-shaking bird has flown?
Dost see thy bulls before the eagles cower?
Thy pigmy foe e'en to a giant grown?
Awake, O Pope, and save thy waning power,
Put on a cloud of wrath and bid thy thunders lower.

CXXXIX

Ye heretics, attend.   The Vatican
Gives forth a sound portentous; he awakes;
Now brave the tempest every one who can;
With sorest wrath his mighty hand he shakes,
And on the startled ear his thunder breaks.
The seven mountains labor,—what comes forth?
A "*mus ridiculus!*" hear what it speaks;
The Syllabus of Pius! hear it South and North,
And East and West proclaim it over all the earth.

CXL.

Poor silly Pope, thou art behind thy time,
The nations do not heed thy piteous cry;
Earth's grand improvements spread in every clime,
Religious freedom breathes 'neath every sky,
And heresy triumphant will not die;
The ghost that frights thee, father, will not down,
For mighty truth is stronger than a lie;
It will not cower beneath thine angry frown,
Nor will it longer wear the martyr's bloody crown.

CXLI.

O Pius, don't despair, but try once more,
And call thy VIRTUES, BISHOPS, PRINCES,
    POWERS,
(*They* surely won't despise thy taurus' roar,)
To help thee stay Saint Peter's crumbling towers,
And shield thee, for destruction o'er thee lowers.
He calls, and thousands hear him, one and all
They hasten from the earth's remotest shores
At their old father's feet again to fall,
And form at Rome a council ecumenical.

CXLII.

" All hail, ye hierarchs of Church and State,"
(The Pope addresses them as he of old
Was wont,) " and all that on your mother wait,
" My many subjects,—if the truth be told,—
" Do not regard me, though I weep and scold ;
" Declare ye my infallibility,
" It will increase my power a thousand fold,
" And greatly add to my tranquility,
" And stay me up while sinking in senility.

CXLIII.

" Make me INFALLIBLE, ye priests of God,"
(At least make doting fools believe him so,)
" I'll make the nations tremble 'neath my rod :
" I'll tread on necks of kings, as long ago
" Rome's hierarchs were wont ; yea, I will show
" The roaring wheels of progress where to boom

"Or stop," (a thing they ought to learn to know,)
"Scare their conductors with some threatened
  doom,
"Or sweep them off the track with my ecclesial broom.

CXLIV.

"Besides, ye saints," (a thing of no account,)
"I'll make our Peter's pence in golden streams
"Ten-fold, flow singing to our holy mount,
"And you shall realize your fondest dreams
"Of wealth and power, as sure it well beseems
"The faithful, and if fallibilitie
"Belongs to me, as sketicism misdeems,
"Infallible shall be my treasurie,
"For all the gold of nations sure belongs to me.'

CXLV.

And can it be a man that has his wits,
Believes himself so favored of high Heaven
That from that tottering throne whereon he sits
Commands infallible can e'er be given?
What if by Papal bulls States once *were* riven!
Or by a mighty crime would he deceive
And hold men down, who for the light have striven,
In sottish ignorance for aye to live,
And bow to his as to Divine Prerogative?

CXLVI.

O blasphemy, how brazen is thy front,
Thus to usurp Jehovah's awful throne;

How long immunity canst thou account
Ere thou'lt be blasted by his withering frown?
Thou seekest still a universal crown.
Say, when thy starving children ask for bread,
What dost thou give to fill their mouths? A stone.
For fish? A serpent poisonous instead.
What crown is infamous enough to wreathe thy head?

CXLVII.

O live there, Heaven, within the light of day,
So many millions breathing thy sweet air,
At such a shrine to throw their souls away,
On such an altar pour unmeaning prayer?
Dumb, driven cattle hasting, anywhere,
At beck of tonsured Priest or mitred Pope,
Believing nonsense stark oracular,
Content in stolid blindness thus to grope,
Now moved by craven fear, and now delusive hope.

CXLVIII.

Almighty Spirit, breathe thy potent breath
Upon these slain, that they may live again;
Cause life to pulsate 'twixt their ribs of death,
That they may stand and walk like living men,
And see what things lie open to their ken;
That they may seek the infallible in Popes
No more, nor yet in any creature; then
Inflame their aspirations with those hopes
Which cheer the saint when he with hell's dark legions
    copes.

CXLIX.

Although the Pope now merits piteous scorn,
And only that receives from thinking men ;
Although the Papal Church is rudely torn
By heresies and factions, still she lives,
And something in her constitution gives
Her great vitality and power, a life
Which, while it wanes, its wasting power retrieves,
And will not yield to reformation's knife
Until it shakes the world with mortal din and strife.

CL.

Fully awake to her great loss of power
In her old seats of empire 'cross the sea,
Upon thy sky her boding tempests lower, [58]
AMERICA ; she calls them up for thee.
'Tis true thou boastest now that thou art free ;
Take warning, Rome is forging heavy chains, [59]
To lay thy sons again in slavery ;
With evil eye she sees thy hills and plains,
And lusts to rule the land o'er which fair Freedom
      reigns. [60]

CLI.

Think not, my native land, that spirit dead,
Which stained her hands with blood, in former
      times,
Think not those bloody hands would spare thy
      head,
Though full the record of her former crimes ;

For she has desolated fairer climes.
If she to her own power can give increase,
It fully with her bloody spirit chimes
To drive from thee all true religion, peace,
And make thy freedom, worship, e'en thy Bible cease.[61]

CLII.

Guard thy Palladium well, America,[62]
The center and circumference of thy power;
THY OPEN BIBLE, which has spread thy sway
O'er realms of mind, increasing every hour:
It is assailed, the flames above it lower,
And threat to take from men its sacred lore.
Thou must not at Rome's haughty footstool cower,
If thou wouldst save thyself, from shore to shore,
Though ballots, bullets, threaten—even seas of gore.

CLIII.

Another of thy bulwarks is assailed—
Thy COMMON SCHOOLS, which e'er have been thy
    pride,
From which the spring Pierian has not failed
To flow to all thy parts, a crystal tide,
O'erflowing thy great country, far and wide;
But Priests would educate thy sons and daughters,
And for thy halls of science would provide,
Corrupting all thy sweetest, clearest waters
With their dark superstitions.   EVIL PLOTTERS.

CLIV.

Let Europe's priest-rid lands a warning give,
How thou entrustest to such crafty hands
Thy dearest boons.　O wilt thou not believe
That groping ignorance on which she stands,
By which she gains consent to her commands,
The only portion she will give to thee,
As to the stolid mass of other lands?
All that she'll give to them who bow the knee
To her, is knowledge to uphold the Roman See.

CLV

She marches on to empire, silent, sure, [63]
Deep-laid her schemes, and strong her outworks
 stand;
She builds as if for ages to endure, [64]
As if her rule no one could countermand;
And myriads are swarming to our strand,
The sworn allegiants of a foreign king—
King Pope—sworn to support, with heart and
 hand;
And to our cherished institutions bring
No love, but hatred in their hearts deep smouldering.

CLVI.

Let none accuse the poet with croaking, when
He augurs yet a conflict sharp with Rome,
Unless we're willing to be slaves again.
To save our dear-bought liberty at home,

We, or our sons, must to the conflict come—
A conflict of opinion it may be,
If we're in time; but by delay, the drum
Shall beat the warning roll, and call the free
To strike with carnal arms again for liberty.

CLVII.

We hear the notes of preparation sounding,
And see portentous heralds of that day,
And while the signs of evil seem abounding,
Behold, the hand of God prepares the way,
And better portents come in blest array.
The high-built walls of separation fall,
And Christian love begins to hold her sway;
Exclusiveness begins to lose her thrall,
And love's blest union banner soon shall wave o'er all.

CLVIII.

The Lord the Christian host begins to mass
For some decisive move along the front,
Beyond the present army lines to pass,
On some stronghold or battlement to mount
His glorious banner; or, in battle's front,
Repel the fierce assault of gathering foes,
Who compass the destruction, as they're wont,
Of all that we hold dear.   He bids us close
With them, and strike their daring front with crushing
    blows.

CLIX.

Hail, Christian union, blessed of the Lord,
Thy trophies now begin to mark our age;
Two mighty hosts are marshaled in accord,
In their united strength, this war to wage,
To stand with breast to breast while battles rage.
HAIL! THE BLUE FLAG OF CALVIN AND OF KNOX,
Of those brave old reformers, glorious badge,
High may'st thou wave upon the eternal rocks,
And ne'er go down in storm, though wild the tempest's
    shocks.

CLX.

God speed the time when all that bear that flag,
In one strong band of union shall be bound;
When none from high emprise their feet shall lag,
And loud their shout of battle shall resound.
ETERNAL SPIRIT, bring the day around,
When other severed Churches shall arise,
And each the other with love's arms surround,
In bonds of union sealed above the skies;
Let prayers and songs united, hell's dark hosts surprise.

CLXI.

And hasten, too, the blessed time when all,
However named, that love our gracious Lord,
As God in man, into one line shall fall,
And, with a shout of high and rapt accord,
Unsheath and wave aloft the flaming sword,
And rain its crushing blows on death's dark towers,

Until his conquering, all-triumphant word,
Shall put to flight the Devil's marshaled powers,
And men and angels shout, " THE VICTORY IS OURS."

CLXII.

But hark! while pæons of triumphant mirth
Rise from our native land, with joy, to heaven,
A muttering storm begins to shake the earth, [64]
Across the sea, as if her womb were riven,
And in her throes most fearful portents given
Of monstrous births.   Hear th' tramp of armed
    men,
O'er fields where maddened hosts of yore have
    striven.
Lo! Gaul sends forth her vulture brood again;
Her martial bugles shake the mountain, plain and glen.

CLXIII.

Behold her glittering pageant proudly wave
Her martial plumes; her armor glitters far,—
A million men go forth.   To what?   The grave.
Ah! see what pride and circumstance of war!
Soon ends the pomp, soon sets her glory's star.
Get ready God's great wine-press of dread wrath,
Heap high a sacrifice piacular,
With vine of earth, reaped from destruction's path.
Death's steeds, wade to your bridles in the gory math.

CLXIV.

Ah! what destruction in this monstrous war!
What bloody torrents deluge that fair land!

What din, infernal thunders, near and far!
In vain the Gauls the German hosts withstand;
Thy day, Sedan, breaks down his high command
Who grasped for empire, though to wade in blood
Unto a throne, or stain his royal hand
With blackest crimes, were needed. There he stood
And sowed the dragon's teeth, to reap a serpent brood.

CLXV.

Proud man! in shame thy haughty pride doth end,
A deep disgrace thy royal purple stains;
No fawning sycophants thy way attend,
Thou art saluted by no martial strains.
A captive, thy forsaken soul complains
Of treachery, when impotence alone,
Joined with that pride of power which filled thy
    brains,
Uncrowned thy head, and drove thee from thy
    throne;
But it is well that thou shouldst for thy sins atone.

CLXVI.

Look at the ruin thine ambition makes;
See how have fallen myriads true and brave;
With war's dread larums thine whole Empire
    shakes,
Near half thy realm is one vast, reeking grave,
And thy proud capital no power can save;—
The cannon thunder at her trembling gates,

And millions there with cold and famine rave;
Poor Paris reels amid her maddening straits,
She falls! *she falls!* forsaken by her fickle fates.

CLXVII.

Look at the myriad homes now desolate,—
Their sun gone down in shades of deepest night,—
What lands made bare! what cities subjugate!
Or laid in smouldering ruins in the fight!
Till La Belle France mourns at her ruined plight.
Where is that valor which at Jena steeled
Her mighty arms, and burned with mad delight
In hell of strife, and shattered Prussia's shield?
Hear France lamenting o'er Sedan's besprinkled field.

CLXVIII.

SEDAN.

The morning sun rose clear and bright,
Which roused these legions with its light;
All gay with life, with vigor warm,
As in long glittering lines they form,
At evening, when its ghastly rays
Are struggling through the battle's haze,
They fall on heaps of slaughtered men,
Which strew for miles the bloody plain.

Look o'er this field, this ghastly field,
Where battle's thunders lately pealed;
How torn and bloody! heaped and crushed!
Where charging squadrons o'er it rushed;

See wreck and ruin, blood and death!
  And tell me, now, if glory's wreath,
And glory's praise, which is but breath,
  Repay the ills which wars bequeath

Where is the soldier's martial fire
  Which burned upon his cheeks at morn?
Where is ambition's costly hire,
  Which nerved his arm in fight upborne?
The fire is quenched upon his cheeks,
  And glory's wreath is rudely torn,—
His praises are the orphan's shrieks,
  His deeds a million widows mourn.

CLXIX.

Ah! France, how fearful is thy bitter cup!
Pressed to thy pale and bloody, quivering lips,
It burns thy soul, yet thou must drink it up,
Though from its brimming fullness madness drips,
And thou must sit in dust, on ghastly heaps
Of ruin. Child of mighty Babylon,
How art thou fall'n into profoundest deeps
Of rage and woe; torn from thy brows thy crown,
And shattered, tottering, fallen, thine imperial throne.

CLXX.

Peace comes; the German hosts from thee retire,
Proud Paris. Ah! now what do we behold? [65]
Thy boulevards flame with revolution's fire,
Fraternal blood bestains thee as of old;

Thy royal halls to mad sedition sold ;
And there in revels bloody riot runs.
Where is the man unscrupulous and bold,
To wake to glory once again thy sons?
Better than this the reign of thy Napoleons.

CLXXI.

Sad nation, to be free thy heart aspires,
But thou canst not the blessed boon preserve ;
Thou hast forgotten God, and burn'st with fires
Of lust, which rob thee of all manly nerve.
Forsake thy crimes, if thou wouldst freedom serve ;
Give to thy land an open Bible's pages,
Nor dare again from God's great law to swerve ;
Give to thy sons the wisdom of past ages,
Restrain thy daughters from those ways which lust
    enrages.

CLXXII.

Corrupt them not with thine abominations,
Nor sell them for the harlot's hire of sin ;—
And to avoid these awful visitations,
At once this reformation's work begin ;
Till then shalt thou be torn without, within,
For God a controversy hath with thee
For thine enormous crimes, and skin for skin
He will require. Ah ! dread calamity
Shall come on thee in protean forms, by land and sea.

CLXXIII.

A changeless God hath said he will, in wrath,
Turn nations that forget him into hell ·—
Trace thou, in retrospect, the gloomy path
Of wicked cities down to hades, and tell
If his vindictive fury never fell
Upon offenders.   Ah! as sure as he
Sits on his throne and wields his scepter well,
Unless thou dost repent, he'll visit thee
With dire destruction —this thine end shall be.

CLXXIV.

Wait not till other vials are outpoured,
Wait not till other woes upon thee fall,
Avoid the plagues which for thee have been stored,
Rise from thy gory bed, to heaven call,
And God in mercy will again install
Thee in thy former glory, purified
From thy deep stains of guilt, and disenthrall
Thee from oppression's power, by which have died
Thy sons by millions, midst destructions wide.

CLXXV.

Ah! France, we do remember, in our night
Of trial, in " those times that tried men's souls,"
When proud oppression sought, with wicked might,
To bind our limbs, enforce her greedy tolls,
And of protection grant us scanty doles;
Thy heart for us beat warmly in thy breast,

Thy gallant soldiers swelled our army rol
Thy La Fayette, in memory ever blessed,
Stood by our Washington, and our deep wrongs redressed.

CLXXVI.

The Tree of Liberty, which now o'erspreads
Our happy land, was watered by the blood
Of thy brave sons who bowed in death their heads,
And, but for them, oppression, like a flood,
Might us have overwhelmed, and spawned its brood
O'er all this western world.   To thee we owe,
For this, a debt of lasting gratitude.
We wish thee well, and pray that thou mayst know,
Ere long, the blessings which to true Republics flow.

CLXXVII.

Great city, on the seven mountains throned,
The storm that deluged France hath shaken thee;
Thou hast not yet for all thy sins atoned,
Though flowing blood hath reddened land and sea,
And plagues have filled thy realms with misery;
From thee not passed the darkness and the pain,
Though from thy woes thy Pope was forced to flee
Thrice, while thy streets were heaped with many
    slain,
And gathering armies choked thy desolate Champaigne.

CLXXVIII.

And Italy, the blow which prostrates France
Doth weld anew the scepter of thy king,

Unbolt those heavy gates and bid advance
His hosts, and over Rome his banners fling,
And make her domes with Freedom's pæons ring;—
Doth make for aye the Eternal City thine,
The bread of life unto her children bring,
The light from heaven upon her darkness shine,—
Shine from THE OPEN BOOK, all glorious, all benign.

CLXXIX.

Victor Emmanuel, all hail!
Thy name, a happy omen to the world,
Means—"God with us," before whom despots quail,
And foes to swift destruction shall be hurled.
See that the banner thou hast now unfurled
Is never stained by foul oppression's hands;—
See that thy crown, with rarest gems impearled,
Shall shine undimmed o'er all thy sunny lands;
And millions shall uphold thee where thy throne now
    stands.

CLXXX.

Poor Pope, alas! we really pity thee,
Dispoiled of all thy earthly realms at last,—
Thou who hast claimed infallibility,
From great pretensions down so quickly cast.
But thou art doomed; hear now the trumpet blast,
For fallen, fallen, is great Babylon!
To blank oblivion thou art hasting fast,
When better days will dawn the world upon.
Thee fallen, Christ shall sit, instead, upon the throne.

9*

CLXXXI.

True, thou mayst call thy minions to thine aid,—
For millions yet before thee bow the knee,—
And thou mayst preach another great crusade
To bring revolted States aback to thee,
T' restore the glory of the Papal See.
But warning take, for warning sure is given,
Filled to the brim thy cup of wrath shall be;
Nor with new crimes inflame the wrath of heaven.
Repent, or with more fires be scorched, more thunders
    riven.

CLXXXII.

But now awhile from these dread tempests sore,
Which did o'er Europe's realms so fiercely rave,
To waste the dragon and cast down the whore,
We turn to where thy floods, Euphrates, lave
The Orient shores, which God in wrath once gave
To the false prophet. See what him befalls;—
For sure, a people God hath there to save,
For whom he breaks the bondage that enthralls
Those realms;—he to his work th' avenging angel
    calls.

CANTO II.

THE FALSE PROPHET.

I.

From Araby, the land of rocks and sands,
There flowed a wondrous river long ago,
And, though it had its source in desert lands,
Far o'er the world its murmuring floods did flow.
'Tis said, great prodigies the earth did show,
When from the rended rocks its waters sprung;—
She was with earthquakes shaken to and fro,
While clouds and darkness in her welkin hung,
And sunk a wide-spread lake her yawning deeps among.

II.

A heathen shrine received attention, too,
Whose fire, supposed divine, had ages burned,
The idol of that fire-adoring crew,
Who, in the East, have true religion spurned.
Its fire is quenched, its light to darkness turned,
And many other portents shadowed forth,
(Though what they were 'tis bootless to have
    learned,)
That, in the East, the West, the South, the North,
These wrangling, swelling waters should o'erflow the
    earth.

III.

We find its symbols in that wondrous book,
In which the vials now outpoured are shown;
You'll find it called Euphrates, if you look—*
The greatest river to the Orient known.
Four mighty angels, in its bed bound down,
Are loosed to bathe the world in fire and blood;
On their fierce prophet's head to set the crown
Of Orient realms; to whelm beneath its flood,
A third of men, while scattering their fanatic brood.

IV.

Its small beginnings soon a flood become,
And whelm Arabia beneath their tide;
It breaks the bounds of its grim desert home,
O'er Palestine its wrangling waters glide,—
That city trembles where our Saviour died,—
And Carmel pales to hear their angry roar,

* And the sixth angel sounded, and I heard a voice from the four horns of the golden altar which is before God, saying to the sixth angel, which had the trumpet, Loose the four angels which are bound in the great river Euphrates. And the four angels were loosed, which were prepared for an hour, and a day, and a month, and a year, for to slay the third part of men. And the number of the army of the horsemen were two hundred thousand thousand: and I heard the number of them. And thus I saw the horses in the vision, and them that sat on them, having breast-plates of fire, and of jacinth, and brimstone: and the heads of the horses were as the heads of . lions; and out of their mouths issued fire, and smoke, and brimstone. By these three was the third part of men killed, by the fire, and by the smoke, and by the brimstone, which issued out of their mouths. For their power is in their mouth, and in their tails: for their tails were like unto serpents, and had heads, and with them they do hurt. And the rest of the men which were not killed by these plagues yet repented not of the works of their hands, that they should not worship devils, and idols of gold, and silver, and brass, and stone, and of wood: which neither can see, nor hear, nor walk. Neither repented they of their murders, nor of their sorceries, nor of their fornication, nor of their thefts.—REV. IX. 13-21.

As, red with blood, all bounds they override;
Across great Lebanon their legions pour,
And roll a sanguine flood on Asia Minor's shore.

V.

See what a numerous host of armed men
Now tramp along in hostile war's array—
The Arab, Turk, the savage Saracen,
In armor rushing to the battle's fray.
They, from their turbid multitude, display
The crescent of the prophet, flaming high;
True to the flag that leads them to the fray,
"Allah il Allah, Allah hu!" they cry,
And with the charge and shout they rend the earth and
    sky.

VI.

Ah! dread array, as couching lance and spear,
Two hundred thousand thousand horsemen strong,
Fly to the charge, to scatter death and fear,
Like whirlwinds, as their squadrons rush along.
SEE! SEE! their horses, maddened in the throng,
From their wide nostrils belch hot streams of fire;
See! in their tails are scorpions, and, when stung,
Their victims, falling, instantly expire,
Ground in the gory dust by horse and horseman's ire.

VII.

Behold o'er Asia Minor's hills and vales,
That torrent roars on its tempestuous path,

And over all opposing foes prevails,
Till e'en on Europe's shores it breaks in wrath,
Resounds the Moslem's shout in march of death;
  And, as the tramping hosts the mountains shake,
  Doomed men in terror mutely hold their breath.
  At last, in siege, Byzantine pillars quake,
Though not for long do they the trembling city take.

VIII.

  But o'er Roumelia's ancient hills and dales,
  And Macedon, the Moslem army sweeps;
  The snow-white peaks of Pindus e'en assails,
  And takes them, then adown their heights it leaps;
  Albania's realm o'erruns, subdues and keeps,
  Where Adria's waters break upon the strand,
  Upon whose breast the tempest never sleeps.
  Thermopylæ, wilt thou not guard that land?
Not shield thy Greece from the invader's bloody hand?

IX.

  Ah! no! for at that pass no Spartans brave
  Stand to resist the Moslem's conquering might—
  To drive him back, or find a glorious grave,
  Preferring death to ignominious flight.
  Thy land, fair Greece, must feel the invader's
      blight;
  In vain thy classic fields are stained with gore;

Thy sun must set in a long, darksome night;
And Greece, dear land, be "living Greece no
    more "—
Thy Corinth, Athens, Sparta's glorious days are o'er.

X.

But not alone o'er Eastern realms this flood
From Araby its wrangling waters poured;
But round Akaba's gulf its path of blood
Was marked; its swelling torrents westward roared,
Across that fatal sea where once were stored
Egyptian treasures, buried in the wave—
A host not smitten by the warrior's sword;
Where horse and rider found a watery grave—
Where God, by mighty wonders, did his people save.

XI.

So onward o'er those fertile lands redeemed
By Nilus from the sands, their armies spread,
As locusts from the pit of hell upstreamed,
Whose clouds o'ershadowed earth with darkness
    dread,
Their mighty king, Abaddon, at their head,
Devouring all where'er their swarms might stray;
Their flaming steeds plunge into Nilus' bed,
Slake their hot thirst, shake from their sides its
    spray,
Then, fierce to snuff the desert air, they haste away.

XII.

Haste madly on o'er Afric's lands afar,
  Along the Middle Sea's resounding shore ;
Old Carthage sees, above, their crescent star,
  While round her walls the Moslem squadrons
    pour,
Then westward rush, resistless as before,
  Until with shout and fiery charger's neigh
Is mingled stern Atlantic's stormy roar,
  And Afric, yielded to the prophet's sway,
Bids millions at his feet their servile homage pay.

XIII.

Not long on Afric's coast the deluge waits,
  But, glancing to the coasts of sunny Spain,
Its fiery squadrons leap Gibraltar's straits,
  To flood that fated land from sea to main.
Fair Andalusia, sweetly decked with plain,
  Hill, valley, thou must feel the Moslem's tread ;
O'er dark Morena's peaks a hurricane
  Breaks, and sweeps down to Gaudiana's bed,
Which cannot quench the fires, for still they swiftly
    spread.

XIV.

Swift o'er Toledo's mountain barriers leaps,
  And down to Tagus' flowery banks doth glide
The thundering avalanche. Still it keeps
  Its onward way, expands its burning tide,

As over hills and vales its horsemen ride;
It climbs the mountain heights of old Castile,
And in Duero's vale lays low the pride
Of Spain, and makes her vanquished armies feel,
Around Segovia's walls, the bite of Moorish steel.

XV.

Nor long its Arab chargers rest upon
Iberian mountains, stretching far away,
But rushing down on proud old Aragon,
Round Saragossa pours the ensanguined fray;
But Aragon repels them from their prey,
And plants upon her high Pyrenian rocks
The cross whose glory never shall decay,
Where it shall never feel war's tempest's shocks,—
Where Moslem never shakes his spear, nor rudely
   mocks.

XVI.

But yet it breaks o'er Pyrenees on France,—
E'en up to Potiers it spreads its power,
Nor stays it in its terrible advance,
Till over half that realm its tempests lower.
But then arises in the North a shower—
A mingled fire and hail of venging wrath;
Rally a host the nation to restore,
To cast destruction in the Moslem's path,
To drive the Moors from Gaul, or lay them low in death.

XVII.

The champion, Martel, leads the avenging host,
In armor dressed for battle's dreadful fray;
Two mighty armies front to front opposed,
Like thunder clouds, stand each in dread array,
To test, in battle's awful brunt, the day.
The destinies of Europe trembling stand,
As there those hostile hosts their ranks display,
All waiting their own leader's dread command,
To join in battle that shall shake the solid land.

XVIII.

There are the lighter-visaged sons of Spain,
With the Arabian and Saracen
Arrayed, and with the sable African;
Full many a pennon fluttering there is seen,
Full many a charger neighs for battle, when
Around their countless falchions shall glance,
And send their lightning flashes o'er their van,
To light upon the steel-clad crest of France;
Behold their feathery plumes in snowy splendor dance.

XIX.

And there o'er many a squadron of swift horse,
O'er many a phalanx with its countless spears,
Full proud the cresent holds its lordly course,
And high the battle's fearful signal rears.
Now here, behold the Christian host appears!
Of heroes come from far, a countless throng,

The flower of France, unknown to craven fears,
Of Germans many mighty thousands strong,
While other peoples swell their numerous tides along.

XX.

Behold their stalwart legions bravely stand,
All covered with the helmet, gorge, and shield,
Like rocks of granite, on the stormy strand,
Whose flinty crests ne'er to the billows yield ;—
Stand 'cross the Moslem's path upon that field,
To stay his progress and turn back his tides.
Hark! HARK! the battle cry, the rattling shield,—
Behold, each horseman to his charger strides,
And then in awful pause the battle signal bides.

XXI.

" Allah, il Allah! Allah hu!" 'tis given,
See how those fiery squadrons bound along,
While with their thundering hoofs the earth is
    riven ;
Now in the air each flashing blade is flung,
Hear, as they dash the Christian hosts among,
To break their living breastwork clad with steel.
Was ever such tremendous clamor rung
With arms, where men in hell of battle reel ?
Did e'er resisting hosts such dread concussion feel?

XXII.

Oh heavens! see how their blood-stained falchions
    crash !
How break on helm and shield the lance and spear !

How blade on blade in maddened fury clash!
Till all along the field, afar and near,
In frightful heaps, the Moslem slain appear;—
Horse, rider, all go down in that advance,
Laid low in that tremendous hour of fear,
When Moorish spear and Arab's balanced lance
Are dashed and broken on the ringing shield of France.

XXIII.

O dread and fearful work of ruin dire!
It broke the power of Islam on that plain;
Like navies wrecked amid the tempest's ire,
Dashed on the rocks and shoals of ocean's main,
It left, alas! full many myriads slain!
'Twas thus the glorious field of Tours was won,
The hammer struck and broke the invader's might,
And crushed beneath his weight Abdalla's son;
And then, when forced into disastrous flight,
He left ten thousand slain in internecine fight.

XXIV.

Nor stops he till beyond the snowy peaks
Of Pyrenees he comes to halt, and stands
Where stern and stormy winter rudely shakes
His frosts for aye, to guard fair Gallia's lands
With icy legions drive his bloody bands
Away, and give to her a long release.
But long their bearded legions shake their brands,
Menacing Europe, giving her no peace,
From Biscay's Bay to where the Danube's waters cease.

XXV.

Long centuries, too, the Moslems hold the sway,
As rulers of the sunny lands of Spain,
Until at length the crescent's powers decay;
The flood that covered hill, and vale, and plain,
Rolls back to Afric's servile coast again,
And she is freed from presence of the Moor.
And in her time, Greece from the Moslem's chain
Strives to be free; the flames which burned of yore
Blaze from her shrines again besmeared with patriot's
    gore.

XXVI.

Fair Freedom flings her banners to the breeze,
Awakes her prostrate sons to nobler life;
Into the fray, which either kills or frees,
They rush, and bravely mingle in the strife,
And strike for altars, children, home, and wife,
And to redeem the green graves of their sires,
Although their land with many slain is rife;
'Tis not in vain,—she gains her fond desires,—
She smothers all her foes in Navarino's fires.

XXVII.

Yet have that river's waters overran
The Eastern Continent from sea to sea.
It rules the Persian still. The Turkoman,
The Afghan, and the roving Belochee,
All serve the prophet. Nor is China free,
Nor Hindoostan, nor Tartary, the wild,

Nor any part of Asia, but may see
The crescent's sign ; and Afric is beguiled
Amid her desert wastes, and where sweet vales have
　　smiled.

XXVIII.

This is the spreading river that was named
Euphrates by that dreaming prophet old,[3]
And widely has its wondrous power been famed ;—
But now its end comes, as by him foretold,
The avenging angel in his flight, behold !
From heaven stoops o'er the oriental land ;
See, o'er its waters dark his wings unfold,
On them he pours the vial in his hand,—
Not long can they its potent influence withstand.

XXIX.

Ah ! high indeed its waters, midst the shout
Of nations, and with seas of blood, had rolled,
And spread before the crescent death and rout,
And on its course for long did hold —
But now its waning floods of power are knolled,
Its deep-worn channels soon shall be left dry,
O'er which the orient kings from empires old
Shall come to offer gifts to the Most High,—
To Zion's King descending from the bending sky.

XXX.

It may be in this wise the work was done :—
The Church, who found herself a Western home,

Where she to Christ had many millions won,
Changed a wild desert into vernal bloom,
Called out a world of light from night and gloom,
Won for mankind a great and glorious crown,
Unfurled the flag of Freedom o'er the tomb
Of slavery, and the despot's throne cast down,
And made his minions in perdition's waves to drown;—

XXXI.

Had sent from thence a faithful praying band,—
The choicest gems of Jesus' earthly crown,—
To preach the Word in that afflicted land,
Where Moslems ruled;—entreat them to cast down
Their idols;—they whose fathers once did own
The sway of Jesus;—to their ancient faith
To win them back;—and wide the seed was sown.
By the dear cross of Jesus, millions found their path
Back to the light of heaven, from darkness grim as
    death.

XXXII.

This roused the Moslem's wild fanatic ire;—
He grasped stern persecution's bloody scourge,
To plunge the Church again in seas of fire.
He by such means, of old, was wont to urge
His faith upon mankind, or in the gurge
Of tribulation drown them. So, with rack
And torture, bastinado, fire, would purge
His realms. Of all such means there was no lack,
So o'er the Church he rolled a tempest wild and black.

XXXIII.

Famine and thirst to them were not unknown ;
To the cross and stake and gibbet they were led
Helpless:—Again to wild beasts they were thrown.
Ten thousand victims for religion bled.
The air was filled with lamentations dread
Of those who cruel murder had survived,
And loathsome prisons echoed to the tread
Of those who rack and torture had outlived
A myriad widows for their murdered husbands grieved.

XXXIV.

Long was the suffering, dire the murderous work
Of slaughter over all that bloody land,
Where Moslem zeal fanatic urged each Turk,
To stain with Christian blood his hostile hand ;
Till, longer, vengeance could not idle stand ;
For loud and wide the cry to heaven was raised ;
Came from the eternal throne the high command,
And the avenging angel, irate, seized
The sword, to smite the foes whose deeds the world
        amazed.

XXXV.

And now is heard in dreadful murmurings loud,
The gathering, hostile armies from afar,
As dread avengers, come a countless crowd,
To wage upon these bloody men a war
That shall of vengeance give them their full share.
Ah, yes, dire persecutors, ye shall feel,

Amid alarums, that the stoutest scare,
The stroke tremendous of His biting steel
Who, as Avenger, doth His mighty hand reveal.

XXXVI.

Lo! in the north is roused the growling bear,
Who leads his countless marshaled warriors down :
The roaring lion, too, would have a share
In fight, and hastens there, from Albion.
Flung to the breeze her flaming gonfalon,
She leads to battle many thousand strong.
And from his eyrie, when the clarion
Resounds, the eagle's cry sounds clear and long,
And o'er Atlantic's wave he leads a numerous throng.

XXXVII.

See how the starry banner flutters there,
O'er brave hearts beating for the world's oppressed;
Where tempests darken in the murky air,
With strife, where many wrongs shall be redressed,
And righteous war shall succor the distressed.
They ready are, when battle-cry is given,
Upon those tyrants' heads who long transgressed,
To launch, as from the stormy cope of heaven,
Hot thunderbolts of wrath with which the world is riven.

XXXVIII.

Staunch Germany, and thou poor La Belle France,
Who once stood breast to breast before the Moor,

While lightnings from your burnished helms did
    glance,
And bolts of war upon the field of Tours,
Say where will ye be ranged, where will ye pour
Your battle hail, in that dread carnival?
What standard follow, till the fight is o'er?
But wheresoe'er your martial bugles call,
Millions are there who low before the prophet fall.

XXXIX.

Ah! yes, the prophet has a strange array:
There the old dragon, stained with martyrs' gore,
Stands ready for the battle's fearful fray,
No thirst for blood has lost since days of yore ;-
Rush his red hosts along the Black Sea's shore.
And there among the tyrant cringing herd,
The Moslem marches in the van once more, —
For him the Persian, Arab, Turk, and Koord
Have couched again the lance and spear and drawn the
    sword.

XL.

Look there! the scarlet flag of Papal Rome,
Is waving too o'er many a supple slave.
She must obey her instincts and must come
To fight against the right, and find a grave
For myriads.   Anti-Christ, he who did rave
Amid the darkness, when himself proclaimed
Himself as high as God though but a knave.
And worse than ever is religion shamed
By him, among that host where heathen gods are named.

XLI.

Yet 'tis a meet alliance tripartite,
The dragon's minions and the scarlet beast,
With the false prophet, all the sons of night,
Who crowd by millions from the swarming East,
While from the West with many a host increased.
Behold them there within their crowded camp,
They marshal many myriads at least,
And earth doth tremble midst their mighty tramp,
While furious horse for fight their iron bridles champ.

XLII.

Behold the Lord's avengers near and far,
Their heavy columns stretching deep and wide,
Swarm to thy fearful work, avenging war,
Across the Bosphorus an endless tide.
Their myriad banners float aloft in pride,
Unfolding now the red, white, blue and gold,
And gleam like rainbows waving side by side.
Their countless guns and bayonets behold !
Earth trembles as their rattling wheels are onward
    rolled.

XLIII.

Ah ! me ! what tumult dread of warlike sounds
Burst forth from yon advancing thunder-cloud,
And bode destruction, death or fearful wounds !
Hear now the tempest's mutterings deep and loud,
As horsemen gather there, a countless crowd,
And on the dreadful flanks of battle form.

Now pause awhile, survey those armies proud,
  Ere wakes the fury of the coming storm,
And those bright blades are dimmed with gore all wet
    and warm.

XLIV.

Ah! think what great decisions hang in poise
Upon the issues of this dreadful day.
There bigotry its enginery employs
To take the heaven-born rights of men away,
The despot's tottering throne from wrack to stay,
Though built on slavery's sighs and tears and
    groans;
For where is Pagan's, Pope's or Moslem's sway,
There may be heard its victims' bitter moans,
Nor aught else would it hear o'er earth's encircling zones.

XLV.

Ah! 'tis a precious right to wield the scourge,
To lay its gory thongs upon man's back,
For bigot superstition grim to urge
Midst torture, stake and wheel, and breaking rack,
Or, with the battle, flaming siege and sack,
Her claims on men, denying heaven to all
Who will not serve the prophet's lustful pack,
Or vilely cringe beneath the Papal thrall,
Or on the name of Boodh and Brahma humbly call.

XLVI.

Pressed by the avengers' gathering power, they know
That the decisive hour has come at last,

To test their rights and to the nations show,
If they may still the chain and fetter cast
On half the world, and all its beauty blast ;—
If they may tread upon the necks of slaves
Who pronely lie beneath their feet aghast,
Or on brave fallen freemen's bloody graves,
Whose fervor drowns in blood or else its country saves ;—

XLVII.

Or if they shall in the dread conflict fall,
Their scepters broken, from their temples torn
Their ancient crowns, destroyed for aye their thrall,
Their purple robes and royal thrones forsworn,—
All ruined, hopeless, to destruction borne.
Say, shall a hundred million own the power
Of Islam ?   Over half the world forlorn
Shall Boodh and Brahma reign ?   Shall millions
    more
Beneath the Papal thunders shrink and vilely cower?

XLVIII.

So, too, with the avenger's gathering host,
If they are overthrown in that dread fight,
Freedom of body, soul and all is lost.
Crushed then shall be the cause of truth and
    right,
Sink down the earth in slavery's gloomy night,
Eclipsed in darkness be the sun of heaven.
Shall all men's choicest blessings take their flight ?
Shall all that science, all that art have given,
Be blotted out when with this storm the earth is riven ?

XLIX.

Shall Freedom, fighting in the stormy van,
Lie prostrate when this frightful fray shall end?
Or shall her banners, in behalf of man,
The skies of every continent ascend,
And their bright flames with starry splendors blend?
O, shall that glorious flag arise on high,
To which the azure skies their tints did lend,
In sign of peace to friends afar and nigh,
Its red, of war to foes, where'er its splendors fly?

L.

Hark! hark! the battle's fearful signal's given,
Loud sounds its echoes to the cope on high.
Then break its flames with fearful flash forth driven,
Full wide its screaming missiles crash and fly,
While its black smoke blots sunlight from the sky.
There cannons roar and muskets harshly bray,
There whiz and screech of ball and shell, and cry
Of death create a hell in sulphur spray,
Whose fires and furies fierce are gorged amidst the fray.

LI.

They glut the grave with food unmeasured, hark!
See there! beneath the cope of battle rack,
Which makes the brightest noonday splendors dark,
The murmuring horsemen form for the attack.
They're falling into lines, dense, deep and black,
See how above their heads their sabres flash,

Like lightnings o'er the tempest's fearful track,
Prepared, like a wild whirlwind's rush and crash,
In the dread melee on the allied camp to dash.

LII.

Ye supple followers of Abdallah's son,
Ye cringing minions of the scarlet whore,
Ye votaries to the dragon's bloody throne,
Prepare to fight as ye have ne'er before.
Behold yon avalanche with thunder's roar
In mighty squadrons rushing to the fray
With sounding hoof, earth shakes as on they pour,
And as they near their grim expectant prey,
The shout of nations rises from their dread array.

LIII.

Ah, me! what fearful work the foemen make,
As on the Moslem ranks the squadrons dash!
Ah! how the hills in the concussion quake,
As through their steel-clad hosts the whirlwinds
 crash ;
Ah! myriads fall beneath the sabres' gash.
In vain the Moslem's volleyed thunder flies,
Amid the racking cannon's frightful flash,—
In vain they drape with clouds the reeling skies,—
In vain the furious soldier falls and bleeds and dies ;—

LIV.

In vain their hungry falchions blush with blood,—
In vain to Allah lift their helpless prayers ;

Ten myriads fall beneath their sweeping flood,
All wounded, bleeding, groaning, dying there.
Dread panic now doth all their minions scare,
Disastrous rout spreads all their ranks among;
They fly in great confusion everywhere
Before the tempest which their hosts o'erhung,—
Dropped down their nerveless arms, aside their falchions
    flung.

LV.

See how in hot pursuit relentless War
Hurls his huge hosts upon the flying foe;
See how they fall by myriads, near and far,—
'Tis thus the power of Islam is laid low,
Thus proud Euphrates' floods, which did o'erflow
The world, were dried in War's dread battle flame.
God's martyrs were avenged in this fell blow,—
Dissolved the spell of the false prophet's name,
Sunk 'neath the vial's wrath in death, defeat and shame.

LVI.

Now, for a season, there is peace and rest,
The gory sword of persecution broke;
Rejoice, the friends of God, in East and West,
Foes crushed beneath his arm's avenging stroke,
And broken now the tyrant's heavy yoke.
Afar the banner of the cross unfurled,
No conquests can its enemies provoke
To blood, and liberty o'er all the world
To worship God, where'er Euphrates' waves have swirled.

LVII.

And so the tale *is* told in many a land,
And Christ proclaimed the Saviour of the race,
Till millions own the scepter of his hand ;—
Till West, East, South, and North, in his free grace
Rejoicing stand before his smiling face,
And sound their glorious anthems in full flood,
As one united Church, in every place,
And tell their triumphs in a Saviour's blood,—
That fountain opened where his cross of anguish stood.

LVIII.

Sweet, O how sweet the gospel work ! to bring
The ransomed captives back to Zion's hill,
And see them bow adoring to their king !
Sweet, too, their hungry souls with bread to fill !
Ah ! how their victor songs our bosoms thrill,
As millions, bought by Jesus' fearful death,
Repentant turn to God ; and angels trill
Their harps, and every creature that hath breath
Sing their loud psalms in heaven, and on the earth
    beneath.

LIX.

For many years the precious work goes on,
While Christian nations, locked in bonds of peace,
Shout their hosannas o'er the triumphs won.
Fair Zion rises bright, her beams increase
So much, and wars and tumults so much cease,
That men expectant now begin to say—
    10*

" The time foreshadowed for the world's release
Has come, the light of the millennial day
Bursts o'er the hills, to chase the shades of night away "

LX.

But yet the groaning world through blood and tears
Must wade, be shaken still by conflicts sore,—
Perhaps for many, many weary years,
Before her Christ shall reign from shore to shore.
Those powers of evil which the hosts o'erbore
Still live, though crushed beneath the mighty tread
Of God's great chariot, in the din and roar
Of war, wrenched from their hands the sword, and
    dead
Their warring hosts, all hushed their shouts and clamors
    dread.

LXI.

Yet other weapons they will surely find
To work sad mischief on the Church of God ;
With other evil powers they will be joined,
By which to seize again the iron rod
Of empire, and, beneath their potent nod,
To bind the world again in heavy chains.
On this vile work three unclean spirits plod,
Vile frogs, to curse the world with bitter banes,
On each bright spot of earth to leave their filthy stains.

LXII.

Forth from the mouth of dragon, and the beast,
And the false prophet, these three spirits came,

Like others from the pit of hell released ;
They call themselves by some pretentious name,
And with great words the credulous inflame,
While with their lying wonders they deceive
The kings and nations, and their homage claim,
Who might their lying miracles believe,
To lead them forth to war, their losses to retrieve.

LXIII.

Philosophy, so-called, essayed to teach [5]
That revelation cannot, *never* comes
From Heaven.   That, what the reason cannot reach,
Cannot be truth ; that man, where'er he roams,
Must trust to nature's light ; no other speech
Revealeth God, whatever man may teach
From sacred books.   He framed eternal law,
And should he turn from that it would impeach
His government, and cause a fatal flaw
In his unchangeability, and ruin draw

LXIV.

Upon the world.   No miracle can be,
Nor change from law.   All forms of prayer are vain,
For even God himself cannot be free
From law.   Man may not ask for sun, or rain,
Or any thing.   Law must its rule maintain
Unchangingly.   If it will rain, it must.
If not, then drouth must parch hill, vale and plain.
And so the law must rule though God be thrust
Out of His world, with naught for us but law to trust.

LXV.

Thus when the law is throned in place of God,
And prayer, the Christian's bulwark, brought to
   naught,
Soon falls his heavenly hope 'neath Satan's nod;
For whosoever harbors such a thought,
Denies God's Providence, and is soon brought
To cast aside his word. Keep men from prayer,
From that dear mercy-seat which they once sought,
And Satan soon can lead them anywhere.
This was one form of unbelief which drew its share

LXVI.

Of blind adherents. Since they could not rule
By force, these unclean devils sought to sneer
The light of heaven from earth; none but a fool
Would hold a faith so built on craven fear,
They said,—that Christ would yet again appear
To save them, since his flesh had been consumed
Two thousand years. How could he uprear
The judgment throne? Could he, so long entombed,
Call forth his sleeping saints for ages now inhumed?

LXVII.

Where of his coming could they find a pledge?
For since their martyred fathers fell asleep,
All things the same continue, they allege,
And as of old their customed courses keep.
Seed time and harvest come and go; men reap,
From year to year, the fields they till and sow.

That God will e'er the world to ruin sweep,
Nor earth nor heaven one portent symptom show;
Yea naught can shake the firm foundations here below.

LXVIII.

These frogs bred lusts in the hearts of millions
    more—
To eat, to drink, to reek and roll in wine, [6]
The lowest forms of license to explore,
And unto sin and shame their souls resign,—
To whatsoe'er men's wicked hearts incline,
Without one honest blush to hide their shame.
Old Sodom did no more. " It shall be mine,"
The young man said, " though blackened be my
    name,
To live in all the pleasures that my lusts inflame."

LXIX.

No matter if he lived to others' cost,
And at the fearful risk of losing heaven ;
Yea, though all hope of heaven to him were lost,
And all those soaring powers to mortals given ;
Yea, not the fear of hell, with thunders riven,
Could from his course his wandering feet restrain,
Though for him many mother's prayers had striven.
All these to rescue him had been in vain.
His short life wasted, sinks his soul to endless pain.

LXX.

Yea, many bent on sin insanely swore
There was no living God, no heaven, no hell,

But this short, fitful life, and nothing more,—
Why should they not enjoy its pleasures well?
Since of a sphere beyond no one could tell,
And earthly good to them and theirs was all
They had, why not submit to pleasure's spell?
Short was their gospel, startling was its call,
" Enjoy yourself, to-morrow die, forgotten fall."

LXXI.

Thus grossest sensualism obtained control,
And held unchallenged an unrivaled sway
O'er many a man, denying him a soul;
Yea, 'twas obeyed by millions in that day.
So strong it grew that it began to lay
The people under ban, and then compel
Them to deny the Lord, and turn away
From faith, neglect his word, the sabbath bell,
And e'en the way to Zion, loved so long and well.

LXXII.

And Mammon, too, regained a mighty power,
In that sad day, and with the hope of gold,
He held his sway o'er many myriads more.
Yea, many million souls to him were sold;
It made the miser's heart so hard and cold,
That he would give no heed to mercy's call,—
Would grasp the widow's mite but small all told,
Cause want and sorrow on her house to fall,
Yea, all the weak he strove to keep in penury's thrall.

LXXIII.

He helped to nerve the assassin's bloody hand,
When he would seek in stealth his victim's bed,
To do a deed of blood, to shock the land.
His love the prowling thief to plunder led,
To rob his neighbor, leave his houseless head
To feel the storm, his wife's and children's cry
Unheeded hear, as they implored for bread.
And he would build the huge monopoly,
To hold the rich man up, and make the poor low lie.

LXXIV.

With law's enactments armed, he steeled the soul
Of heartless minions, to the devil sold,
To put the cursed and fiery, damning bowl
Unto their neighbors' lips for sordid gold,
That they, their feet enthralled, might be controlled
By spirits lost, prone in the filth to crawl,
To drag to penury and woe untold
Those mothers and their children, who should fall
From happy homes to hovels, where rum's demons
    brawl.

LXXV.

O! if damnation's loudest, direst knell
Sounds in the ears of any guilty man,
If there are hottest flames in deepest hell,
And hugest chains to hold his soul in ban,
They are for him whate'er his tribe or clan,
Who sells the burning contents of the bowl

To friend or neighbor, say he what he can
In self-defense : he damns the life and soul
Of every one who falls beneath the fiend's control.

LXXVI.

The power of alcohol was truly great ;
Deep did its widening, withering influence blend
With social life, and with the powers of State,
With strength that made the people cower and
    bend
In suppliance, with which few might dare contend.
For millions paid their homage at his feet,
And men, though longing for his reign to end,
In open conflict dare not with him meet,
His power had grown so strong, his mastery so complete.

LXXVII.

'Twas by the liquor league defiant, bold,
He seized the reins of power and under ban,
Would lay, and in his shameless clutches hold,
For purposes political, th' outspoken man
Who durst propose and advocate some plan
To rescue liquor's victims from the jaws
Of frightful death ; with hands of ruffian
Would throttle him, if he durst plead their cause,
And seek to abate the infernal work by wholesome laws ;

LXXVIII.

Yea, in the dark would aim at him the blow
Of the assassin ; would his buildings burn,

If he its villainy should dare to show;
His walls and fences e'en would overturn,
And with mean spite that common thieves would
　　spurn,
Turn loose the hungry herd into his grain;
Would gird his trees and vines, with hate inferne;
With snares and traps would seek his hurt and pain,
In every way that craft Satanic could attain.

LXXIX.

And when in open power it was arrayed,
It laid its hand on any one who dared
To raise his voice against the wretched trade,
With mulct and heavy bonds and prisons scared
The timid; all the friends of temperance shared
A common portion of its hate and wrath.
But, if it failed of suffrage, it upreared
The flag of treason o'er its burning path,—
With fire and sword of war would scatter hurt and
　　scath,

LXXX.

If it might thus its baneful power retain.
For civil rights sought opportunity
To send its plagues all o'er the land and main.
It claimed unchallenged, free immunity
To blight the life of each community;
Its monstrous claims uphold with bloody hand,
And, if it could, with bold impunity,
No law so sacred it would not withstand,
Which sought to make its deathful traffic contraband.

LXXXI.

'Twould skulk in secret, crawl, and lie, and steal,
To thwart restraining power of government;
And at such villain practices could feel
No shame, 'twas so intently, fiercely bent
On its curst errands, by the devil sent:
No evil power had wrought such hurt before:
And thus by false religion with it blent,
And lingering tenets of the scarlet whore,
An evil power was gathering, unsurpassed of yore:

LXXXII.

Lo! now these three foul spirits, at the head [7]
Of millions, ranged in hostile league once more,
Again o'er Christendom their armies spread,
To drown the Right in seas of crimson gore.
Since they have felt the truth's great pressure sore,
They know that they must win or lose their sway
Amid the fearful battle's din and roar,
And so they'll stake their all in one great fray,
To win, or dash the pillars of the world away.

LXXXIII.

They gather now their hosts in countless throngs,
To the great battle of Almighty God, [8]
Innumerous nations, peoples, tribes, and tongues,
Where they shall feel Jehovah's crushing rod.
The kings of earth send their commands abroad,
And call great captains on the lists of fame

By thousands, who the world have overawed,
And thus by daring deeds have won a name ;
And common hosts by millions, their hot zeal inflame.

LXXXIV.

In their great camps are royal robes and crowns,
And glittering tinselry of grand array ;
And there are many pontificial gowns,
Which lend their presence there to fire the fray,
Amid their armies stretching far away.
Then revelry is heard within that camp,
And lustful passions have unbounded sway,
All mingled with their minions' ceaseless tramp,
Or when they rest at eve, or wake at morning's gray.

LXXV.

Hark ! how their loud blasphemous curses rise,
As madly boast they of their mighty power,
Defying God enthroned above the skies,
While counting all their numerous legions o'er,
Swearing that now their foes shall be no more ;
They send defiance to the very stars,
And call creation's hosts from shore to shore,
To meet them there upon the field of Mars,
And test their rival powers amidst the battle's jars.

LXXXVI.

To banish Right and Truth from every land,
They wake again the noise of civil strife ;

With martyr blood would stain the murderous
    hand,
Would hold at every Christian's throat the whetted
    knife,
And aim the assassin's blow at every life,
- Until the seas with gore again be blent,—
Until the cry, amid the fearful strife,
Rings up to heaven by prayer's strong groanings
    rent,
And to avenge the Right Jehovah's hosts are sent.

LXXXVII.

THE WICKED WARNED AND THE FAITHFUL CONSOLED.

Behold, ye despisers, and wonder and fear,
For now, as avenger, the Lord doth appear,
Like a thief in the night,* when your legions are still,
In drunken sleep hushed, in the vale, on the hill.
Ye have seen, when the tempest was gathering its
        power,
When its legions in blackness of darkness did lower,—
Ye have known, when the earthquake was ready to
        shake
The nations, and merge their great cities' wreck,

That the silence of death, o'er the land and the sea,
Ruled the world, till the powers of the tempest set free,
Should burst in wild fury on hamlet and town,
And with thunder the clamor of myriads drown;

*Rev. xvi. 15.

When death rides in fury on earth and in air,
And faces are pale with the looks of despair,
As expectant they wait in the turmoil of wrath,
Which scatters destruction in every path.

Just so shall Jehovah of battles come down
    In silence, till ready to burst on your lines;
Then your legions, as chaff in the whirlwind is blown,
    Shall be scattered, with death to your bloody designs.
Ye will not remember what plagues he has poured
On the beast and false prophet, abhorred of the Lord;
Ye despise his long-suffering, blaspheme his great name,
Take warning, take warning, he'll whelm you in flame.

Ye servants of Jesus, be faithful and true,
For behold! I come quickly a Saviour for you;
Watch, watch and be sober, with garments untorn,
Unstained by the world, and in comeliness worn,—
That you may not in nakedness walk and proclaim
To the world what would ever redound to your shame.
If coming he find you in righteousness clad,
With salvation's strong helmet surrounding your head,

With truth as your girdle, with feet duly shod,
With the gospel of peace to protect on the road,
And the breastplate of righteousness, glittering and
        bright,
And faith's mighty shield over all in the fight;
With the means of aggression, the spirit's great sword,
To vanquish your foes, e'en the Word of the Lord;
With all perseverance and prayer to the end,
That God will his saints in the battle defend :—

If coming he find you thus armed for the fight,
In you, as his soldiers, he'll take great delight;
Your arms, in the conflict, he'll clothe with his might,
With confusion the minions of darkness to smite;
His shield he'll stretch o'er you in that fiery day,
And bring you in safety through battle's fierce fray;
While he whelms all his foes in eternity's night,
You shall shine as his saints, clad in garments of white.

Yea, when he to judgment in triumph shall come,
With life's crown on your heads he will bring you safe
          home.
But watch and be sober, Jehovah's great day
Is coming with haste, and the battle array
Will be set when the beasts and the fowls of the air
   Shall be called by the angel who stands in the sun
The flesh of great captains and warriors to share
   In the supper of God which will soon be begun.

LXXXVIII.

Forth from the throne a fearful mandate goes,
For now to Armageddon's fatal field
Jehovah gathers all his wicked foes.
Yes, yes, ye rebels, ye must to him yield,
When earth and hell in furious fires annealed
Hurl their dread thunders in the face of God,
And answering, heaven's artillery shall be pealed
In greater fury from the tempest's cloud,
And earth shall quake with clamor huge and loud.

LXXXIX.

Such issues on a battle never hung.
Shall be religion in the world suppressed?
Shall fall the Saviour's name unheard, unsung?
Shall all the world as cringing slaves confessed,
By tyrants be forever more oppressed?
O say shall the sweet reign of Jesus cease,
And his dear Church be torn and ne'er have rest?
Shall never come the reign of joyful peace?
And Jesus' glorious kingdom have no more increase?

XC.

Sweet name of Jesus, say, shall men not hear?
That name! than which none other under heaven
Is given to save the soul and hush each fear,—
That name for which those hero souls have striven?
Must hush those praises which to God are given,
That roll so sweetly down from Zion's hill?
Shall Satan's bonds no more from men be riven,
Saved souls with joy the heart of Jesus fill?
Shall all the world be doomed forevermore to ill?

XCI.

Shall set the sun of Freedom's glorious light,
Amid the gloom of endless night and storm?
With her shall end fair Science's reign so bright;
The works and triumphs swallowed by that swarm
Of foes? Shall shrewd Invention come to harm,
Who always showed herself the friend of man?

She with her scepter's wondrous, magic charm,
Called from their chambers subterranean
The occult powers of Nature, man's great artisan

XCII.

She bade her railroads gird the rotund world,
And made her thundering cars of commerce great
Along their iron tracks be swiftly whirled,
To bind the world's great peoples State to State.
She bade the ocean's billows boil irate,
Beneath the glorious steamer's wide recoil;
She did the world with wire reticulate,
To make highways where heaven's lightnings toil
For man, to be his couriers in life's brunt and broil.

XCIII.

She wove his garments, sowed in spring his grain,
And reaped his fields; and from the flinty rocks
She crushed his golden wealth; naught could restrain
Her work. With wondrous speed she made his books.
To all she lent her hand with kindly looks,
On every work she set her glorious seal.
Shall sadly perish all Art's beauteous works?
Shall all things bright and sweet that bid men feel,
Be blotted out amid the tempest's crash and peal?

XCIV.

The voice of millions stoutly answers, No.
Wide let the martial trumpet send its blare,

Above let right its streaming banners show,
Fling on the foe defiance near and far,
Arouse Jehovah's hosts and call to war,
And fill his camp with swarms to seize the prey.
More than before shall light the battle's glare,
More reel in fight for God.   Now comes the day
When hell is balked in one tremendous conflict's fray.

XCV.

Listen, O blood-stained earth from far and near,
Ye rocks and hills, ye murmuring floods and air,
Six vials, full of wrath and trembling fear,
Have on the earth been poured.   But stored with
    care,
In heaven, a seventh awaits its summons there.
Awhile these marshaled armies wait, before
They test in fight the fearful fate of war,
Then God the last dread vial doth outpour,
Earth pales and shudders wild with fear on every shore.

XCVI.

DEFIANCE ON THE FOE.

Now, ye oppressors of truth and the right,
Howl your defiance on Jesus with might,
Call forth your legions to battle's fierce fray,
Roll out your engines, tremendous array,
Though strong your armies when marshaled for war,
The God of battles is mightier far;

11

You may not, cannot escape his great hand,
When red with vengeance it shakes o'er the land.
The angel commissioned the vial to bear, [9]
Pours out its contents into the air;
Wide it diffuses itself o'er the world,
Into commotion all nature is whirled.
Hark! how the thunders fill earth and the sky,
Jehovah's alarums resound from on high.

XCVII.

Above these gathered hosts a dismal noise
Is heard, loud sounding from Jehovah's throne,
In deep, heart-thrilling accents; a loud voice
Portentous tells the world " THE WORK IS DONE." [10]
Ah! yes, 'tis done, oppression's power is gone,
Its blight shall curse the sons of men no more.
Wrong shall be crushed, and right shall rule alone,
While light shall banish darkness nature o'er,
And unbelief, pride, lust shall fall, on every shore.

XCVIII.

The prince of evil cowed with hideous fears,
Beaten in fight on many fearful fields,
Shall clank his ponderous chain a thousand years.
But ere he to the great Avenger yields,
The direst war must rain on upturned shields
Hot bolts, and bathe the sword in blood yet more,
Though worlds have fallen 'neath the power he
    wields.
Prepare again to see red streams of gore
The mountains, valleys, plains and streams becrimson
    o'er.

XCIX.

Now awful voices in the air are heard,[11]
Surely portentous of some dreadful doom,
Most fully ripe for wicked men prepared,
While clouds and tempests lower in deepening
    gloom,
And fearful thunders shake the skies, which loom
In wrath, and redden with the lightning's glare.
On comes the storm, its distant chariots boom,
Men's hearts now fail with fear and dark despair,
The earth and sky are thick with portents everywhere.

C.

Hark! hark! Do ye not hear that saddening wail,[12]
Raised by the sighing winds in fitful puffs,
As if tasked nature's weary powers would fail?
It rises; dies again in mournful soughs:
The sea, uneasy, heaves in waves and troughs:
The trees moan sadly in the dying wind,
The grain waves solemn to its soft rebuffs,
While frightened birds and beasts of every kind,
Fly madly here and there with terror undefined.

CI.

Dire apprehension fills each trembling heart,
All cheeks turn pale beneath the vaguest fear;
What may be coming none can tell: they start
At every sound: and signs to all appear,
That earth with fear and trembling, far and near,
Awe-struck, awaits some dread award of heaven.

Hark! hark! that dreadful sound! Do ye not
    hear? [13]
It jars beneath, where giant powers have striven:
It comes! with earthquake's crash the solid world is
    riven.

CII.

It heaves the ocean from its briny bed, [14]
Rolls the great billows high upon the land,
Wrecks navies, dashed by waves high overhead,
Its Titan shocks the rocks cannot withstand;
It mocks the mightiest works of human hand—
Convulsed is tortured nature everywhere—
Uplifts the valleys, sinks the mountains grand,
Engulfs great cities in its treacherous snare,
The frightened world forebodes the end of all things
    near. [15]

CIII.

Never before was work so fearful known
Since the young earth received her tenant, man,—
When she was into such confusion thrown,—
No, never since the reign of sin began.
Ah me! there rushed the hostile stormy van [16]
Of armies; midst the earthquake's fearful fray,
Mad into the red hell of strife they ran.
As thunder-clouds bedazed with blood-red spray,
They hurl huge hosts together, ranged in wide array.

CIV.

Ah! there ten thousand cannons belch and crash,
And many million muskets harshly bray,

While midst the smoke ten myriad sabres clash
So loud they cannot hear the earthquake's fray;
And scarcely would, though earth should pass
    away.
But God and nature aid the powers of right,
They win the field on that decisive day,
The foes are broken, routed, put to flight,
And myriads of them slain by God's avenging might.

CV.

And now behold the fruits that war has won,
On Armageddon's fearful field of blood!
Ah! me, ah! me, what fearful work is done!
Where, with his sword unsheathed, Jehovah stood,
And drove his foes before a fiery flood.
There to the blood-stained harlot he hath given
A wound which shall destroy her murderous brood,
To rob none more of the sweet light of heaven:
While with her wailings hell's dark pit is fiercely riven.

CVI.

For lo! while hills and mountains reel and shake
Beneath the earthquake's fearful shock and roar,
The city's strong foundations rock and break,[17]
And fall in shattered wreck, to rise no more.
By fissures deep, of fathoms many score,
Into three parts the city hath been rent,
Each faction stained by internecine gore,
Its armies but a fierce, mad rabblement,
Munitions, strength, and blood in mutual conflict spent.

CVII.

No more, as once, thou standst the nation s dread,
Proud city of the hills,[18] with trembling filled,
And never more shalt stand the tyrant's head,
Bereft of might, with coward terror thrilled,
The rushing of thy chariots now is stilled ;
And to increase the sorrows of thy fall,
The cities of the nations, who fulfilled
Thy high behests in the dread carnival,
Are wrecked, or turn on thee to fill thy cup with gall.

CVIII.

Begrimed and torn thy scarlet robes of state,
Stripped thy tiara from thy helpless head,—
Dishonored now is thine uncovered pate,—
Cast out in scorn of thine unholy bed,—
Wrenched from thy hand with gore of martyrs red
Thy scepter, fall'n thine ensigns of command,
With all thy mighty men, great captains, dead,
Expelled with loathing hate from every land,
Come down and sit in dust, and wait the avenger's
　　hand.

CIX.

Ah me ! in that commotion of the sea,
Before the tidal wave's high swelling wrath,
Behold the terror-stricken islands flee [19]
In haste away from the dread tempest's path.
The mountains shake beneath the fear of death,
Fly from their ancient seats to 'scape the storms

Which frown upon the rebel's heads beneath.
See how their legions gather now in swarms
The spirits of the tempest, grim, terrific forms.

CX.

THE TEMPEST OF HAIL.

Behold, O men, the gathering clouds,
  Surcharged with whirlwinds, fire, and hail,
Behold how fear on terror crowds,
  As winds and thunders loudly wail.

O God, thy judgments were severe,
When in that carnival of fear,
With battle's din and earthquake's shock,
Thou didst the startled nations rock.

When millions in the strife were slain,
Which smeared with blood vale, hill and plain,—
When bruised and dying, with their cries
And lamentations, rent the skies.

Must now the sons of men bewail
Wide slaughter by the wrathful hail?
O may not thine avengers rest,
Since earth is with thy plagues oppressed?

Ah! no; comes on the dreadful storm;—
On, on its countless legions swarm;
Its whirlwinds through the forests pour
With rattling din and crashing roar.

They break the forest trees asunder
Like frailest reeds, with bolts of thunder;
As reapers lay the fields of grain,
All things they reap from hill and plain.

They fiercely plow the watery deep,
Its waves their 'customed bounds o'erleap,
Which mingle with the cloudy skies,
And hailstones form of fearful size.

These from the roaring heavens are cast
On earth by whirlwind's rattling blast,
And scatter ruin all around,
Till scarce a living thing is found.

CXI.

Hark! what alarm! for midst that fearful fight
Of elements, blasphemous curses roll
From out the heaving womb of blackest night,
Poured forth in torrents from the burdened soul
Of men, who curse the hail with bitter dole.
So God may thunder through the shaking sky,
Down from the clouds, his mighty chariot roll,
The nations feel his lightning strokes and die,
Yet see not 'tis his hand uplifted from on high.

CXII.

Mistaken men, why will ye madly brave
The God, whose hand the earth's foundations
    shakes;

O why blaspheme his name and madly rave
Against his power, which earth's great kingdoms
  breaks,
Whose Providence in quick obedience makes
The winds and waves serve him, and wrath of men
To praise him, and from the remainder takes
The power to hurt.   Repent, or else again
Prepare for fiercer wrath, sore blight, and deathful pain.

CXIII.

But ere that last dread storm of wrath shall burst
On her rebellious, proud, defiant head,
Recall to mind the woman God hath cursed,—
Behold her ere her minions all have fled,—
And think how, by her hand, the saints have bled,
And how against them she has long prevailed;
E'en till God's thunderbolts shall strike her dead
She at their torments will have fiercely railed.
Hear now her story, and how God her power assailed.

CXIV.

*MYSTERY OF BABYLON, THE GREAT, THE
MOTHER OF HARLOTS AND ABOMI"
TIONS OF THE EARTH.*[21]

Lo, in the wilderness of earth,*
Behold what wonder had its birth,—
A woman full of all that's bad,
In purple and in scarlet clad;

* Rev. xvii. See Lecture XI.

11*

And decked she was with precious stones,
And pearls around her glittering zones,—
In hand a golden cup she held,
With vile abominations filled.
That cup with filthiness o'erflowed,
Her unclean fornications showed.

She sat upon an evil beast,
Which had been once from hell released.
His color was of scarlet hue,
And well, for million saints he slew;
While on his gory skin were shown,
Names of blasphemies all his own.
He was a monster, for he bore
Seven heads and ten great horns of power.
The woman's forehead bore a name
Which loud proclaimed her sin and shame.
Though beautiful, she burned with lust
And trampled virtue in the dust;
For with the kings of earth she played
The harlot, and with them she made
A league of death, to draw the sword
Against the servants of the Lord,
Till drunk with blood and carnage she
Rolled in her sin and infamy.

This woman is the Church of Rome,
Which hath the nations overcome,
And formed alliance with her kings,
Till earth to her its tribute brings,
And lays it at her bloody feet,
Her ghostly favors to entreat.

And like the waters of a flood,
Swarm to her seat a multitude.
The beast is ancient Pagan Rome;
For on her did the woman come,
And Rome's idolatries she taught,
Her idols to her temples brought,
Baptised as saints to them she prayed,
As Rome had to her heroes paid
Her homage.   She to cross and shrine,
And pictured saints, bowed as divine;
To them paid adoration blind.
As Rome to such things was inclined.
And she to vilest lusts would creep,
That she might thus her votaries keep;
She stumbled not at any crime,
That ever stained the book of time,
As Rome, in her licentious fanes,
On lustful passions laid no chains.

The seven heads upon the beast,
Are seven mountains on which rest
The city of the harlot's power,
Which kings had given her for her dower.
The city of the seven hills
With story many ages fills;
To her swarm kings and potentates
Of peoples, empires, kingdoms, states:
They traffic with the impious witch,
By whom their merchants have grown rich,
To purchase scepters, crowns and thrones,
Silver and gold and precious stones.

And costly raiment of all hues,
  They buy; with wine, oil, odors sweet,
All kinds of food which nations use,
  With steeds to jostle in the street.
And chariots, too, full many score,
With which to bolster up her power,
They bought, and slaves and souls of men,
In which she bartered for her gain.
Indulgence, too, for any sin,
She sold to them who sought her shrine.

The horns are kings which shall have power
To prop the beast up for an hour.
They with one mind united stand,
Sworn to support the woman's hand.
Their gathering hosts with war inflame,
Against the followers of the Lamb;
Of kings the King, of lords the Lord,
They cannot stand against his sword,
But worsted, beaten in the fight,
Their legions all are put to flight.
And then they turn in deadly hate,
To make the harlot desolate,
To strip from her her glittering zones,
And tear the flesh off from her bones;
To scorch and burn her in the fire,
As hot as her own fierce desire:
For they agreeing do fulfill
The will of God in good or ill.

They serve the purposes of God,
Bring on his foes his scourging rod,
Whether they fight against his word,
Or pierce the harlot with their sword.

CXV.

Behold! another wonder still appears,
Filling the world with blank astonishment,
While all that serve the harlot shake with fears.
A mighty angel from the heavens is sent,
With clouds of glory, his habiliment.
Hark! as above the earth he wings his flight,
The firmament with his great voice is rent,
The inhabitants of earth turn pale with fright;—
These are the portent words he utters forth with might—

CXVI.

LAMENT FOR BABYLON.

Babylon is fallen, is fallen from power,
Low lies her strong ones to rise nevermore,
Her robe and tiara with carnage are soiled,
Her temples are crumbled, her palaces spoiled,
The vile habitations of devils become,
Where every foul spirit may find him a home;
Of birds all unclean and most hateful, the cage,
A warning most fearful to every age.

All nations have drunk of the wine of the wrath,
Which the Lord surely pours in the transgressor's path;

* Rev. xviii.

In her vile embraces the kings of the earth,
Have indulged in their revels of unholy mirth,
Till their sins have enkindled Jehovah's strong ire.
And the merchants of earth have waxed rich on her
  hire,
By their traffic in dainties forbidden of God,
For which they shall feel the strong weight of his rod.

Come out, O my people, her blasphemy see,
Saith Jehovah, that ye from her plagues may be free,
For her sins up to heaven have reached, and they call
For the great sword of wrath on her head now to fall.
Reward her as she has rewarded your sires,
Around her enkindle redoubled the fires
With which she slew them, and the cup that she filled
Redouble to her, from strong wormwood distilled.

As much as she lifted herself in her pride,
As much by her crimes as she heaven defied,
So much, in full measure, to her now be given
Of plagues, till her bosom with torment be riven.
For she saith in her heart, "Lo! I sit as a queen,
And no sign of widowhood e'er shall be seen
Around my habitation, nor shall I see sorrow,
As to-day is great plenty so shall be to-morrow."

For this, in one day famine, mourning and death,
Shall fall as dread plagues on her desolate path,
And she shall be burned in unquenchable fire;
For strong is the Lord who arises in ire.

Now the kings of the earth who have seen her great
        power,
And rolled in her dainties for many an hour,
Bewail her sad fate from Jehovah's fell stroke,
As they see all her glory ascending in smoke.

And the merchants, grown rich from the sales of her
        ware,
Afar from her stand lest her torments they share,
With weeping and wailing and sounds of great woe,
That the source of their wealth to destruction should go,
That a city arrayed in such costly attire,
With its gold and its gems should be doomed to the fire,
Saying, "Woe worth the day, it surpasses all thought,
In one hour such riches should thus come to naught."

The masters of ships and the whole company
Of those who for traffic go down to the sea,
Stand afar from her plagues and lament to discover
The smoke of her torment arising forever.
"Alas! O alas! that she in one hour,
The source of all mariner's riches and power,
With direst distress is made desolate!"
Casting dust on their heads they bewail her sad fate.

Rejoice over her, O ye heavens, with praise:
Ye prophets, apostles and martyrs now raise
Your songs of redemption from her dreadful thrall,
For God, your avenger, now makes her to fall.
And then a strong angel took up in his hand
A stone, like a mill-stone, which lay on the strand,

And cast it with violence into the sea,
Saying, " THUS THOU GREAT CITY IT SHALL BE WITH
        THEE."

With violence sudden she shall be thrown down,
While the cry of her torment the tempest shall drown,
As the stone is entombed by the waves on the shore,
So she shall be found on the earth nevermore.
Now hushed is the voice of the harpers she cherished,
Her music of pipes and of trumpets is perished,
All palsied the hand that has swept the sweet strings,
And dead is the rapture that melody brings.

Her craftsmen are gone that supplied her rich store,
And the sound of the mill-stone is heard there no more,
Her light has gone out in the darkness of night,
And the joy of her festals has taken its flight.
The board where the bridegroom was wont to preside,
At which, in her beauty, attended the bride,
Is desolate, round it are silent their songs,
For the stroke of Death's angel has palsied their tongues.

CXVII.

Rejoice, the battle's o'er, the day is won.
In arms and panoply victoriously
Rides forth upon his chariot the Son,
His banner o'er his head waves gloriously ;
The earth, long rent with pangs laboriously,
Is now from the red harlot's power released ;—
Ring her high anthems meritoriously,
Exultant that her agony hath ceased,
While with the voice of floods the music is increased.

CXVIII.

Hark! hark! there sounds from heaven a mighty
    voice [22]
Of many people swelling high and strong—
Rolls up and bids the starry worlds rejoice,
And join with men in one resounding song
Of triumph, full, clear, loud and long,
While angel's harps with harmony are trilling,
And all are jubilant amidst the throng;—
Hark to their strains with joy so sweetly thrilling,
The full choired heavenly hosts with deepest rapture
    filling.

CXIX.

*THE TRIUMPHAL SONG.**

Hallelujah to God,
Who sits on the sky,
And breaks with his rod
His foes far and nigh.
Salvation, and honor, and glory, and power
Ye nations give to him, in songs evermore.

True and righteous his ways,
His judgments severe;

---

* And after these things I heard a great voice of much people in heaven, saying
Alleluia: Salvation, and glory, and honor, and power, unto the Lord our God: For
true and righteous are his judgments, for he hath judged the great whore, which did
corrupt the earth with her fornication, and hath avenged the blood of his servants at
her hand. And again they said, Alleluia. And her smoke rose up for ever and ever.
And the four and twenty elders and the four beasts fell down and worshiped God
that sat on the throne, saying, Amen; Alleluia.—REV. xix. 1-4.

O join in his praise,
With trembling and fear;
For on the corrupter he visits the blood
Of martyrs, shed by her in streams like a flood.

Hallelujah again!
Send the shout through the skies;
Let the mighty amen
In thunders arise,
In anthems loud pealing from heaven's vast throngs,
With symphonies swelling from angelic tongues.

Ye elders fall down
And worship the Lamb
Who sits on the throne,
With loud-sounding psalm.
Amen! hallelujah! let it sound forth again
Through the heaven of heavens, hallelujah! Amen!

CXX.

Thus Heaven's high-sounding anthems rang aloud,
With all its golden harps' delicious clang,
At sight of ruin of the harlot proud,
Whose smoke doth o'er the pit of blackness hang.
Hark! hark! as once the stars together sang,
Another louder burst of rapture thrills
The hosts than when creation's anthems rang;
It rolls a deluge from the heavenly hills,
And all the earth with its harmonious music fills.

CXXI.

THE UNIVERSAL ANTHEM.

Praise Jehovah, praise Jehovah,
  All ye bright, angelic throngs,
Shout his praises, shout his praises,
  Earth, with thy ten thousand tongues;
Tell the glad and thrilling story,
  Ocean, with thy thunders loud;
Show his glory, show his glory,
  Tempest, flashing from the cloud.

Lo! his kingdom,—lo! his kingdom,
  Stretches now from shore to shore;
He is mighty, he is mighty,
  He shall reign forevermore.
In the dust his foes are fallen,
  All their mighty heads lie low,
Crushed to earth and ground to powder
  By his last tremendous blow.

Let rejoicing, let rejoicing
  Fill our hearts with gladness now;
Give him honor, give him honor,
  And before his footstool bow,

---

* And a voice came out of the throne, saying, Praise our God, all ye his servants, and ye that fear him, both small and great. And I heard as it were the voice of a great multitude, and as the voice of many waters, and as the voice of mighty thunderings, saying, Alleluia: for the Lord God omnipotent reigneth. Let us be glad and rejoice, and give honor to him; for the marriage of the Lamb is come, and his wife hath made herself ready. And to her was granted that she should be arrayed in fine linen, clean and white: for the fine linen is the righteousness of saints.—REV. xix. 5-8.

For the long-expected marriage
  Of the glorious Lamb has come,
And the bride hath made her ready
  To attend him to his home.

Church triumphant, Church triumphant,
  Ne'er shall sink again thy head
In the dust, beneath the footsteps
  Of thy foes, forever fled ;
Clothe thyself in finest linen,
  White and clean as fallen snow,—
Robe of righteousness adorns thee,
  Stain of sin shall never know.

Once again repeat the wonders
  Of the triumph of the Lord,
Shout the song with pealing thunders,
  All his mighty acts record ;
Let hosannas, loud hosannas,
  From creation's countless throngs,
Roll in surges like the ocean,
  Filling heaven with sounding songs.

CXXII.

"BLESSED ARE THEY THAT ARE CALLED TO THE MARRIAGE SUPPER OF THE LAMB."*

Sweet are the words that fill our ears,
  Like heavenly music to the soul,
Changing to smiles our falling tears,
  And bidding broken hearts be whole.

* Rev. xix. 9.

Blest are the men that hear the call
    That bids them to the wedding feast;
O what delights await them all,
    Of fruits delicious to their taste.

A glorious vision fills their eyes:
    The fairest of the sons of men,
The Lamb who was their sacrifice,
    Doth now the kingly state maintain.

They look upon his glorious face,
    Bright shining as the morning sun,
And sweet assurance there they trace
    Of everlasting joys begun.

There they shall see, in stainless dress,
    The bride adorned with all her charms,
As, coming from the wilderness,
    She leans on her belovèd's arms.

O there forever shall they rest,
    And feast their souls on heavenly bread;
With all heaven's dainties now possessed,
    Which on the festal board are spread.

There with united hearts and tongues,
    And golden harps' delicious sound,
They all shall sing triumphal songs,
    While heaven with rapture shall resound.

CANTO III.

I.

THE LAST PREMILLENNIAL CONFLICT.

Look yonder! in the clouds of heaven uprolled
A vision full of wonder and surprise,
Mid gorgeous tints of purple, white, and gold,
A way to heaven lies open through the skies,—[1]
A way down which full many a cherub flies,—
A *beaten way* down from those heights sublime,
So bright, what mortal looks upon it dies;
Those walls which tower above the wrecks of time
Appear: their open gates reveal that glorious clime.

II.

A rider on a milk-white horse comes forth,*
Most glorious of all visions we have seen,—
His eyes flash fiery flames upon the earth,
And many crowns cast their resplendent sheen
From his white brow. A sword with edges keen
Flames from his mouth, with which to smite.
"FAITHFUL AND TRUE" his name hath ever been,
His wars he wages in behalf of right,
In truth and righteous judgments always takes delight.

* Rev. xix. 11.

III.

He hath a written name, to man unknown,
Which none but he himself can apprehend;
A character, yet to his saints unshown,
Must with his many names its glory blend;
Though PRINCE OF PEACE, he can his Church
      defend
With fire and sword. A vesture dipped in blood
He wears, which bolts of hell can never rend.
Another name he bears, "THE WORD OF GOD;"
His mission is to spread that message all abroad.[2]

IV.

Still other name wrote on his robe and thigh
He bears,—"THE KING OF KINGS AND
      LORD OF LORDS."
He thus arrayed, in mien and bearing high,
What office now with him so well accords
As leading them who wield Jehovah's swords?
Behold them there! the armies of high heaven!
On milk-white chargers mounted, while each girds
His sword o'er linen white as snows new driven;
To them, to wage the last great war with hell, is given.

V.

By these he rules the world with iron rod,
And with them war's red, recking wine-press
      treads,—
The "wrath and fierceness of Almighty God."
Preached from his mouth, the gospel widely spreads

O'er earth's great nations, and its glory sheds
Upon the world.   But wicked kings combined
To fright it from the earth with bloody deeds;
They and their minions to its mission blind,
Shall to the sword and flame of battle be consigned.

VI.

Behold! a mighty angel now uprears
Himself upon the sun's broad, flaming face,
So bright, his form in that great disc appears;
His brightness e'en those splendors doth displace,
Which on a thousand shores their footprints trace,
And through their open, massive, golden bars,
Those floods no finite distance can efface,
Fling their white banners flashing to the stars.
Hear now his proclamation: hell's huge hosts it scares.

VII.

"Come, gather together, ye fowls of the heaven,
" For your countless legions a supper is given;
"The Lord hath prepared it, come ye to his board,
"Where food in abundance for you he has stored.
"For lo! on the battle-field, steeped in their gore,
"The flesh of great captains, full many a score;
"Of kings that have fallen, and men of renown,
"Their lofty heads shorn of both helmet and crown;
"The steed from whose nostrils life's fervor is fled,
"The rider all pale with the hue of the dead;
"Where the freeman and bondman lie down side
        by side,
"As in the dread onslaught of battle they died;

12

"Where in death's gory arms lie the small and the
    great,
"With no kinsman left to bewail their sad fate.
"Come, come to the banquet of carnage and blood,
"Ye fowls, to THE SUPPER OF ALMIGHTY GOD.

VIII.

Exalted now on high prophetic ground,
Like that on which the prophet took his stand
When from Mount Pisgah's top he gazed around
Upon the desert and the promised land,
In retrospect what visions we command!
Ah! what a journey through the wilderness
The Church has made, though led by his right hand,
As now outstretched behind us we may trace
Her path from where she started up to this high place.

IX.

See yonder where she rode upon the flood,
Anon begirt around with flames of fire,
Then onward marching, wading seas of blood;
And then assailed and tossed by tempest's ire;
Attacked by myriad foes, with fierce desire
To hurl her to destruction; on she came,
Though round her wrangled conflicts fiercer, higher;
Still she, now merged in floods, now scourged with
    flame,
Held ever loyal to that only saving name.

X.

What sandy, barren deserts she has crossed!.
O'er what high, craggy mountains she has toiled!

Now in the wilderness her way seemed lost,
And now by lying landmarks almost foiled—
Though there were pastures green that were not
   spoiled,
Where her young lambs in safety might lie down,
And there were quiet streams by foot unsoiled,
Which through these pastures had forever flown,
By which a gentle shepherd led them as his own.

XI.

Along that weary, toilsome way were seen
The rack, the torture, and the blackened stake,
Where, midst the burning, God's dear saints had
   been,
And there were dungeons where for Jesus' sake
They suffered all their weary bones to break
Beneath the Inquisition's torturing rack.
And often they a spectacle did make
For thousands filled with lusts demoniac,
Where bravely they received the wild beasts' fierce
   attack.

XII.

Yet on, through floods and flames and conflicts sore,
O'er mountains, deserts, wildernesses' waste,
Midst tortures, where she bled at every pore,
O'er fields of strife, where she was forced to taste
Most sore defeats, by foes relentless chased,
She held her way, and from her hardest thralls
Arose, increased in strength and unabased,
Her numbers multiplying, and her walls
Enlarging, till their shadow over millions falls.

XIII.

Yes, she endures while all things pass away.
On that long journey since her race begun,
She saw the youthful nations growing gray
With years, great empires, when their race was run,
To ruin fall, and cities which had greatness won,
With power and riches, sink beneath the shock
Of arms, or earthquakes, all their warrings done,
While tottering thrones did hoary monarchs mock,
And wrecking revolutions wrangling nations rock.

XIV.

Ah! what a desert waste is that behind!
How barren, thirsty, bloody, conflict torn!
A perfect rest and peace she could not find,
While thus by sorrow, toil and suffering worn.
Now is she to this favored height upborne,
In numbers numberless, her tents outspread
O'er many a rood, with banners of the morn
All waving gloriously above her head:
To the last conflict she is waiting to be led.

XV.

Now nations, empires, rally to her call,
And Jesus' name is sung in many tongues,
Thrones and dominions at his footstool fall,
While continents are thrilled with Zion's songs.
O what a prospect fills these marshaled throngs!
The world outspread in all its riches, power,

To Jesus and his toiling Church belongs;
And now comes on the great decisive hour,
When it shall surely fall the bride's rich marriage dower.

XVI.

Behold! behold the glorious scenes before us,
Send up the shout, all hail! the promised land,
Let all the armies swell the sounding chorus,
Inspiring fealty to his high command,
Who leads the sacramental host.   We stand
Upon the border which divides the night
From day; the desert from that region grand
Where, in effulgence beams celestial light,
" Sweet fields in living green and rivers of delight."

XVII.

But yonder rises a black cloud of wrath,
Which spreads its murky wings from pole to pole,
And casts its gloomy shadows o'er our path,
And veils the day-star in its outstretched scroll,
As on its fearful convolutions roll.
It makes the darkness just before the dawn
More fearful and depressing to the soul,
Than when night's car is to the zenith drawn,
And to engulf the world the deeps of midnight yawn.

XVIII.

Religious despotism was shorn of power
By that fell stroke on Armageddon's field,
And Islam did before the avenger cower,
When proud Euphrates' flood was forced to yield.

In vain, in other strifes upon the shield
Which overspread the Church, had Satan hurled
The heaviest bolts his mightiest power could wield:
On every field his bloody flag is furled,
And, now, religious freedom rules the Christian world.

XIX.

The dragon, which had symbolized before
The persecuting power of Pagan Rome,
When crushed, was superceded in his power,
By her that in a harlot's dress did come,
And on the seven mountains fixed her home;
Again revived, he on his back did bear
This woman covered with the odium
Of fornications vile, till God did tear
Her from her seat and hurl her minions to despair.

XX.

"The beast that was and is not and yet is," *
Is this red dragon, now the last of foes,
Dread symbol! all the Pagan world is his,
And has been since from hell's dark shades he rose,
And will be till the last tremendous blows
Of God shall fall upon his hydra-head;
When in the last great struggle they shall close,
For ever falls the monster horned and red,
By whom so many prophets, saints and martyrs bled.

XXI.

Behold! two worlds are front to front opposed,
The Christian and the Pagan, all prepared

* Rev. xvii. 8.

For war, and soon in conflict shall be closed ;
That rider with his flaming falchion bared
Now calls his saints who have his kingdom shared,
To rally all their legions for the war.
Wide have the dragon's martial trumpets blow'd
To summon all the nations, near and far,
That own his power, to swell the battle's fearful jar.

XXII.

How then shall these two worlds in war collide?
The Son of God arrayed in mightier power
Than he has ever shown before, shall ride
Upon his foes, with myriad saints, and shower
His mighty blows, increasing every hour,
By that sharp sword delivered from his mouth,—
The blessed gospel, heaven's most precious dower,
The Spirit's weapon, all-prevailing truth,
On heathen lands,—till all shall hear of love and ruth.

XXIII.

Thousands shall fall in every country, slain
By that sharp sword, but slain again to rise
To new and nobler life, to break the chain
Of sin and death and hell, and to the skies
Be borne,—when struggling with the agonies
Of the last hour, an endless life to feel,—
On that great day to hear the symphonies
Which angels sing when their loud anthems peal,
And th' burden of their songs the heavenly worlds
     shall thrill.

XXIV.

As from the sun, the fountain of all light,
The angel's last dread invitation came
To all the fowls in their remotest flight,
So war, where'er his beamy arrows flame,
Shall rage and roar, with nation's loud acclaim,
In East, West, North and South, and everywhere,
Wherever men are sunk in sin and shame.
High burn the fires and wide their lightnings glare,
Angels and devils in the conflict all shall share.

XXV.

Behold THE MAN WHOSE EYES ARE FLAMES OF
　　FIRE!
Who wields resistlessly the sword of God,
With gorgeous banners streaming in the air,
Preparing now to rule, with iron rod,
The nations, who shall quickly own his nod;
When, in the reeking wine-press,* he shall tread
In fierceness of his wrath, with vengeance shod,
Till higher he shall raise his jeweled head,
And over all the world his conquering armies spread.

XXVI.

What wondrous armies follow in his train!
Heaven's glorious chieftains famed in wars of old!
Their countless cohorts swarm o'er hill and plain,
Wide through the air their glittering ranks unfold,
Yea, on the clouds their daring way they hold;
Yes, see the earth, the air, the rolling clouds

* Rev. xix. 15.

Alive with warriors on their chargers bold,
With ranks wide, deep, and high, in countless
    crowds,
While sheen of banners, plumes and swords, the heav-
    ens enshrouds.

XXVII.

These are the warriors which the conqueror led,*
When first rebellion shook the heavenly world,
As from his presence thrones, dominions fled,
And fallen hierarchs to hell were hurled.
Lo! on the right, with banners all unfurled,
Great Michael illustrious comes in arms;
Far to the north, white as the snows upwhirled
By boreal winds, his countless army swarms,
Outnumbering the snowflakes in that realm of storms.

XXVIII.

While on the left, down to the furthest pole,
Next, Gabriel commands the heavenly hosts;
Princes and potentates, neath his control,
Guard with their legions all those Southern coasts,
E'en from where Capricornus holds his posts,
And turns the torrid summer northward back,
When it hath reached its bounds, t' Antarctic
    frosts:
Outspread and wide his armies, as the wrack
Which rises from the ocean, in the sun's warm track.

* Rev. xix. 14.

12*

XXIX.

And he who bears the sword, the center holds,
Which stands outstretched across the burning
    zone:
The mightiest columns his command unfolds,
Wide as the ocean, towering toward the throne,
On which the Great Eternal sits alone,
In numbers far too great for men to show
With earthly signs—to God they're only known:—
As countless as the aqueous drops that flow
In all the ocean tides throughout the world below.

XXX.

And mighty Abdiel and Uriel,
His great lieutenants, hold direct command
With him, who knows their power and valor well,
For each has led in fight a numerous band,
And each with mighty foes has tried his hand
On many a hard-fought field of strife and din,
Where heaven's great sons contended to withstand
The powers of darkness, Satan, death, and sin:
Ranged now in line, they wait the battle to begin.

XXXI.

But there are others in that vast array,
Not less beloved of him who bears the sword,
Who, over thorny paths, have made their way,
With faith, in life or death, to own their Lord;
Ten million saints in white, with one accord,
Join with the angels, their last war to wage

Against the beast, so much by Heaven abhorred.
Behold the Church triumphant there engage,
Apostles, prophets, martyrs, saints of every age.

XXXII.

These are the hosts, invisible, that come
To this last conflict, which, when won, shall end
The wars before the blest millennium.
These, Church of Christ, doth thy Redeemer send
To guard thee day and night, and thee befriend,
Since to the post of honor thou art called,
In battle's front the banner to defend,—
To plant on every fortress, grim and walled,
The lifted cross, by which are millions disenthralled.

XXXIII.

Now Jesus sends his proclamation forth
Again,—" O Church, gird up thy loins anew,
" Go to the East, the West, the South, the North,
" And preach my gospel to the Greek and Jew;
" Gird on thy sword which once its thousands slew,
" And wield it with a faith that ne'er before
" Hath nerved thine arm; and keep my cross in
          view.
" Go tell all men its precious story o'er,
" And offer pardon, heaven, to all from shore to shore."

XXXIV.

" Go, I'll be with thee, and those countless hosts,
" Around and o'er thee, covering van and rear,

"Shall guard thy goings to those distant coasts,
"Which thou shalt traverse, then dismiss thy fear,
"And sound the trumpet for the world to hear."
The Church responds, and feels intenser zeal
Thrill through her limbs and members far and
    near—
The mission spirit, love for others' weal—
She feels more strong desire to save a world from ill.

XXXV.

They go by thousands, now, instead of twos,
Dear missionaries of the precious cross,
For Jesus' sake, a weary life they choose.
The Church begins to count her gold but dross,
And all her richest gains as so much loss,
If she the glorious kingdom may not aid;
And to the winds her doubts and fears doth toss:
She gives her millions where before afraid
To give her tens, for this she learns her gold was made.

XXXVI.

Soon missionaries swarm the heathen world;
In sufferings, prayers and labors, they abound,
Until Jehovah's banners are unfurled
On every mountain top, the world around,
Till every nation hears the trumpet sound,
And myriads haste the precious cross to own
While casting their dumb idols to the ground:
They burn to make the cross to others known
And bring the world to bow before Messiah's throne.

XXXVII.

Now he who wore the vesture dipped in blood,
Sounds his great trumpet, makes its thunders roll
From the high zenith, upward many a rood,
Round the whole heavens and down to either pole:
It stirs his armies, thrills them to the soul.
They know his signal, bidding them to haste
To counsel with him : quick as thought, the whole
Celestial army, numberless and vast,
Upstand in grand concentric circles round him massed.

XXXVIII.

" Archangel, cherubim and seraphim attend,
" Dominions, principalities, give ear,
" And to my words your quick obedience lend :—
" On yonder outspread battle-field you hear,
" Midst mortal strife, the sounds of hope and fear,
" My struggling Church contending with the beast,
" Must fight his minions, gathering far and near,
" Until the chosen are from him released,
" And he cast down to hell, the grievous war hath
        ceased.

XXXIX.

" Round every soul, now struggling for release
" Upon that field, a thousand demons wait
" To hold him back from Wisdom's paths of peace,
" And bind him down to their own fiery fate.
" Once angels like yourselves, in high estate,
" Though fallen, mighty yet, they will prevail

" To drive each sin-sick soul from yonder gate,
" Unless your equal powers their ranks assail,
" And pour upon their heads Jehovah's burning hail.

XL.

" Great Michael, renowned for lofty deeds,
" Put on thy shield, thy sword upon thy thigh,
" Conduct thy legions, on their flaming steeds,
" To yonder empire where in conclave high,
" The king and princes of the land draw nigh ;
" Where fallen potentates elate for fight,
" Still hope celestial thunder to defy,
" To bind that mighty realm in ruin's night ;
" Go, with your flaming weapons, all their armies smite.

XLI.

" And Gabriel, second in your high estate,
" Go, lead your hosts where Boodh and Brahma
        reign,
" Who on the beast as servile minions wait ;
" Launch all your thunders on their heads amain,
" Drive them in dire confusion from the plain.
" While Abdiel, Uriel, warriors tried and bold,
" Be it our part to bind a ponderous chain,
" Upon the limbs of him who once of old
" Stirred mightiest war :—in lasting bondage him we'll
        hold.

XLII.

" Ye spirits of the just made perfect, dear
" As apple of mine eye, be this your part,
" Our struggling brothers yet on earth to cheer ;—
" When fighting, ward away the fiery dart,

" When wounded, soothe the bitter pang and smart,
" When weary, gently lead them into rest,
" When fainting, re-inspire the sinking heart,
" When dying, in ambrosial garments dressed,
" Go, bear their franchised souls to regions of the blessed."

XLIII.

He spake, and quick as light's swift arrows fly,
In mighty arcs back to their stations wheel
Innumerable armies, filling earth and sky,
While loud the hoofs of heavenly chargers peal,
And with their rattling wheels the heavens reel.
They pause awhile as forming their array
Till each division hears its chief's appeal.
Behold!   Imagination can convey
No thought of visions seen in such a grand display.

XLIV.

There a white cloud, ten thousand leagues around,
Uprears so bright that moon and stars grow pale
And hide their faces in the deeps profound,
While e'en the sun's resplendent banners fail.
It is alive with warriors, clad in mail,
With shields outspread broad as the orb of day,
Helms from whose crests hath glanced hell's fiery
    hail,
And swords that flash their own intrinsic ray,
And milk-white steeds that rush like whirlwinds to the
    fray.

XLV.

Now swift as morning, on their squadrons roll,
Their sounding hoofs upon the empyrean break,
Like seven-fold thunder, shaking either pole,
While tramp and shout and thundrous clamor make
The highest heaven and earth's foundation quake.
Songs of high daring swell from rank to rank,
While tramp and trump and shout no discord make,
But blend harmonious song or saber's clank,
And one all-thrilling anthem sounds from flank to flank.

XLVI.

Thick as autumnal leaves swept by the wind,
They scatter o'er all lands of Pagan night,
Swarm round each soul by thousands, to unbind
The chains of sin, to ope blind eyes to light,
To worst hell's struggling legions in the fight
Which soon with double fury rages round,
Where'er th' awakened soul would take its flight
From Death's dark door; it loudly will resound,
Till Satan flies and leaves the captive's limbs unbound

XLVII.

It is a wondrous, solemn thought indeed,
That round each sin-sick soul such conflict rages,
As that to it the heavenly powers give heed,
And angel with archangel there engages,
Momentous more than long historic pages
Unfold.   Yea, there the great destroyer Death

Doth dash his floods against the Rock of Ages,
To drown the soul, e'er it is moored beneath
His shade—in deep despair to merge awakening faith.

XLVIII.

But yet we will remember what that soul
Possesses, that its worth is vastly more
Than many worlds like ours ; as ceaseless roll
The ages more than sands on ocean's shore
It lives, and heights, unmeasured, shall explore,
Of knowledge, virtue, happiness and peace ;
Or merged in shades where storms forever roar,
Where endless pains forever shall increase,
And pangs of worm that never dies, shall never cease.

XLIX.

O, if the possibilities of hell
And heaven are hanging in the dreadful poise
Of battle, wonder not that angels dwell
Upon the conflict, and, with bold emprise,
Cross swords with fallen cherubim, midst noise
Of rattling shields.   What is an empire's dower?
What the whole sum of all terrestrial joys?
What are ten thousand crowns and thrones of
     power?
Stark nothing when compared with life forevermore.

L.

O then, ye warriors, spur your steeds afresh,
Dash your bright squadrons on the powers of hell,

And with the glance of lightning 'gainst them flash
Your swords of high celestial temper, fell
Their huge, misformed battalions, ring their knell
With your resounding, helmet-crushing blows;
On, *on*, their horrid insurrection quell,
And save the people from devouring foes,
Go, hurl sin's legions down to everlasting woes.

LI.

The conflict rages far o'er hill and vale,
In country, village, seaport, inland town,
In cities great, where'er is heard the wail
Of millions sinking under wrath's dread frown,
Of beggar and of him who wears a crown;
But everywhere God's warriors prevail,
While Satan's shaken bulwarks topple down
Beneath the truth in storming rain and hail
As everywhere in huge defeat his armies fail.

LII.

Now millions own the Lord, in every land,
Snatched from idolatry's debasing thrall,
While songs and praises rise on every hand,
And east to west, and north to south do call,
To tell the news, proclaim, to great and small,
The precious gospel's joy-inspiring sound.
So many come, 'tis thought again that all
Will soon obey the truth, the world around,
And Christ will reign where'er the race of man is found

LIII.

Thus hell is worsted, on ten thousand fields,
And its dark warriors fly before the sword,
Which smites and crushes all their orbed shields,
And cleaves the brazen helmets which begird
Their scowling foreheads, yea, with zeal bestirred,
It thrusts through every stony, hating heart,
Those piercing pangs which they who hate the
    Lord,
Forever feel, while writhing with the smart,
Of worm that never dies and fires that ne'er depart.

LIV.

The fallen hierarch, o'erthrown in fight,
Now fled from battle's dread disastrous rout,
Betakes himself to yon lone mountain height,
And there, in his dark soul, is tossed about
With mighty passion, while he belches out,
Like a volcano, hatred, scorn and pride:
Now he laments, and now he curses stout
The Prince against whose shield he vainly tried
His sword, when on his ranks the milk-white steeds did
    ride.

LV.

He groans, and, with the sound, the mountain
    shakes,
As Ætna, when its adamantine base
Is heaved with hidden fires and inly quakes,
As in convulsion, it would strive to raise

The flaming vomit, its sore pangs to ease.
" Alas! alas! and has it come to this
" That scorned and beaten, filled with deep disgrace
" .Great Lucifer, who once was throned in bliss,
" Must now receive both men's and angels' gibing hiss.

LVI

" Must I, to whom both thrones and kingdoms
        bowed,
" Whom seraphim and cherubim obeyed,
" Before the Almighty's minions scourged and
        cowed,
" And by my craven followers betrayed—
" These sons of men against me now arrayed—
" *Must I* be driv'n from this mean earth, the last
" Of my once great possessions, and afraid
" Of venging wrath, fly at his trumpet's blast,
" And, with my limbs enthralled, in deepest hell be cast.

LVII.

" By all the fiends that rally round me, NO!
" By all the storms that in the abyss may lower,
" *By all the thunders in the world of woe,*
" BY ALL INFERNAL ENGINES OF DREAD POWER,
" BY ALL THE DEEDS WHICH MADE THE NATIONS
        COWER,
" Before me, who am styled the prince of air,
" BY ALL THE TEMPESTS WHICH FROM HEAVEN
        I'LL POUR,
" IT SHALL NOT BE, naught shall my purpose
        scare,
" I'll win or lay the world in ruins everywhere."

LVIII.

So saying, filled with bitter rage and hat '
He grows a monstrous form, black, swoll'n, immense,
And darkens earth and sky, as clouds dilate
When gathering, in their caverns dark and dense,
Their tempests, fires and floods, with violence
To scathe and scatter all upon the gale :
So he to measure with Omnipotence
His powers again, doth fire and winds inhale,
And with hell's stormy night doth cover mount and vale.

LIX.

He sounds his horrid signal far and near,
To call his hosts from each disastrous field,
The mountain groans and shakes, as if with fear,
And belches flame, the growling thunders yield
Their lungs to sound the trump as pealed
They once o'er Sodom, winds and tempests wail
With dismal hiss, like flying serpents, nealed
In fires, thus all combined, the ears assail
With dissonance ne'er heard before, unless in hell.   '

LX.

His minions hear on every hill and plain,
And quick as thought, as locusts swarmed of yore,
They rise from myriad fields where they have lain
In dire defeat, amazed, appalled and sore,
By angels' strokes amidst the battle's roar,
And fill the air above, below, around

.The mount, a hundred leagues and more,
While with the clouds their dark battalions crowned,
Rise rank o'er rank above where Satan sits enthroned.

LXI. .

With satisfaction high the fiend surveys
His armies, thus so ready at his call,
He brings to mind the scenes of other days,
Ere he and his did from the empyrean fall.
He sees the same great chieftains, one and all,
Have come, with 'tendant armies, numerous
As forest leaves, now rallying great and small,
As once they hung on battle ruinous,
When first they sought with God rebellious swords to
    cross.

LXII.

Their swarming legions darken e'en the sun;
They dry the dews and rains with their hot breath,
O'er all that land whereon their armies run,
Their footsteps wither, blast, and lay in death
Green grass, and shrub and tree, and all beneath
The horrid cloud, and make the land a waste
A thousand roods around, a barren heath,
Whose blistering sands, nor dews, nor rains may
    taste,
Where, through the choking air, the poison samiels
    haste.

LXIII.

Look on that vast array of fallen spirits,
Each in his own etherial essence lives,

(For there is none but endless life inherits,
Though doomed to hell, and many a time receives
Great sword thrusts, such as high archangel gives,
Which wound, but cannot kill.) But how deformed
Their horrid shapes, whose features naught relieves!
Distort with hate, and now with fear alarmed,
Or shriveled with hot bolts, as in the fight they
    stormed.

LXIV.

Soon as this grizzly host is gathered round
The seat, pavilioned by the sulphur smoke,
Where Satan sits, again the hills resound;
He speaks, as many a time of yore he spoke:
"Once more, O comrades, we have felt the stroke
"Of the Almighty in his power and wrath,
"As erst upon our ranks his thunder broke,
"And we were writhing with the pain and scath:
"Fled we have hence, aside the Son's victorious path.

LXV.

"But not to hide ourselves in craven shame;
"No, no, to nurse our injured pride and hate,
"To brave again the terrors of. his name,
"For we will ne'er this stormy war abate
"While we can strike; let prince and potentate
"Recall the grievous wrongs they have received
"From yonder upstart Son, who rides in state
"Upon that ghostly horse, and is believed
"The king decreed of all the earth, from us retrieved.

LXVI.

" Think how, upon the heavenly hills, we waged
" An equal war with twice our numbers told,
" Of angel hosts ; think how the conflict raged
" For many a day, till o'er our legions bold
" This enemy his thunder chariot rolled :—.
" How thick and fast his hurtling missiles cast
" Upon our heads with fury uncontrolled !
" Unused to such dire war, we stood aghast,
" Till to the abyss we fled before the flaming blast.

LXVII.

" This Son hath balked my plans a thousand times :
" Once, when upon the earth the deluge came,
" And we had grasped all men besteeped in crimes,
" Foredoomed to death ; above the flood and flame,
" In that great ark, he snatched from death and
    shame
" A remnant of that doomed and hated race,—
" Which now by millions rally at his name,—
" That he might save their sons by his free grace,
" And safely make them dwell for aye before his face

LXVIII.

" He hath cast down those heathen gods of yore
" Who rallied hosts obedient to my nod ;
" And that false prophet, rallying millions more,
" Hath bowed his head transfixed beneath his rod :
" And Pagan Rome, beneath the scourge of God
" Hath fallen, and with her, Rome's high Pontifex,

" And hoary prelates the same path have trod,
" Who with the rack, and flame, and death would
    vex
" God's servants, e'en high heaven's deep counsels would
    perplex.

LXIX.

" And Sensualism, Atheism, o'ercome and shamed,
" Which once called millions our strong cause to
    aid,
" Are now cast down where'er his sword hath
    flamed.
" The despot's throne, which once our flag upstayed,
" And Mammon's, too, which many soldiers made
" For us, are fallen prone 'neath his attack,
" And all our helps, of low or lofty grade,
" Are sunk, o'er half the world, in ruin's wrack:
" Our cause is lost unless we drive his armies back.

LXX.

" Let us recall how we have balked his power:
" Once, when our hosts were into prison hurled,
" We broke his bonds, and, in a Stygian shower,
" Poured countless armies on this new-made world,
" And, in the pall of death, its beauty furled;
" Drew man from his allegiance to his God,
" Laid all in ruins dire, by tempests whirled,
" Spread sickness, pain, and sorrow all abroad,
" With wounds, and blood, and death, where'er our
    feet have trod.

13

LXXI.

" And once, when yonder victor came to save
" This wretched race from our supreme control,
" We caught and held him in the gloomy grave,
" And down to hell did send his groaning soul,
" And, though he from our gloomy prison stole,
" What has been may be yet again, we may
" This warrior seize, and 'gainst his prison roll
" Mountains of granite, which, to roll away,
" Not all his hosts have power, with all their great
          array.

LXXII.

" And, as the trophies of our numerous wars,
" Behold yon mighty host of ruined men
" In the abyss, outnumbering the stars,
" Doomed to eternal pains and sorrows, then
" Consider what vast hosts we'll capture when
" Our squadrons rush again to hostile arms,
" And tell me, warriors, have our wars been vain ?
" Those hosts now doomed to yonder realm of
          storms
" Are nearly equal ours when first we felt hell's harms."

LXXIII.

To whom Beelzebub, in prompt reply :—
" Great King, thy faithful subjects all say No !
" 'Tis not in vain we've raised the sword on high,
" For we have been avenged for all our woe,
" In this great host of captives from our foe ;
" My suffrage still is, war e'en to the knife,

" Lead on, great chief, into the fight we'll go,
" And sate our lust and hatred in the strife,
" Or in the blaze of battle quench this wretched life.

LXXIV.

" But, first of all, methinks thou shouldst be wise;
" Behold our foe, in his triumphant trains,
" Leads forth his saints by thousands from the
    skies,
" Whilst thou hast kept thy followers bound in
    chains, ·
" As helpless captives on yon Stygian plains;
" Unbind their fetters, habit them in arms,
" And I'll engage, by all the racking pains
" Which they have suffered, they will come in
    swarms,
" And swell thy train, and fill thy foes with dread
    alarms."

LXXV.

Apollyon next, the Great Destroyer, spake :—
" Fools we have been as we have ne'er before,
" In this last fight; why did we fail to take
" Our carnal arms, and call from every shore
" Obedient kings,[8] and stain the earth with gore?
" My counsel is, the scourge, the burning stake,
" The rack, the torture, with the wild beast's roar,
" To conflict let earth, heaven, and hell awake,
" We'll win, or with the shock of arms creation shake;

LXXVI.

" Yea, with the smoke of fight put out the sun,
" And veil the reeling sky in blackest night,

" Unhinge the stars, which in their orbits run,
" And make them fall like rain, the world to fright;
" Yea, wreck the world in one last mortal fight,
" And make the stormy heavens together roll
" As one black scroll, and pass from mortal sight;
" And while the earth doth shake from pole to
          pole,
" The flames shall, covering land and sea, devour the
     whole."

LXXVII.

Surceased the crafty fiend, when round him broke
Applauding thunder, at his braggart boast;
Upflash a million spears amid the smoke,
Which seethes in sulphur stench throughout their
     host,
Echoes through all that land, from coast to coast,
The noise of rattling arms prepared for wars,
Defiance huge from rank to rank is tossed;
Impatient chieftains in the camp of Mars
Now clamor for a conflict that will shake the stars.

LXXVIII.

Behold what tempests bode within that cloud,—
The heavens grow black beneath their scowling
     hate,—
The wrangling winds with passion shrieking loud,
Groaning in limbos of the storm, inflate
The clouds, their pregnant caverns agitate,
While far, from flank to flank, the frowns of wrath

Light up their glancing fires infuriate,
Where fiends of blood incarnadine their path,
As whirlwinds, hail, and tempest scatter wreck and
    death.

LXXIX.

Arises now the prince of power of air,
And sounds again his trumpet in the din,
His minions hear his signal from afar,
And pause ere they the battle may begin ;
They catch a voice discordant far within
Their ranks, and to it all attentions lend.
" Well spoken, faithful servants, if we win
" We must to battle all our forces bend,
" And in the dread attack let men and devils blend.

LXXX.

" Great Beelzebub, go with this brazen key,
" Push back the massy bolts which hold yon gates,
" And set that numerous host of prisoners free ;
" Tell them their captain now in armor waits
" Their coming here, that he may put to straits
" Our common foe ; for empire of the earth
" We fight ; the wrathful conflict ne'er abates
" Till we win back the country of their birth,
" Where all shall dwell forever free from blight and
    dearth.

LXXXI.

" And thou Apollyon, words so bravely spoken,
" Must needs have weight, go thou to every king

" And prince who with us have not broken,
" And stir them up to deeds of blood, and bring
" Them here, their greatest armies gathering
" From all their realms, roll up their cannons'
        thunder,
" Let lance and spear and sword and saber ring,
" And muskets crash the rolling rack from under,
" We'll gather force and win, or cleave the world asunder.

LXXXII.

" Go thou with hell-born vengeance on thy brow,
" Stir all our furies far o'er hill and vale,
" Again to flames these praying Christians throw,
" Bid Moloch make their roasting infants wail ;
" Upon the cross their writhing bodies nail,
" As once, in better days, we nailed their Lord,
" With torture, rack, ten thousand deaths assail
" The rebels 'gainst our power, of hell abhorred.
" Exterminate them all, as once by Nero stirred."

LXXXIII.

He ceases, then as quick as tempests dash,
His ready servants on their missions haste.
Soon hell re-echoes with the sounding crash
Of bolts withdrawn, the gates, before the blast
Of quick explosion, backward open cast,
And from the dread abyss outpours a tide,
Black as the smoke of furnace hot and vast,
And, like an inundation deep and wide,
It rolls along through air and halts at Satan's side.

LXXXIV.

High acclamations shake that vast array
Of fallen angels, when those spirits damned,
Whose murky clouds shut out the light of day,
Swarm to their aid, by hell's fierce fires inflamed,
Won to that course by lying words unshamed ;—
Lost souls, once cheated out of heavenly bliss
By this apostate, the old serpent named,
Now hope to gain, in such a world as this
A place, to mend, by fighting Christ, their fatal miss.

LXXXV.

To Beelzebub is given the command
Of this array, an army woundrous great,
To spread throughout the world in every land,
Against the Church to stir up wrath and hate,
And urge to blood each evil magistrate
No bloodier armies, Satan ever had,
Than these lost souls with wrath insatiate :
Not even fallen angels are as bad
As they, since they in arms against the Church are clad.

LXXXVI.

Apollyon hastes through all the earth to stir *
Each king and prince to wrath against the saints,
Assisted by the beast, to wage a war,
So bloody, that imagination faints
At its dread picture, which she vainly paints,
To crimson earth and sea with running gore,

* Rev. xix. 19.

To fill the pregnant air with mournful plaints,
To shake the mountains with the battle's roar,
And light war's conflagrations wide on every shore.

LXXXVII.

HARK! hear the call to arms throughout the
    world, 9
Roll its alarums over land and sea,
Behold! war's crimson banners wide unfurled,
Hear sounds portending dread calamity,
The bugle call, the rumbling chariots, see
Yon RIDER comes, upon his milk-white steed,
To meet these hosts of hell-born chivalry;
His earthly Church in this great war to lead,
In carnal armor clad for this last time of need.

LXXXVIII.

Now heaven, and earth, and hell, for fight arrayed,
On battle's awful brink, expectant stand.
There have the kings of earth their flags displayed,
With many nations massed at their command,
Outspread, for many a league, on either hand,
While far in rear their deepening columns form,
In numbers vast as grains of desert sand,
And overhead, around, on wings of storm,
Lost souls of men and fiends in countless armies swarm.

LXXXIX.

Outnumbering these, by far, the hosts of God
Are ranged for fight, o'erlapping their wide flanks,
With steeds of battle for destruction shod,
While to the rear outstretch their bristling ranks,

For many a mile where gun or saber clanks,
And overhead, far to the zenith rise
Celestial warriors, filling boundless blanks
Of space, the guardian armies of the skies,
To cover front, flank, rear, where winged danger flies.

XC.

Now wake the sounds of carnal strife again, [10]
More loud and fearful far than e'er before.
Along the front burst fires of death amain,
While like exploding worlds the cannons roar,
And through the sky their iron tempests pour,
While leaden rain torments the sulphurous air:
Come wounds, and death, and floods of running
   gore,
Mid glancing steel of sabers, in the glare,
Where iron tramp of steeds the wounded do not spare.

XCI.

E'er wnile, above this mortal din and strife,
The powers of hell fight with the hosts of heaven,
Where whirlwind gusts and thunderbolts are rife,
Hurled back and forth as to the battle driven,
At whose tremendous strokes the sky is riven,
Where host meets host in huge concussion crashed
(Such hosts in battle ne'er before have striven)
With such commotion, e'en the stars are dashed
Down from the sky, as flaming swords on shields are
   clashed.

13*

XCII.

Along the north, where Michael's claymore flames,
Thrones sink in ruins, hoary empires fall,
Kings lie in death, who wrote in blood their names,
Great cities shake, lies prostrate every wall:
In vain the princes on their subjects call.
Down sink, ye gods, your temples stained with
    lusts,
Your grisly powers are wavering one and all,
Below, before a million saber-thrusts,
Above, before the angels' awful thunder-gusts.

XCIII.

Meanwhile along the south where Gabriel fights,
Is heard the dismal crash of falling towers,
The rush of heavenly hosts the beast affrights,
And Boodh and Brahma yield their waning powers,
Prone in the dust, each smitten minion cowers,
Their ancient kingdoms sink in ruins dire;
No more their gods shall bask amid their bowers,
Their prophets fall beneath Jehovah's ire,
All soon to be o'erwhelmed beneath the lake of fire.

XCIV.

But in the center where, in battle closed,
Hell's potent hierarch arrayed in arms,
With heaven's most choicest warriors is opposed,
His mightiest powers are gathered round in swarms,
There, in the shock, as swept by myriad storms,
The mountains tremble, shakes the solid land,

The heavens grow pale amidst the dread alarms,
Sun, moon and stars in fear expectant stand,
As if the end of all things earthly were at hand.

XCV.

Now Satan's armies, shattered in the shock
Of battle, fly and leave him all alone,
But yet, uncowed and firmer than a rock,
He stands and hurls defiance at the throne,
And scorns to fly, though all his troops are flown.
The heavenly hosts divide and swift advance
Sheer past the spot where his dread form is shown,
Then close behind him quick as lightnings glance,
And leave him helpless quite, to mend the dread mis-
    chance.

XCVI.

And now their wide extended flanks outspread
In curve concentric round his routed host,
A flaming crescent, by the archangel led,
Pursues them, now with pain and terror tossed,
Their idle swords no more in battle crossed.
Chased by a mightier power than whirlwind's blast,
They know the day, that *everything* is lost,
So, like autumnal leaves by tempest cast
To th' winds, they fly, in huge confusion thrown, aghast.

XCVII.

On rush the horsemen, roar the chariot wheels,
And rain hot thunderbolts by angels hurled

Upon their writhing shapes, creation feels
The shock.　Then upward, by tornado whirled,
They're lifted far above th' astonished world,
And borne in ruin dire unto the brink
Of that abyss of fiery billows swirled
By hot recoil, 'neath scoria black as ink,
Down in whose horrid deeps the foes of God must sink.

XCVIII.

Hell hath enlarged itself a hundred fold :
Farther than eye can reach, that sulphur sea
Extends its dread expanse, with smoke uprolled
In pitchy blackness, where eternally
The tempest groans, whence none can flee.
High flaming walls do everywhere enclose
This realm, and fires to all eternity
Shall rage unquenched : its lowest deeps disclose
Still lower deeps enlarged for all Jehovah's foes.

XCIX.

They halt in horror's dread recoil, at sight
Of that tremendous lake of flaming fire,
As if again they would renew the fight,
But charged with heaven's ten-fold avenging ire,
They're swept across the brink in ruin dire,
And down the horrid height, a deluge pours,
Than of Niag'ra's endless cat'ract higher
Ten thousand times ; nine frightful days it roars :
The shock is heard and felt on earth's remotest shores.

C.

In huge astonishment erst Satan stood,
To see the ruin of his armies vast;
Outstretched around him, on that field of blood,
Lay kings who, in his service, armies massed,
Great captains, too, laid low by tempest's blast;
The horse and rider, bond and free, all slain
By heaven's devouring fires, in vengeance cast,
While mountain heaps of bodies choke the plain:
The fowls of heaven unto their supper haste amain.

CI.

E'en while the foe of God and man surveys
The wrack and ruin of this last great fight,
Lo! in the east a wondrous cloud displays
The True and Faithful, on his charger white,
By heavenly guards attended in his might.
With them had he from swift pursuit withdrawn,
To seize this wily foe, disdaining flight,—
When all his armies into rout had gone,—
And bind and cast him where hell's fiery caverns yawn.

CII.

Whom Satan sees, he feels within his breast
Hot fires enkindling envy, wrath and hate,
His swelling rage by naught can be repressed,
The heavens grow dark with frowns infuriate,
His eyes flash lightnings, thunders fulminate
From his dark bosom, earth grows black

And quakes with terror, lest her fate
Should be destruction, midst the threatened wrack
Of fight, as this great chieftain waits the dread attack.

CIII.

As onward the victorious horseman rides,
He gathers heaven's hot lightnings in the cloud
On which, with sounding hoof, his charger strides,
Flings from his hand ten thousand thunders loud,
And calls his guard around, a numerous crowd:
Nor pauses when he nears his raging foe,
But hurls his sword upon his forehead proud,
Whose swift descent cleaves helm and buckler
    through,
Nor stays its fall until it cleaves the fiend in two.

CIV.

Now once again with monstrous pain he quails,—
Though quick his essence part to part returns,—
At sight of such fierce anguish heaven e'en pales;
And so black hell would pale, where hottest burns
Its fire, if it were there, although it spurns
All thoughts of pity for the pangs it makes.
Swift flight this chieftain now no longer scorns,
But to his aid the wings of whirlwind takes,
And flies the frowning cloud, whose thunder on him
    breaks.

CV.

Like some vast meteor, through the midnight
    gloom,
Discharging loud explosions, jets of flame,

The dragon flies, as if to 'scape his doom,
Pursued by him who bears the unknown name.
Nor does he seek his clamorous flight to tame,
Till on far Afric's sands he's brought to bay
By heavenly guards, uncowed by fear or shame,
Surrounded, yet through many a well-fought fray
He braves angelic arms and stems the vast array.

CVI.

Far in the desert stands a mountain high,
Of strongest granite built, with furrowed brow,
Whose hoary turrets lean against thy sky.
With back against that mount the fiend doth vow
To brave extermination, ere to bow
Submiss to him who bears the sword of God,—
Not all heaven's angels shall his spirit cow,
Grim death alone shall make him own that nod,
And death can only come by the Almighty's rod.

CVII.

Now heaven's stern warriors their artillery wield
Against him fearless, e'en upon him cast
The mountain tops, yet on his rocky shield
The avalanches thunder harmless; last
They seek to overturn the mountain, blast
Its strong foundations, hurl it down in wreck,
And bury him 'neath rocks to hold him fast.
But he, perceiving what they'd undertake,
Doth balk their counsels, all their meshes break:

CVIII.

For, as his wont was, he with rage, and hate,
And stark defiance, swells his monstrous form,—
A nameless shape of cloudy wrath elate,—
Begirts the mountain with a wreath of storm,
And shakes loud thunders with his great right arm.
Vain is the fight, till " HE WITH MANY CROWNS "
Rides to the front and stays the work of harm,—
Confronts the mount, from which the tempest
    frowns,
And sounds his signal trump, which all the thunder
    drowns.

CIX.

Now from the bending sky, on sounding wing,
The warrior, Abdiel, stoops at his command,
Ithuriel, disenchanter, following,
And both before the Lord obedient stand,
The first a chain and key holds in his hand.
Says Christ: " Ithuriel, take thy wondrous spear,
" Go touch yon monster who doth so expand
" His large proportions, and himself uprear
" So high,—in his appropriate form he'll soon appear."

CX.

No sooner said than done,—the frowning cloud
Ithuriel smites ; with quick collapse it takes
Its pristine form—the fall'n archangel, proud—
Though shorn of glory, still with wrath he shakes,
And on the ear his stern defiance breaks.
" Go, Abdiel, bind his rebel feet and hands

" With thy great chain, for earth now groans and
    quakes
" To be released from his enslaving bands;
" Go shut him up in prison beneath the burning sands."

CXI.

The mighty angel grapples with the foe,
But short the struggle with superior might;
Soon hell's archangel in the dust lies low,
And, held by giant hand, he yields the fight.
Quick bound in chains, he is prepared for flight
To the abyss; fast in the whirlwind's track
He's borne away, far out of mortal sight,
And, with the rush of tempest, hurried back
To that grim world of death and stark destruction's
    wrack.

CXII.

Beneath the wall that guards the burning lake,
On side the furthest off from earth or heaven,
A horrid path, two severed mountains make,
Through fearful gorge, by some great earthquake
   . riven,
Leads down to that dread place, where vengeance,
   driven
By dire rebellion, hath in wrath prepared
A prison-house, where fiends of yore have striven;
Its ponderous gates have open stood, unbarred,
Since when the powers of hell the new creation marred.

CXIII.

Unto those yawning gates is Satan borne,
Through them, upon a fiery tempest, whirled
Into the soundless deep, forever torn
By wracking torments: then the gates are hurled
Together with a crash that shakes the world
Below.   The ponderous key drives home the bars
That hold in prison him who first unfurled
The rebel flag, and plowed the earth with wars,
And scattered wounds and death o'er all beneath the
   stars.

CXIV.

Shut in his adamantine prison round,
With the archangel's seal upon him set,
No more the cheated nations shall be drowned
In wars; yea, sword and spear they shall not whet,
And even war's dread arts they shall forget.
They shall enjoy this rest a thousand years,
With all that peace and plenty can beget;
Exempt from war's alarms, its deaths and fears;
Dried up the fount of orphans' moans and widows' tears.

CXV.

Hail, conquering Jesus, hail, all hail to thee!
Comes on thy kingdom now with peace and joy;
Earth sings thy praises over land and sea,
And in thy service finds her sweet employ—
No more shall foes thy heritage destroy:
Now from the east the gloomy clouds are gone,

Wide for the advance the heavenly hosts deploy:
Lo! through the gates, by milk-white coursers
    drawn
The Eternal Son of God brings in the glorious dawn.

CXVI.

Ah, me! what visions fill my raptured eyes!
The Conqueror, arrayed in robes of state,
Outshining all the glories of the skies,—
The rainbow on the cloud where fulminate
His thunders loud. —his eyes, whence radiate
The light which pierces to creation's bounds,—
His locks,—his brow,—his form,—the hosts that
    wait
Upon his path,—the choir that him surrounds,—
Their myriad harps:—a psalm from earth to heaven
    resounds.

CXVII.

BEHOLD OUR CONQUERING JESUS COMES.

Behold our conquering Jesus comes,
    In triumph from the skies;—
Now, from our homes and temple domes,
    Let our loud anthems rise.

Thou earth, lift up thy smiling face,
    Ye mountains, skip like rams,
As bathed in glory by his grace,
    Ye little hills,—like lambs.

Ye forests, clap your hands for joy,
    Ye murmuring rivers, sing,
Ye oceans, all your waves employ,
    To praise our glorious King.

Ye nations, hail the blessed Lord,
    The glorious Prince of Peace ;—
Beneath his reign, in sweet accord,
    Shall wars and tumults cease.

Oh ! gracious Sovereign, hail ! all hail !
    We welcome thee to earth :—
Thy righteous scepter shall prevail
    Wherever men have birth.

We'll fill thy courts with sounding praise,
    The world with holy song,·
And heaven shall echo back our lays,
    Our joyful notes prolong.

CXVIII.

He listens, smiling, to our faltering strains,
His scepter waves in answer to our joy,
His countless choirs, arrayed in glorious trains,
Will all their sweetest minstrelsy employ,
Earth to salute in notes without alloy
Of discord. O, what harmonics descend,
As rank by rank, their glittering hosts deploy,
And, earthward, all their shining squadrons tend,
While all the melodies of heaven in concert blend.

CXIX.

THE ANSWERING SONG OF THE ANGELS.

We're coming, we're coming, on pinions of love,
  With chariots and horses, innumerable throng,
We haste with sweet rapture from regions above,
  And we send you our greeting in heart-swelling
    song.

We have heard of your sorrows, your fears and your
    pains,
  Your conflicts and triumphs for Jesus' dear name,
As, in the dark valleys and drear desert plains,
  You breasted the tempest of war, flood and flame.

We have stood by your sides in your weakness and
    woe,
  Invisible spirits to strengthen your souls ;
Now, as earthward in glorious triumph we go,
  We catch your loud anthem as heavenward it rolls.

We join in your songs of Salvation to God,
  To Jesus, all glorious, our own blessed King ;—
With loudest hosannas we'll spread all abroad
  His praise while creation its tribute shall bring.

CXX.

O, never was the earth so bright before,
Since Eden's morn, when God with men did dwell,
Never such music sound from shore to shore,
Never such raptures from men's bosoms swell ;—

Too deep and strong for human speech to tell,
The angel hosts descend on Zion's mount,
And mingle with the hosts of Israel,
In unison the praise of Christ recount,
And shout the song that thrilled his armies militant.

CXXI.

CHRIST'S CORONATION HYMN.

"All hail the power of Jesus' name!
    Let angels prostrate fall;
Bring forth the royal diadem,
    And crown him Lord of all.

"Crown him, ye morning stars of light!
    He formed this floating ball;
Now hail the strength of Israel's might,
    And crown him Lord of all.

"Ye chosen seed of Adam's race,
    Ye ransomed from the fall,
Hail him who saves you by his grace,
    And crown him Lord of all.

"Let every kindred, every tribe,
    On this terrestrial ball,
To him all majesty ascribe,
    And crown him Lord of all."

CXXII.

The hymn is hushed—yet one more swelling wave
Of song rolls up from those attendant throngs,
So loud, its liquid measures even lave
The throne of God—the grandest of all songs,
Its theme alike, to heaven and earth belongs—
It fired the souls of heroes for emprise,
And heavenward raised their thoughts; and e'en
    the tongues
Of angels chant its measures in the skies;—
Like ocean's, and the thunder's voice, its clamors rise.

CXXIII.

" Praise God, from whom all blessings flow ;
    Praise him, all creatures here below ;
    Praise him above, ye heavenly host ;
    Praise Father, Son and Holy Ghost."

THE END.